The Wolf and the Favour

The Wolf and the Favour

by Catherine McCarthy

The Wolf and the Favour

Edited by Carrie Allison-Rolling
Proofread and formatted by Stephanie Ellis
Cover illustration and design by Tony Evans

First Edition: October 2023

ISBN (paperback): 978-1-957537-73-3
ISBN (ebook): : 978-1-957537-72-6
Library of Congress Control Number: 2023944639

BRIGIDS GATE PRESS
Bucyrus, Kansas
www.brigidsgatepress.com

To Daniel, the little boy who taught me as much as I taught him.

The Lane

February, 2012

If only Hannah could find the courage to take one more step, it would be the furthest she'd ever been. But a moment ago, the long finger of a winter-bare ash had tugged at her hair. Like a witch's finger it was—all bony and gnarled—and it hadn't wanted to let go. Eventually, after lots of twisting and turning, she'd managed to set herself free. Several long strands of Titian hair waved at her from the malicious twig, as if to say, *don't worry about us,* and willing her onward. She put up her hood, her snuggly fur-trimmed hood, but instead of pulling her hair, the branches knocked on her hood, demanding to be let in over and over again, until she didn't know which was worse.

She stood hands on knees, gathering her breath as it tried to escape in little wispy clouds. Maybe the branches were jealous of the twig for the way it displayed the red strands like a rhythmic gymnast. Or perhaps the branches weren't being mean; maybe they were clinging on to stop her going any further. She froze on the spot, undecided.

If only *she* were still here. Hannah hadn't been afraid of The Lane like this for some time, but with *her* gone it was all scary again. Hannah's heart beat fast, like the little robin whose wing had broken some weeks ago. Never mind, the robin was all better now, she and Dada had made sure of it.

She'd been in the garden and there—right there by the holly tree—she'd spotted it. And it wasn't any old robin; it was Hannah's robin—the one she'd fed since autumn. It stumbled around, holding its left wing lower than its right. And Hannah knew it was in pain. Dada carried it into the kitchen in a cardboard box and carefully wrapped a long, thin strip of bandage around it to hold its little wing against its tummy. And that was when she felt its heart beating fast–when Dada asked her to hold it still and not to panic if it tried to move. She did her best, though it was crazy tricky. The robin's beady, black eyes never left her face—not once. She'd known by the way it relaxed that it trusted her to do a good job.

They'd kept it in a cage until it was all better, before setting it free. The memory was still warm, like a buttered crumpet. Ah, she was so proud of herself. She spun a half turn, and through wind-teared eyes, peered back the way she'd come. Her footprints looked brave in the snow. There was only one direction they were heading, and it wasn't back home.

From where she stood, Hannah could just make out the slate-grey roof of her cottage. Just see the twirl of smoke rising from the chimney. She did a pirouette, like a ballerina. She was the smoke! She giggled, then froze, awash with guilt. Dada would be sitting at his computer, furiously bashing away at the keys, oblivious to the fact that she was out here again. In The Lane. All alone.

She loved that word–*oblivious*, despite it being difficult to say. She'd only learned it the week before, when Dada had said she was oblivious to how dangerous the road in front of the house was. The word would get stuck around her tongue, again and again. So they'd practised, her and Dada, with Dada splitting the word into bits and her repeating it after him until eventually she was able to blend the bits together. Now, as long as she took her time, she was able to say it perfectly. "*Ob-li-vi–ous.*" It meant Dada would be *in the dark* as to what was going on around him. Dada called such sayings idiots, or was it idioms? In any case, if he didn't know, then he wouldn't need to worry, would he? She shrugged once, twice, three times, enjoying the squeaky sound the coat made as it rubbed against her shoulders.

It was at this point in The Lane that Hannah always got stuck. It was the bend's fault. Not knowing what was around the bend scared her. And what was more, she knew without a shadow of doubt, that once around the bend she would no longer be able to see her cottage, no longer be able to scream for Dada should something bad happen, and no longer recognize every tree and every stone beneath her feet as she did these—because she'd come this far *so* many times. She was as familiar with this path as she was with the single crease that ran across the middle of her own small palm. She often wondered why the doctors seemed so fascinated by that line.

As to what was around the corner—well, she had no idea. All she knew was the time had finally come for her to find out. She stood up straight, hands on hips, determined and defiant. She felt like a snowman in her padded, silver coat and thick fluffy mittens, and she knew her nose was red. Okay, so it was red—not orange like a carrot—so what?

Perhaps the trees believed she was a snowman and were wondering how she had come to life. She twirled again to prove to them that if it wanted to, even a snowman could dance. She was reminded of the film, *Jack Frost*, the one where the boy's father dies and comes back to life as a snowman. Her Dada wasn't going to die, never, ever, ever! And there were other films about snowmen—scary films—that Dada didn't even know she'd heard of. Jack from drama club had told her about one last week, except he shouldn't have watched it because you were supposed to be eighteen.

Snowmen were brave!

She took a deep breath and fixed her gaze ahead.

Come on Hannah, you can do it.

It wasn't Hannah's own voice that spoke, not even the one in her head. And it wasn't Dada's voice, even though she'd heard him say those exact words so many times. And it wasn't *her* voice, because she'd been gone for such a long time. She sniffed and wiped a cold trickle of snot onto her coat sleeve.

See, that's what frightened her about The Lane—it spoke to her. It had always spoken to her. It wasn't a scary voice, but an *encouraging* voice, a gentle, *persuading* voice. Oh—there were so many words she loved! Musical words. Words you could split into parts and clap a rhythm to. "*Per–suad–ing*." That one had three claps.

A few more steps …

Too frightened to look up. Instead, she stared down at her wellington-clad feet as they came to life without her even telling them to. On and on they plodded, with a mind of their own, leading her farther and farther.

And her heart continued to beat faster and faster with each step—just like her little robin's.

Wolf

Three years earlier

Bleddyn stood at the school gate, watching, waiting. Hannah was always the last one out. Her teacher, Miss Blain, accompanied her to ensure she left safely. The noisy throng jostled past him unnoticed. There was a knot in his stomach today. He'd know the moment he saw her whether or not it was good news. He hoped it might be, but in reality, he doubted it. He'd not wanted to badger Miss Blain—it wouldn't have seemed fair—and besides, tough as it was, Hannah had to learn. If he didn't want her treated differently, both of them must accept that things didn't always go according to one's wishes.

As soon as she spotted him, the floodgates opened.

"Dada!" She threw her arms around his waist and howled. "I got Grandma!"

His heart sank. Peeling her away, he held her at arm's length. "That's wonderful, Hannah. You clever thing." He tried hard to make his voice sound convincing. And it was true, he was proud, especially considering she hadn't spoken her first word until she was almost three, and until fairly recently had still used telegraphic utterances and addressed herself in the third person. Being given a main part in the school play was a huge achievement.

"'Su-su-ppointed," she managed between sobs.

"I told her how proud you'd be." Miss Blain raised an eyebrow.

Hannah scowled and cocooned herself beneath his jacket.

"Thank you … for giving her the opportunity I mean," he said, attempting to unravel Hannah from the garment.

"She did a fabulous audition. Put her heart and soul into it, didn't you, Hannah?"

Hannah ignored Miss Blain and continued to howl, but the howling seemed fake now. Bleddyn knew she was calming down.

"Come on, Missie. I've left the car at the park—thought you might like a few turns on the slide before we go home." He'd kept this ace up his sleeve, ready for playing, just in case. "Say thank you to Miss Blain," he said, taking hold of her hand.

She hiccuped and rubbed her nose with a sweaty palm. "Thank you. Bye," she said with a scowl, before turning away with a sour look of indignation.

Dishes were cleared away and there was an hour or so to spare before the usual bedtime routine kicked in. Although Hannah had bounced back to her usual exuberant self at the park, during dinner, Bleddyn sensed the sullen mood slip in through the back door.

Since babyhood, she'd had a good appetite, one thing he didn't need to worry about. She wasn't picky, but this evening she played with her lentil shepherd's pie, mashing it to a paste with her fork and spearing the peas spitefully with the prongs. He didn't reprimand her—he would wait until dinner was over, until she calmed down, then they could discuss things sensibly.

They sat together at the kitchen table, positioning the final few, satisfying pieces of the jigsaw. It depicted a scene from *The Wizard of Oz*—the one where the lion eventually finds its courage. How many times had they watched the film? And they'd completed this puzzle almost as many. Still, she learned a lot from repetition. "I think starting from tomorrow you and I should begin rehearsals, Missie."

"There!" she said, slapping her palm a few times on top of the last piece to ensure it didn't pop back out. He always let her place the final piece. She swiped her hands together several times, as if brushing away invisible crumbs. She'd ignored his comment—about rehearsing—even though *he* knew that *she* knew what the word meant. She sidled away from the table.

"Hannah." He called her back, his voice calm but firm. She hesitated, before reluctantly returning to stand by his side.

She held his face in her hands, rubbed his stubble against her warm palms, and kissed his nose. She knew how to win him around.

He laughed and tickled her chin before lifting her to his lap. She was growing so quickly. Soon she would be too grown up for him to do this, to sit with her like this. He would need to make a conscious effort not to baby her beyond her years. Glossy Titian strands of hair clung to the corners of her mouth, sticky with dry tears and food. Although she was seven—almost eight—she still displayed some immature habits such as sucking a tendril of hair as she concentrated. Removing the damp strands, he planted a kiss on her forehead. He knew she didn't want to talk about it. My god, she could be stubborn.

Through narrowed eyes they watched each other, both wondering who would be bold enough to make the first move and reignite the subject of *the part*. "All the better to *eat* you with, my dear!"

Hannah laughed out loud, despite herself. She leapt from his lap and stood facing him, bottom lip pouting. "But I wanted to be the wolf," she said, stamping her foot and making her face all sullen again.

"Hannah, the wolf's an old meany. You're not an old meany. The part of Grandma is much better … and the lines will be easier for you to learn." He stole a glimpse, to see if she seemed convinced … perhaps half convinced. He'd need to try harder.

"But I wanted to be the wolf—like you."

Bleddyn frowned. "What do you mean, like me? I'm not a mean old wolf."

"You told me you were." Her face was all pinched round the mouth, and her elven-green eyes squinted up at him.

It was then he remembered … it must have been a year or so back. She'd asked how she came to be called Hannah. He'd explained about when she was born, how the doctors had told him and Mamma that Hannah had a few problems and would probably need help with certain things because she had a condition called Down syndrome. He never wanted to lie to her—had always intended to tell her when the time was right, and he'd been confident it had been the right time.

"Well?" She waited for an answer.

It jolted him back to the present. "I remember. You clever thing. Dada'd forgotten, but you hadn't." He laughed, though his eyes were sad from remembering.

Hannah giggled. She hadn't forgotten. "Hannah's a favour; Dada's a wolf."

And she was right. He'd explained how the name Hannah meant *a favour,* like a gift. He told her she was the most precious gift he'd ever received, then they'd googled the meaning of his name. Of course he knew it was Welsh, his whole heritage was Welsh, but never before had there been any reason to discover what his name meant. *Bleddyn—like a wolf*, it had said. Now he understood why she wanted to play the part of the wolf.

"Oh Hannah, you're so funny. I'm not a real wolf—it's what my name means, that's all."

And they laughed together, all soft and warm. She never ceased to amaze him. Despite all her challenges, sometimes her memory was incredible. He didn't doubt for one moment that she would learn her lines well and steal the show.

My Fair Lady

September 2010

Hannah spotted it on her iPad, darted to his office, and stood red-faced and panting. "Look, Dada! Mamma's in London. We need to go see her." She held out the iPad to show him what she was so excited about.

Bleddyn's stomach hit the floor. He was already aware that Emily had secured the part of Eliza Doolittle in *My Fair Lady*, but he also knew her well enough to know she would not welcome the prospect of either Hannah or himself watching the performance. Emily knew how much Hannah loved music and drama, yet not once had she ever invited her to a show. Were her acting cronies even aware of her past life, the one that included a husband and daughter? Was she embarrassed by Hannah? Whenever the thought crossed his mind he swatted it away, like a pesky fly, because it was too painful to acknowledge.

A squeal of excited delight brought him back to the present.

"We must! We must! We must!" Hannah chanted, twirling in a circle and clutching the iPad to her chest.

"Oh, I don't know, Hannah. It will be very expensive … and it's an awful long way to travel." He knew his protest was lost before it even began. He had always known this day would come, and that one day, when she had enough grasp of reading, she would track down her mother in some show and ask to see it. Had she googled Emily's name? The idea stung a little. It peeved him, the fact that Hannah adored Emily so, considering she only had contact with her once or twice a year. Still, he hid it well, at least in her presence.

She watched him closely, her myopia encouraging her to look directly into his eyes, the way she always did when she wanted to read his feelings. "Please, please, pleeease!"

Exasperated, he took the iPad from her to read for himself. Why on earth couldn't it have been an adult play? He'd have a good enough excuse to refuse her, then. The show dates ran from early October to November, just weeks before their intended move to Wales.

Hannah bounced up and down, waiting for confirmation. "Mamma will be pleased to see us, won't she Dada?" The question was rhetorical—more a statement of fact.

He made one last ditch attempt to persuade her otherwise. "The date is close to when we move, Hannah. We'll be ever so busy."

"But Dada—Pleeease!"

"Oh well, I suppose—"

"Yes!" She spun in a circle, then lost her balance and fell to the floor. No tears. Instead, she sprung to her feet and laughed. She'd not cried for quite some time. In fact, the last time he'd seen her cry was the day she'd landed the part of Grandma in the school play, and that was such a long time ago. Of course, that didn't mean she was always happy. Far from it. She had her moments like any child, but preferred to express her frustration by pouting rather than tears.

Later that night, when he was certain she was sound asleep, he retreated to the kitchen—the room furthest away from her bedroom—and dialled Emily's number.

"Oh, I don't know, Bleddyn. It's my first lead role, and I'm not feeling all that confident. I'll be even more self-conscious with you and Hannah in the audience."

"For goodness' sake, Emily. You expect me to believe that's the real reason?" His voice was an angry whisper.

Emily whined on and on in her childlike voice—the one she used when she was being defensive—trying to come up with all kinds of excuses, but he stopped her in her tracks.

"Well, if *you* want to tell her no, you can do it yourself! You know how much this would mean to her, but if you're not going to make her welcome, and if you're not prepared to meet us, then fine." He detected a sigh of relief down the line. Had she taken his words to mean they wouldn't be going? If so, she was very much mistaken. "I'll book the tickets myself."

She didn't answer.

He put the phone down quietly, so as not to wake Hannah, and stood trembling. He'd be glad when they moved to Wales—at least the physical distance from Emily would aid his excuses as to why Hannah was so infrequently allowed to see her mother. He was sick of playing the bad guy. It was always him who had to make up some excuse about how busy Mamma was; how she was in America at the moment; how she had an important role lined up and needed to work hard and so on.

There were times when all he wanted to do was to tell Hannah the truth—that her precious mother, the person she idolized and aspired to emulate when she grew up, wanted as little to do with her as possible. But no matter how angry Emily made him, he would never hurt Hannah. And so that night he booked the tickets, and the following morning, before she was up, slipped a printout of the online confirmation in a little envelope and placed it beside her cereal bowl.

***

They spent the previous night in a hotel, and took a taxi to the theatre in Covent Garden in time for the matinee performance. He reserved a box for the two of them. It cost an arm and a leg, but he wanted Hannah to feel special.

Back home, she'd taken ages deciding on the right outfit, but he'd tried his best to feign interest. Eventually, she decided on the cream taffeta dress she'd worn to her Christmas party the previous year. "It looks a little tight under your arms," he'd said. "Are you sure it's comfortable?" She'd insisted it was fine.

He'd taken her to the hairdresser in the morning to have her hair coiled in a ballerina bun before catching the train to London. He had to admit, it was the one thing he failed at—styling Hannah's hair. She rarely wore it up, other than in a straightforward ponytail, and he could just about manage that.

He watched her reflection as she preened in front of the hotel mirror, her almond eyes glinting like emeralds. She was his princess—simply beautiful.

Having warned her to be careful not to distract her mother on stage, he had to smile when she leapt to her feet the moment Emily appeared.

"Mamma!" she shouted, waving frantically, but she soon remembered his warning. Clasping her hand to her mouth, she sat back down, red-faced. It was the excitement of the moment that made her forget.

She watched the whole performance, enthralled. Even her popcorn remained untouched, and she was so busy emphasizing how wonderful Mamma was during the interval that she refused ice cream.

He was still seething though, underneath the smile. As usual, it was he who had to admit they would be unable to talk to Mamma after the show, he who had to explain she would be busy changing and preparing for the evening performance. Yes, it was him, as usual, not Emily. Never Emily.

Hannah accepted the fact. She was so thrilled at having the opportunity to see her mother perform that she didn't question him further.

Encore over and lights up, she turned to face him. "I love you, Dada. The most in the whole wide world." It brought a lump to his throat. Was it her way of saying that deep down she knew?

And so to Wales

Uprooting Hannah at such an impressionable age consumed Bleddyn with guilt. He had to admit, he'd been feeling out of his depth lately. Swamped. Juggling the demands of his writing career, as well as Hannah's needs, without any support, had become increasingly difficult this past year. And in any case, she was up for it, she loved Wales. They'd holidayed at his sister's farm near Llechryd twice a year ever since Hannah was born. So for him it was a homecoming.

He wasn't one for self-pity, but as the little green Fiat pulled up in front of the cottage he had a lump in his throat. His sister Ffion, and brother-in-law Aled, had already collected the keys from the estate agent and were there to greet them.

Hannah squealed with delight as her cousin, Evan, ran towards her, closely followed by his energetic border collie, Jipp. Evan took Hannah's hand and the two of them dashed off to explore the garden.

A few minutes later the removal van arrived, and by lunchtime most of their belongings were unloaded. It wasn't as if he had much to bring. Emily had pretty much cleaned him out when they'd split up, at least of anything of worth. But it didn't matter, he wanted a fresh start. This old cottage demanded vintage, not flat-pack. He looked forward to attending a few auctions and antique fairs in order to kit it out.

"Come on, kids, Ffion's got a picnic waiting,' he called from the back door. The garden—if it could be called a garden—for it consisted of almost an acre of wilderness, meant neither child was visible. However, Jipp's bark, accompanied by the sound of giggling, soon reached him. A wave of utter contentment washed over him. As much as he'd fought to cope on his own over the past eight years, life was bound to get easier with a loving support network so close by. Already this old cottage already felt like home. Heart and soul this place had.

***

Hannah and Evan had been counting the fish in the pond, which was tricky because not only did they keep moving but some of them looked the same. Some were gold, some were silver and black. In fact, they were all sorts of colours. Dada had warned her not to get too close to the edge, but she wasn't stupid, and in any case, she already knew how to swim. Jipp had been watching the fish too, when all of a sudden something caught his attention. He shot off, more like a hare than a dog, and all they could hear was an excited bark that grew more and more distant. Evan called him, but Jipp didn't listen. "Stay here, Hannah. I'll be quicker without you," he said, before dashing off towards the front of the cottage and disappearing.

Hannah inched her way through the long grass, until she reached the gap where Jipp had disappeared. Her garden was bordered by a wire fence that was almost invisible through the tangle of bramble and sticky willy that clung to it. Sticky willy was easy to identify because it did exactly that—stuck to your willy—or, if you were a girl, your— She mustn't say the word because Dada said it was rude to talk about private parts. Nevertheless, it had to be the coolest plant name ever.

She stood at the spot where Jipp had escaped. The gap was big enough for him to squeeze through, but too small for her or Evan to follow. It was suddenly silent—that was how she heard the squeaky sound her chest was making. She put her hands to her cheeks in an attempt to cool her skin, and her tummy did a flip. But she needn't have worried, as soon the rapid thud of Evan's feet came running in her direction on the other side of the fence. He was hardly out of breath, even though he ran like the wind. She knew the reason—he was wearing his new Converse trainers and they made him superfast.

"How did you get over there?" she asked, but he didn't answer.

"Here boy!" he called, in the direction of Jipp's bark. His voice sounded all anxious.

Within seconds, Jipp came bounding down The Lane towards them, his tail wagging and his eyes all wide and shiny—mad almost. Evan made a grab for him, but Jipp was too quick. He dodged Evan's arms and skidded back through the fence and into the garden, like a rugby player scoring a try. He spun round and round in a circle, growling, and when Hannah tried to cuddle him, he refused to let her near. Hannah thought he seemed a bit upset, but seconds later Evan was back and Dada called her to wash her hands for lunch.

After Aunty Ffion and Evan left, Hannah returned to the spot where Jipp had disappeared. She grasped the wire-topped fence with both hands, taking care not to cut herself on the bramble that had woven itself in and out of the diamond-shaped wire. This part of her garden was steep and wild. Grass as high as her knees, still sodden with dew. There, on the other side of The Lane, stood a dark wood.

"Ooh!" Hannah's curiosity got the better of her. Without telling Dada, she crept around to the front of the cottage. Right there, at the furthest corner, was the start of The Lane. She stood at the bottom and squinted along its steep path, peering into the distance. Late afternoon, and the sun sat low in the sky, its glare making her eyes water. She shielded them with her right hand. The Lane seemed to go on and on for ever and ever, all the way up, until it reached the sky. And it didn't end there. When it got to the top it disappeared around the corner, reminding her of the magic beanstalk. To the right of The Lane was her garden, and to the left, nothing but woodland stretching as far as the sky.

She considered walking along it like Evan had, as far as the hole in her fence, but resisted the temptation. She'd better ask Dada first, in case it belonged to someone else. For now, it might be best if she went home and drew a picture of Evan and Jipp.

That night Dada tucked her in, just like he used to when she was small, though he hadn't needed to do so for a long time because she was all grown up now. She'd let him though, because he probably thought she was afraid, what with it being the first night in their new home. But she wasn't afraid. Far from it.

After he'd gone, she got out of bed. Quiet as a mouse, she crept towards her window—the little one facing the garden, not the big one facing the front—and peered out. Never before had she seen the night sky so dark, not even when she'd stayed at Aunty Ffion's farm, because at the farm, a light always shone from the barn. She giggled, and put her hand over her mouth to suppress the sound. Dada mustn't know she was out of bed.

A sliver of new moon grinned at her from the corner of its twisted mouth. It had come to say hello. She counted the stars in the sky—five, six, seven. One particularly bright star flashed at her, on and off, on and off, trying to send her a secret message. She didn't know how to read secret messages like Penny from *Inspector Gadget*, so she had no idea what it was trying to say.

The garden itself was invisible. So dark that neither of the sheds, nor the picnic bench where they'd eaten lunch, could be seen. The tops of the big trees were all she could identify. Trees so tall their bare, creaky branches were silhouetted against the moonlight. They waved gently in the breeze, their old limbs all bent with arthritis, like the grandmas and granddads who came to cheer at sport's day. Except she didn't have a grandma or granddad, only a Dada to cheer her on.

Hannah watched as one by one the clouds scudded across the sliver of moon, snuffing it out like a candle for a moment. But the moon was clever, like one of those birthday candles you couldn't extinguish, no matter how hard you blew.

Her feet were freezing. She wiggled her bare toes. Better get back to bed, before Dada heard her. Her face felt sad when she thought about Dada. She'd noticed how tired he seemed lately. His eyelids had crinkles on them; kind crinkles though, not like Rumpelstiltskin's.

A few more seconds … She pressed her nose to the window, watching her steamy breath form its own cloud on the glass, before swiping it away with her fingers. She wanted to look at *it* before she went to sleep. She wanted to see what *it* looked like in the dark. So she strained her neck to the left, towards the back of the cottage, in the direction of The Lane.

On the second day, Hannah was busy helping Dada unpack the boxes, so she forgot all about The Lane. Her bedroom was already painted her favourite colour—golden yellow—so Dada wouldn't need to change it. It wasn't a boring yellow like the sun she'd painted when she was in nursery. No, this yellow was warmer, like corn on the barbecue before it got its brown bits, and smothered in melted butter. How had they known … the people who lived here before her? How had they known she would choose this as her bedroom? And how had they known to paint it her favourite colour?

Dada wanted to put up curtains that Aunty Ffion had made to fit. They were white and sprinkled with little yellow buttercups—beautiful. Hannah let him put them on the big front window, but not her side window.

"The light will wake you very early, especially in the summer. You know what a grumpy boots you can be if you're woken too early," he'd said.

She didn't care. She didn't want the window overlooking the garden to be hidden—not even by beautiful yellow-and-white curtains. She wanted to be able to see the garden at all times, both day and night.

He tried a different tack. "It won't be private, Hannah. Anyone in the garden will be able to see you."

She didn't worry about that either. After all, who would be in her garden at nighttime? No one would see her. They finally compromised on a piece of floral lace, that way she would still be able to still see out, but no one would be able to see in, not even if they stood in her garden at nighttime. And the spare curtain? Well, she was sure Aunty Ffion wouldn't mind if she used it as a cloth for her dressing table.

And so it wasn't until the third day that Hannah remembered about The Lane.

She'd fed the fish, a little sprinkle of food. They were all lazy because it was coming close to winter. One by one they popped their heads out of the dark water, gulping air rather than food, disinterested in her offering. Her reflection watched her from the still surface, all disappointed. She felt nervous because today was Thursday, and she was due to start her new school on Monday which meant—she counted on her fingers … Friday, Saturday, Sunday. Three. Just three more sleeps until the big day. Realising her mistake, she huffed and counted again … Thursday (of course, she still had to sleep tonight), Friday, Saturday, Sunday. Four sleeps left. Well, at least it meant she had a bit longer.

It was as she straightened again, she noticed it. Something moved, swiftly, darted—right by the gap in the fence. Hannah didn't see it, but she heard the sound it made. She tiptoed through the long grass towards the spot, taking care not to make too much noise, and peered into The Lane. Nothing … Nothing but the wind in the trees. It must have been a rabbit, or perhaps a squirrel. It was the right time of year for squirrels. She hoped it was a red one as she didn't particularly like grey squirrels. Dada said they bullied the red ones. Jason Fletcher from her old school was a bully, but he didn't have grey hair … yet. She stood stock-still, watching, trying not to breathe. How strange. The birds had fallen silent. Had they seen it, too?

She returned to the pond, but the scurrying sound itched at her. Would Dada worry if she went for a little walk? It was only around the back of the house, and she was almost ten. Stealthy as a robber, she stole around the cottage.

The Lane stretched ahead into the distance, a thick carpet of autumn leaves for its bed: gold, crimson, auburn. A gust of wind blew, lifting the dead ones from the ground and making them dance like a mini tornado. It appeared as if they were doing the Viennese waltz on *Strictly*. She giggled. It made her dizzy trying to follow their dance with her eyes.

Still no birdsong. She was certain a few minutes earlier, while she'd been feeding the fish, they'd been calling to one another.

From where she stood, the bottom of The Lane was in shadow, but higher up it was bathed in sunlight. The shady part appeared dead without the sun on it—all sad—whereas a bit further on it seemed so alive and inviting.

She listened … No Dada calling. He must be busy setting up his new office in the spare bedroom. She'd been helping him earlier, and there'd been wires everywhere. He'd seemed stressed—all frowning and sweaty. That was how she knew he wasn't likely to notice if she went outside for a bit.

Counting her strides, five … six … seven, she began to climb. Twenty, twenty-one … Only then did she notice the wall. It was invisible from inside her garden because it had disguised itself with a coat of moss and ivy, but from The Lane it was plain to see. Hannah picked her way towards it. The wall was as high as her knees and made from the same stone as the cottage. It separated the back of her garden from The Lane and continued for some distance. She knelt on the ground and poked its mossy blanket, inhaling the damp, earthy scent. She loved moss—all wet and springy.

She turned her focus towards the back of the cottage. The little landing window, the one with the slidy opening with pull ropes and lots of square panes like in the olden days, was spying on her. Eight eyes, the same number as a spider, recorded her movements so that later they might tell Dada where she'd been.

Even though she'd taken twenty-something steps, there were at least that many more before she'd reach the spot where the sound had come from—the spot where Jipp had escaped. She chewed her bottom lip. That part of The Lane appeared so much nicer. The sun was happy there because the cottage wasn't blocking its way. She'd go as far as the gap in the fence, though she must remember to ask Dada if The Lane belonged to them later.

The sound came again—the same quick rustle she'd heard while standing at the fish pond, only this time it was right behind her, causing her insides to flutter. Placing her hands on the ground for support, she pushed herself to her feet and turned around. Nothing. It must be a rabbit because the sound was bigger than a squirrel. Was it watching her from the wood? The Lane was so narrow, a mere five or so paces from one side to the other. She peered into trees that climbed into the distance. It made the back of her neck all achy when she tried to see to the top. No rabbit; no squirrel; nothing other than trees creaking in the wind. She'd better get back—Dada would be worried if he couldn't find her, despite the fact she had not strayed far.

And yet it seemed as though she were far away … almost in another world.

Rhiamon

Deep within the heart of the wood, Rhiamon sat cradled by the bough of an alder, her bare legs swinging in the chill of the evening air. So, the old house had new occupants? She tilted her face skyward, relishing the cool breeze that blew in her favour. It was good to see new faces. And a child, too. How enchanting! About time this place had new life breathed into it. The previous occupant had provided her little entertainment over the past decade. An elderly woman, who had never visited the lane, nor the wood. Not once.

In comparison, the child had only lived in the house three days, but had already summoned the courage to pay her first visit. Rhiamon's pulse quickened at the thought of making a new acquaintance, especially one so fragile. She clenched her fists tight, imagining the girl's warmth in her arms. But she would take her time. The last thing she wanted to do was scare the girl off. Such a delicate thing. Hair the colour of flames and eyes like jewels. And there was something else about the girl, too—Rhiamon sensed her vulnerability.

On the day the new family moved in, Rhiamon had watched the comings and goings from her woodland hideaway. Such a rumpus! She was glad only the girl would be living at the house permanently. She hadn't liked the look of the boy, or his dog. The boy had seemed too agile. Too suspicious. She'd witnessed the speed with which he'd run after the dog, and the way his eyes had darted here, there, everywhere. He was protective of the girl, too; that much was obvious. How sweet. And that hound of his. It had snarled at Rhiamon, causing her to scare. She'd been tempted to snap its neck. It had taken such a lot of willpower to resist teaching it a lesson. Instead, she'd issued a warning, a reprimand of sorts, and the hound had soon scarpered.

She dismounted the branch with the grace of a gymnast and tiptoed towards the boundary, where wood met lane. The girl was at play again, safe within the realms of her own garden. She'd noticed how the child had crept past the back of the house when she'd visited the lane earlier, her eyes darting towards the little window at the back. So she hadn't told her parents of her wandering, then.

Rhiamon sat on the grassy bank at the edge of the wood, watching. Parents. Come to think of it Rhiamon had only seen the woman once, the day the new occupants moved in. Perhaps she wasn't the girl's mother. Perhaps she was the boy's. In that case, did the girl live alone with her father? Interesting.

A little more observation would surely provide the answer. Observation, and a little help from the creatures of the wood was all Rhiamon needed. There would be ample opportunity for her and the child to get to know one another.

Rhiamon watched the child at play, sensing the child's loneliness. An array of garden gnomes, abandoned by the previous occupant of the house, sat in a row in front of the fish pond.

"You will be going to your new school soon," she heard the child say. "You mustn't worry. I won't let anything bad happen to you."

Rhiamon smiled. The girl was lost in her own world. Attempting to draw comfort by acting out her own fears on the spiritless. Hadn't she done the very same as a child? A shimmer of reminiscence. A memory. A doll, made in the image of Rhiamon's own mother, and by her father's hands. A mother in miniature. Raven haired, each strand lovingly woven from the barbules of a crow's feather. Pale complexion, fabricated from the bleached skin of a foal, and piercing, painted eyes of celestial blue which captured the glint in mother's precisely. The paint had faded with time, as had Rhiamon's memories of her, until by the time she'd reached adulthood, her mother was no more than an indistinct impression.

She knew what it was to grow up without a mother. As ruler of her realm, her mother had been destined for great things, as had Rhiamon. But those dreams had been quashed for both of them. Trampled into the ground by some villainous heel and spat upon. And Rhiamon's heart had been tainted ever since. Plunged into a lake of ice. It had never thawed.

Rhiamon was so entangled in the memory, she failed to notice the child retreat indoors. The air chilled as the sun dipped in the sky. The child must have grown cold. She stood and brushed the earth from the back of her tunic, before retreating into the comforting heart of the wood.

Remembering had made her mournful. The child wasn't the only one to have suffered rejection. She, too, sometimes longed for company, but what hope did she have here? She would have to make do with the company of the woodland creatures. The speck of warmth they provided was better than none.

FIRST DAY

Hannah was good at pretending she wasn't nervous. Mr. Andrews, her new teacher, had a kind, smiley face and bushy eyebrows with bits of grey in them like Dada's. He showed her where she would sit, and introduced her to two girls, Erin and Millie, telling them to look after her and show her around the school. They were both pretty, but Erin had neater handwriting.

Mr. Andrews was nice, but Miss Morgan was even nicer. Miss Morgan was going to be her helper. Mr. Andrews explained that Miss Morgan would sit next to her every morning and help her with her work, and sometimes Miss Morgan would take her out of the classroom and they would work together in the library. She was used to that, because the same thing had happened in her old school, except her helper hadn't been called Miss Morgan; he had been Mr. Robbins, and sometimes he seemed a bit grumpy, especially on Monday mornings.

Miss Morgan was a bit plump, with blue eyes the same colour as Hannah's favourite crayon—aquamarine—and the blue part even had a dark circle round the edge like the crayon's paper wrapper. Hannah wondered if the circle was there to stop the blue running into the white. She didn't like to ask, as they hadn't long met. If she had, Dada would have told her not to be personal.

She didn't mind if Miss Morgan knew personal things about her, in fact she'd prefer her to know from the start. So before break, when she and Miss Morgan were in the library setting up a laptop for Hannah to use, she told her.

"I have Down syndrome." Hannah watched the blue crayon eyes to see what they thought. She was always able to tell by doing that.

"Yes, I know Hannah. Mr. Andrews told me, but don't let it worry you. I'm here to help with your work, and I'm also here to help you if you have any other problems."

Hannah only heard the first bit, the bit about Miss Morgan already knowing. She'd better tell her some more. "Dada says my sittums are mild—you know, like the nice cheese."

Miss Morgan laughed, *really* laughed, and Hannah laughed too, though she didn't see what was so funny. Miss Morgan's whole face laughed, not just her mouth.

"Your symptoms are mild like nice cheese and fair weather, Hannah. That's good to hear."

***

Bleddyn stood at the gate. Watching, waiting. Hannah would probably be the last one out. He wondered whether or not anyone would accompany her, to ensure she left safely. Maybe not, after all she was in Year Five. One more year and she'd be in High School. The thought made his stomach twist.

Lately, he'd considered whether or not to discourage her from calling him Dada. Was it too babyish? At twenty-six months it had been her first spoken word and had meant so much to him—a sign the potential for verbal communication was finally beginning to develop. Until then, he'd attempted to use some Makaton sign language with her, but she hadn't seemed all that interested. On the other hand, years of regular speech therapy had paid dividends. He was so grateful for it, even though Emily used the fact that she paid for it as a *Get out of Jail* card. He took a deep breath. It still stung a little.

The noisy throng of children moved past him unseen. He'd know the moment he saw her whether or not it was good news.

She ran up and threw her arms about his waist. "I got my own laptop!"

A young woman, who he imagined to be in her late twenties, caught up with Hannah, a little breathless. She was about to introduce herself when Hannah spoke. "This is Miss Morgan, Dada. She's my helper."

Miss Morgan held out a hand for him to shake, flushing a little as she did so. "I'm Hannah's classroom assistant. She's had a great first day, haven't you, Hannah?"

"It's got proper letters on it, not capital ones like yours."

"That sounds grand! So you had a good day?"

Hannah beamed. "The best!"

What a relief. "I'm so glad. I've been thinking about you all day."

Hannah took hold of Miss Morgan's hand and shook it. "See you tomorrow."

***

For tea, Dada made her favourite veggie sausage and mash to celebrate her first day.

"Dada, Miss Morgan's eyes have a ring around the blue part. Is it to stop the blue running into the white when she cries?" She'd been itching to know all day.

He smiled. "No, Hannah. Some people's eyes are like that. The colour can't run. So tell me, what was your favourite thing about today?"

She tilted her head. "Lots of things." A sausage dangled between mouth and fork. "I know. Getting my own computer."

"You're so lucky. You never had your own in your old school, did you?"

"Mm-mm. And I've got two friends, Millie and"—she tapped her temple—"forgot."

"Ah well, it doesn't matter. You can ask her name again tomorrow."

She remembered something else she wanted to ask him. It was about The Lane and who it belonged to, but as she was about to ask the phone rang.

"Great, just great," she heard Dada say. "She came out all excited because they've given her a laptop of her own."

It had to be Aunty Ffion. She was one of the few people who would care about Hannah having her own laptop.

They still told bedtime stories, except now Dada didn't tell them when she was tucked up in bed. Instead, he told them while she was drinking hot chocolate on the sofa and cuddled in her peachy blanket, the one with teddy bears all over it. Evan had bought it for her as a housewarming present. Did it mean when someone moved to a different house you had to buy them something to keep them warm? Weird.

Dada didn't tuck her in any more either, he just gave her a kiss and said goodnight. It had only happened since she was nine, and she knew it wasn't because he didn't love her. He wanted to help her to grow up, see. And anyway, she knew he'd creep in and check on her a little while later, that was why she waited until he'd gone again before getting back out of bed and tiptoeing over to the window.

Amber Eyes

Each day over the past week she'd asked Dada, "Is it today?" and each and every day he'd replied, "Thursday, Hannah. You have to wait until Thursday." Thursday wasn't coming quick enough.

She told Miss Morgan all about it, and Miss Morgan told her Megan also went to the same drama club. Megan from her class. Funny Megan. Miss Morgan shared Hannah's news right there in the playground at break time, and Megan spun her around and said, "Goody, goody, goody! You can be my partner for *Add a Freeze*. We always play it at the beginning of the session."

And it made Hannah's day.

When Thursday finally arrived it was raining, and it wasn't any old rain because this rain had bits of ice in it that Dada called sleet. She worried the sleet might turn to snow, and Dada wouldn't be able to drive her to club. She kept looking out the classroom window to check, until Mr. Andrews got a tiny bit cross with her. She knew he was cross by the way his bushy eyebrows bunched up in the middle. She grinned. "All right, all right, keep your hair on," she said, which made him laugh, despite himself. The same trick always worked with Dada, too. She wouldn't tell Dada what she'd said though, because he would take Mr. Andrew's side.

Back home, three or four mouthfuls of dinner was all she managed. Her stomach was in knots. The sleet had turned to rain—ordinary rain, without the icy bits—so at least she was sure Dada would drive her to club. Should she choose pink leggings or denim? She decided on the denim ones and a navy and white T-shirt. She deliberated over which socks to wear. Were the white ones with little blue bows on the side cool enough? She'd stick to plain, and wear a navy headband. The reflection in her bedroom mirror approved with a thumbs-up.

When she arrived at the drama club hall, the door to the entrance lobby stood wide open, the light from within welcoming her approach from the car park. Hannah's cheeks burned hot with anticipation as she stepped inside the building, Dada in tow. She'd allow him to come inside with her this time, but not next time, it would be too embarrassing.

From the lobby, the excited sound of chatter carried to where Hannah stood, frozen to the spot, her feet refusing to go any further.

"In you go," Dada said, placing a gentle hand on the small of her back.

All week she'd looked forward to this, but now she was on the threshold she was close to backing out. Both hands placed flat against either side of the door frame, she stood—rigid. Her heart beat like a drum.

"Hannah!" Finding herself grasped tight around the middle from behind, she was forced to drop her arms. She turned to see who her assailant might be.

"Megan!"

Hannah found herself whisked into the hall without so much as a goodbye to Dada.

Drama club was so much fun that she was too exhausted to get back out of bed, which was a bit of a shame because she was sure she'd seen something shining in The Lane when she'd peered out the previous night.

***

Dada said it was okay for her to play in the garden. He was at a crucial point in his writing, so if he got carried away and didn't check on her for a while, she must remember to let him know she was all right every now and then. She didn't know what crucial meant, but it sounded important. In any case, it was probably important enough to keep him from calling her for a while. She knew he was working on a play at the moment, though he wouldn't tell her much about it. It was for adults—a comedy. She knew it meant it was supposed to be funny, but she wouldn't mind betting there'd be kissing.

Thursday's sleet had cleared, and Saturday dawned bright and breezy—like her on Thursday mornings. Aunty Ffion was bringing Evan round later, so she knew she didn't have much time. Aunty Ffion always brought a cake. Hannah hoped it would be a chocolate one. She hoped Jipp would stay at the farm, just in case.

She climbed as far as the gap in the fence and sat on the low stone wall panting hard, unable to decide whether The Lane was soothing or scary. Whenever she thought about The Lane lots of words popped into her head, the same as they did when she played the picture game in drama club.

She sang quietly to herself. It was her favourite song, "Pack Up," by Eliza Doolittle. It was her favourite for lots of reasons. One—because the words made her think about how *she* felt lots of the time, especially the bit about not caring about what people say about you. Two—Eliza Doolittle was her favourite singer because she had the same name as Mamma in the play, and three—when Dada had helped her google Eliza Doolittle, she'd discovered they had lots in common, such as Eliza's Dada was also a writer, and her mother was an actress like Hannah's, plus, Eliza's parents had split up when she was little, just like her Dada and Mamma.

She reached the chorus when a rustle in the wood caught her eye. She fell silent and fixed her gaze on a large oak that stood a little distance into the wood where she was certain the movement had come from. A huge smoky-grey head peered round the trunk. Two amber eyes locked hers—green to amber, red for danger.

Hannah was too frightened to move; too awestruck to call out. Its head was enormous. As she stared, transfixed, it revealed itself entirely—its handsome, intelligent eyes never leaving her face. A wolf. Narrow shoulders, a thick coat in various shades of brown and grey, its bushy tail hung low as it approached. Its muscles flexed and relaxed in rhythm with its footsteps as it came closer and closer …

Hannah froze, her heart raced. *Run*, the voice inside her head said, but she failed to convince her feet to move. She stood one side of The Lane, the wolf the other—opponents, ready for the tackle. How long they observed each other she could not say. Long enough for her to read its mind. Curiosity, sadness, anger—they were all there. Breaking eye contact, the wolf gave a high-pitched yelp, turned and ran. She watched it climb higher and higher into the wood, its powerful hind legs and huge paws pounding the earth until it reached the top, the place where she needed to strain her neck to see. It glanced at her, before disappearing out of sight.

The spell was broken.

That night, Hannah stared from her window towards The Lane, where the tops of the tallest trees were silhouetted against the moonlit sky. Why had she not told Dada? She never kept secrets from him. Was it because he might be cross with her for wandering The Lane alone? If she was honest, it wasn't the real reason.

EAVESDROPPING

On Wednesday, Hannah brought home a letter addressed to Dada. She remembered to hand it to him as soon as she emptied her school bag, which pleased her, as she usually forgot such things. Dada said it proved she was becoming more independent by the day. Independent … Hannah knew it meant doing things for yourself.

Dada's hands were wet from washing dishes, so he didn't open it straightaway. Hannah wasn't interested in what the letter said because she was certain she hadn't been naughty at school, so it wasn't like Mr. Andrews was splitting on her or anything.

In fact, it wasn't until the following Saturday afternoon, when Aunty Ffion came round, that the letter was mentioned. It poured with rain, so she had to stay indoors. She was in the living room, watching *Horrid Henry* on Netflix, and Dada and Aunty Ffion were in the kitchen, when she heard him tell Aunty Ffion about the letter. He tried to make his voice quiet, but Hannah still heard him.

"She brought this home, Ffi."

Hannah's ears pricked up, and she turned the volume on the remote down a level. There was a pause, then she heard Aunty Ffion say, "Would you like me to have a word with her this afternoon, Bleddyn? You know, woman to woman."

Hannah was confused, because Aunty Ffion was the only woman in the house. Dada told her it was his job, and he'd speak to her that night. "Call me old-fashioned, but it seems a bit young to me. Does she need to know about periods and such yet?" he said.

Aunty Ffion laughed. "Get used to it, mate. They learn about everything these days."

Hannah would wait then, to see who he would phone later to talk to about the letter and the periods thing.

Aunty Ffion and Dada carried on talking in their normal voices. Within seconds, the periods thing was forgotten as she heard Aunty Ffion ask Dada about The Lane.

Dada said it belonged to a farm high up on the mountain. He told her the previous owner of their cottage had explained it wasn't a *public right of way,* and that in all the time she'd lived in the cottage, not once had she seen the farmer or anyone else use it. He explained to Aunty Ffion that back in the olden days, it had been used for transporting milk churns down from the farm to the road that ran in front of the cottage, except in those days it would have been a dirt track rather than a road.

So Hannah had two puzzles to solve, the periods puzzle and the public right of way puzzle. How might she ask Dada about either of them? She wasn't supposed to have been listening to his conversation. She decided that instead of asking Dada, she'd ask Miss Morgan on Monday … if she remembered.

Saturday night was always special. She and Dada would watch *Strictly* together and finish what was left of Aunty Ffion's cake. Dada also drank red wine on Saturdays, but Hannah wasn't allowed red wine, and in any case, she'd stolen a sip one night when he'd been in the kitchen and it had tasted disgusting.

Hannah loved *Strictly*, though she wasn't sure if Dada did. His smiley mouth seemed to like it, but his eyes didn't. And sometimes, after he'd drunk his wine, he'd nod off in the chair beside her while it was still on. Hannah loved it because she loved dancing. She danced in the house all the time, and in drama club, too. When she grew up, not only did she want to act, but she wanted to dance on the stage like Mamma as Eliza Doolittle.

Since Aunty Ffion had left, Hannah sensed Dada wasn't right. He seemed a bit on edge, a bit far away. She knew what those sayings meant because he often said them about her. She hoped nothing was worrying him. She'd keep a close check on his eyes—then she'd know. However, once she got caught up in *Strictly*, she forgot to check Dada's eyes, and anyway, after his second glass of wine, Dada seemed back to his normal self.

Usually, after *Strictly*, her bedtime routine would kick in, so Hannah was surprised when as soon as the *Du, du, ru, du, du, du dah* of the final music played, he switched off the television.

"I need to talk to you, Hannah. About something important."

She remembered him talking to Aunty Ffion about The Lane, and felt a bit guilty. Perhaps he knew she'd visited it. Was it possible Dada also knew about the wolf? Surely not. If he'd known, he'd have warned her to stay away.

But Dada didn't talk about The Lane, and he didn't know about the wolf. Instead, he told her about something called *puberty* and the *periods* thing. He seemed a bit embarrassed at the start, but she behaved like a grown up and asked sensible questions when she didn't understand what the heck he was on about, even though a giggle bubbled inside her, and she had to force herself not to say, *Pubey, dubey doo*, in her Scooby Doo voice. So after a while he seemed okay, talking about the periods. Hannah felt a bit sorry for him, though. It should have been Mamma's job to tell her about those girly things. Would Mamma tell her when she saw her next? She doubted it.

She lay in bed, unable to sleep. She still didn't know who the woman was that Aunty Ffion had mentioned, nor had Dada phoned anyone. Could they have meant her? Of course not. She was hardly a woman.

At least he hadn't mentioned The Lane—just the periods, and she was glad. To Dada, The Lane was simply a disused old track that led to a farm except she knew it was more … far more.

Second Sighting

As far as Hannah could remember this was the first Christmas she'd ever spent in Wales. As usual, she phoned Mamma in the morning to thank her for the gift. Mamma was busy with the theatre at Christmas, but Hannah didn't mind because she couldn't remember a Christmas with Mamma anyway. They didn't talk long. She thanked Mamma for the Pandora charm, and said she would add it to her bracelet. It was a little red house and looked a bit like Hannah's cottage—except her cottage was white. Mamma must have thought about it a lot before she'd chosen it, knowing Hannah now lived in a cottage.

Dada didn't believe in expensive jewellery. He said it was superficial, which was strange because Hannah imagined all words with super in them meant something especially good. Anyway, he hadn't said it to her, he'd said it to Aunty Ffion when they went for lunch at the farm.

Hannah and Dada were vegetarians, and Aunty Ffion made them a special strudel in place of turkey. As she helped to dry the dishes, she repeated the word quietly to herself—*strudel.* It wasn't an easy word to say, but she liked it because it rhymed with poodle. Hannah had never seen a poodle so wondered what one looked like. Megan told her she had a half-poodle called a Cockapoo. The word Cockapoo made her laugh a lot because she loved rude words.

Dada bought her lots of useful things to occupy her mind—those were Dada's favourite presents to give.

Aunty Ffion bought her new dance shoes, which were amazing. They had gold straps and a little heel. She insisted on wearing them all day long, even when she went to feed the ducks with Evan.

Back home, Dada got the log burner blazing and lit lots and lots of candles. They cuddled up on the sofa, under her teddy blanket, and he told her a story. Usually, when he told her stories from his head—not from a book—she would fall asleep, not because he was a boring storyteller, quite the opposite. Dada told wonderful stories, full of magic and mystery, but Dada's voice was soothing, like a creamy mug of cocoa, and Hannah would find herself drifting … drifting … until she always seemed to wake up right at the end, which was very annoying.

But she didn't fall asleep on Christmas night when Dada told this story. It was about a dog named Gelert who belonged to Prince Llywelyn—a Welsh prince. The prince loved and trusted Gelert so much, he left him to look after his baby son while he went hunting.

When the prince returned, he saw the baby's crib upside down and Gelert lying beside it covered in blood. Llywelyn assumed Gelert had killed his baby son. In anger, the prince took his sword and killed Gelert, but when he overturned the crib, there was his baby son, safe and sound. Lying close by was a dead wolf. The prince realized his mistake. Gelert had killed the wolf to protect the baby, and that was why he was covered in blood. The Prince was full of regret, as he loved the dog. He buried Gelert in a special place outside the castle walls.

Dada told the story with all the sound effects, like the wolf howling, and the baby crying which was brilliant.

"Gelert's grave is still there, Hannah," he said. So they made a pact—during the next school summer holiday they would travel to North Wales and visit Gelert's grave.

"Did they make a grave for the wolf, too?" Hannah asked, but Dada said nobody knew what became of the wolf, and they probably used his fur to make a coat and threw his bones to the dogs. Hannah preferred to believe it had come back to life and might even be the wolf living in her wood. North Wales wasn't all that far away, so it would have been able to walk the distance.

Dada tucked her in that night because Christmas night was special. She clutched her hot water bottle close when he left and went back over the story in her head. She didn't get out of bed—it would have felt like cheating after the wonderful day they'd had. Exhausted, she closed her eyes. The howl seemed far distant, but she hadn't yet fallen asleep, so it wasn't a dream.

***

The remainder of the Christmas holiday was far less cheerful as it did nothing but rain. Between the weather and the short days, Hannah had little opportunity to visit The Lane.

If she was honest, she was also a little afraid. She wondered if she might have been mistaken and that the animal she'd encountered was not a wolf at all. Perhaps it was nothing more than a big dog. She was sure she'd seen one similar when she'd been at the park ages ago. It had been on a lead, so she hadn't needed to be afraid, and besides, Dada had been with her. And yet something deep inside told her it really was a wolf she'd met that day in The Lane.

There were other clues too, such as the howling at night, and also, when Evan brought Jipp to visit on the weekend, Jipp seemed nervous in the garden. He sniffed and scurried all around, sometimes whimpering, and he stayed well away from the gap in the fence. Even Evan seemed to notice and made a fuss of him.

She still hadn't mentioned anything to Dada about The Lane, and she'd forgotten the exact words he'd said to Aunty Ffion in the kitchen—something about pubic, or public. She got mixed up after the periods talk she and Dada had, so she wasn't able to ask Miss Morgan after all.

And so it wasn't until the middle of February that she found herself returning. It was half term week, and luckily the weather had finally decided to improve. Dada complained she'd been driving him crazy lately, and she had to admit to being a bit of a pain, except on Thursdays because then she had drama club.

She was playing in the garden. There were twenty-three fish in the pond, and she'd given each of them a name so she could speak to them individually, except some of them looked the same, so she sometimes ended up having the wrong conversation with them. Did they mind when she got their names wrong? She doubted it.

Earlier that morning she'd annoyed Dada by charging indoors wielding a hammer and shouting, "Help! Come quick!" He was putting the vacuum cleaner back under the stairs at the time, and stood up too quickly, banging his head on the low beam.

"Jesus Christ!" he said, rubbing his head, and she almost laughed because he'd sworn.

"Quick, Dada! You need to rescue the fish. They're dying!"

Hannah could tell he didn't know what to do first—see to the painful lump on the back of his head, or see to her. And it was all because the water in the fish pond had frozen over, and she'd thought the fish couldn't breathe. They'd looked so pathetic beneath the surface, swimming as slowly as the oldies in the leisure centre. When Dada finally got to the bottom of the reason for the mayhem, he'd not been impressed.

"They don't need to breathe air like us, for god's sake!" he'd shouted, a bit unnecessarily she thought. "Put the bloody hammer back and don't go smashing the ice—you'll give them a heart attack!"

She'd forgiven him for shouting, because the lump on his head looked painful, and he'd needed to sit for a minute or two holding a bag of frozen peas to it.

Anyway, she was feeling a bit lonely, because he was busy working in his office. Also, she suddenly remembered about Connor in her class calling her *moon face* the week before and how it made her feel sad. Even though she loved looking at the moon, and watching how it changed shape and mood, she didn't want to have the same face as it. She'd told Mr. Andrews, and he'd made Connor say sorry, but Hannah had watched Connor's eyes as he said it, so she knew he hadn't meant it.

It made her feel different when she got called names, and she didn't want to be different. Sometimes she wished she had neat handwriting like Erin, or she was quick at answering maths questions like James, or even that she was able to plait her own hair like Millie. "Never mind," she said to the fish, "I'm a lot like Eliza Doolittle." Saying it out loud made her feel a bit better.

She heard a tapping sound coming from The Lane. She picked her way over to the gap in the fence, from where the sound had come, and listened. It came again … a rapid drumming noise. She was sure it must be a woodpecker, only woodpeckers made a sound like that, but she was too far away to see.

A tiny flip of guilt leapt in her tummy as she ran around the cottage to The Lane. In no time at all, she reached the other side of the gap in the fence. She sat on the ground and listened. Nothing— then a scurry as a grey squirrel sped along a fallen branch a little distance into the trees. It sat there, munching on whatever it held in its paws, and watched her defiantly, daring her to try and take its food away.

"*Drrrr, drrrr.*" There it was again. It sounded like a jar of marbles spilling over. The bird perched high up on the branch of an oak, and it *was* a woodpecker. Black-and-white, with a red tummy, it drummed its beak against the branch as fast as one of those drills used to break up roads—the really noisy ones—except it wasn't as loud, so she didn't need to cover her ears.

Hannah watched in fascination as it drummed at incredible speed. "Cnocell y coed," she whispered. It was one of the few Welsh words she'd managed to learn so far—woodpecker. She remembered it because she liked the sound of the word, though she had to practise it quite a few times before she got it right. In Welsh, the word for woodpecker sounded like the sound it made, cnoc—knock.

Dada worried about her having to learn Welsh. She knew it was one of the reasons they hadn't moved to Wales sooner, but he needn't have worried. Most of the time they spoke English in school, and Mr. Andrews told her she wasn't to worry if she didn't pick it up. He explained that many of the children in her class had been learning Welsh since they'd started school, so they were bound to be streets ahead of her. She didn't know which streets most of them lived in, and in any case, she wasn't worried about it.

"Cnocell y coed, cnocell y coed," she repeated over and over. The woodpecker flew to another tree, further up The Lane. Without a moment's hesitation Hannah followed, stealthy as a spy, because she didn't want to frighten it off.

It wasn't Hannah who scared the bird away, nor was it the squirrel. It was the wolf. All of a sudden, she found herself face to face with it, and froze. Only the width of The Lane separated them. Where had it come from? She hadn't heard it approach. Her heart beat loud and fast in her chest. Dada would worry if he could hear her heart, because she'd needed a little operation on it when she was a baby. *Stupid Hannah!* She should never have returned to The Lane alone. Her chin quivered. But she was unable to move, unable to run away. It crossed her mind that she might never see Dada again.

The wolf approached, one huge paw at a time. It didn't look frightened at all. So close now. Hannah could see the droplets of moisture on its big black nose and smell its steamy breath as it greeted the cold air. She heard a small sound—like a mewing sob—and realized it came from her.

The wolf was within touching distance. Hannah froze and covered her face. Her legs trembled and threatened to give way. Other than its rhythmic breathing—in-out, in-out, it made no sound as it circled her. It pushed against her with its nose. *Sniff, sniff, sniff.* She squeezed her eyes shut tight. It pushed its sniffing muzzle into her tummy, her back, her legs and then it happened. She couldn't help it. Her bladder let go, and a trickle of warm wee flowed down her legs and pooled inside her wellies. She began to cry—out loud this time—but she was still unable to scream.

Then something strange happened. The wolf sniffed her wet legs, curiously, before squirting its own scent over the puddle forming at her ankles—sickly sweet, yet bitter, like the dark-green plant that grew in the far corner of her garden. Then it stretched and yawned, as if bored, and skulked off back to the wood, this time without even giving Hannah a second glance.

***

Bleddyn was concerned. She hadn't wet herself in almost two years. Perhaps she was ill—a water infection, maybe. She'd always been prone to them. Or was she worried about something? Perhaps the move was proving too much for her to cope with. He should never have uprooted her at such an impressionable age. And he was sure she'd been crying. Her eyes were still red, and dried snot streaked her nose and cheeks.

She wouldn't have it; she insisted what upset her was the fact she'd wet herself. She'd got stuck in the shed—that was her excuse. The door handle had jammed, and she wasn't able to turn it to get out in time. It had frightened her, the thought of being stuck and him unable to hear her call. She wouldn't look him in the eye as she said it though, and she was quiet for the remainder of the day.

He ran his hands through his hair, exhausted. The pressure from his editor to get the latest piece finished seemed like a mountain to climb at the moment. He'd been so busy with the move and trying to ensure Hannah was ferried to school and drama club and so on. Perhaps he hadn't paid her enough attention of late. He'd have to make a conscious effort to watch her more closely from now on.

He tossed and turned, mulling it over. Perhaps he should talk to Ffion—see if she'd noticed anything.

The following morning Hannah was back to her usual bright and cheerful self, and he felt more at ease.

"Hey, Missie, how about we have a day out?" There were two days remaining of half term, and he'd been so tied up with work, he hadn't taken her anywhere so far.

"Ooh, yes, yes!" Hannah clapped her hands, and beamed at him across the breakfast table.

"Where do you fancy? Any ideas? We can ring Aunty Ffion and invite Evan if you like."

"Oh yes, Dada. Ring her now, ring her now!"

"Perhaps we should decide where we're going first, so Evan can make his mind up."

She paused for a second. "I know! I know! The Gelert place. Let's go see the Gelert place."

He'd been about to protest. The village of Beddgelert was more than a two-hour drive away, and they'd made a pact to wait until summer. He saw her beaming face and knew she would not have considered the length of the journey, nor the time it would take to get there and back.

Oh, what the hell. It was a beautiful day. If they set off soon, they'd have time to see it before dusk. He didn't mind driving back in the dark.

BIRTHDAY

With a week to go until Hannah's tenth birthday, Bleddyn was disappointed Emily had not yet made contact. Since they'd separated, when Hannah was two, Emily would invite her to visit two or three times a year, except for Hannah's birthday, which was the one consistent occasion she'd spend time with her mother.

As the years progressed things became more and more strained, and Hannah seemed less enthusiastic with each visit. Afterwards, it often took a week or so for her to return to her usual self.

This year was no different—if anything it was worse—for Bleddyn sensed Hannah's anxiety increase throughout the week. He assumed, correctly, the older she became, the greater awareness of time she had, so was able to anticipate the forthcoming visit. As the date came closer, he lost count of the number of times she'd asked whether or not she was going to see her mother on her birthday. "Would you like to?" he'd asked, to which she'd merely shrugged.

He found it strange, as despite her seeming reluctance, Hannah still appeared to worship Emily. Did she love her mother, or was it admiration of her career choice—hero worship almost? Perhaps she loved her but at the same time found it difficult to be away from home, away from routine and him. He knew such anxious behaviour was a common trait for children with Down syndrome, nevertheless it concerned him.

Whatever her reasons, he had resolved from the time of the split to encourage a positive relationship between Emily and Hannah, while at the same time refrain from forcing Hannah to do something she didn't want.

He was relieved when two days later, his agent, Tom, rang to ask for a face-to-face meeting the following week. It would mean having to travel to London two days after Hannah's birthday. Hopefully they could kill two birds with one stone, plus it would mean her spending her actual birthday at home with him. He pondered over who he should discuss it with first—Hannah or Emily. He knew once Hannah had an event planned in her head, she found it stressful if the plan was thwarted, and so he decided it best to speak to Emily first, though why she'd left it so late this year to make arrangements was anyone's guess. He'd send her a text, to test the waters, rather than phone.

Busying himself with preparing tea, he awaited Emily's reply. He'd begun to suspect she might be beginning to relinquish ties altogether. His stomach churned at what it might do to Hannah. If Emily intended to push her aside it would have been better to do so when Hannah was still too young to understand. All he could do was to hope this was not the case.

Reaching for the salt, his eye caught sight of the pile of photographs sitting on the kitchen shelf where he'd left them after she'd brought them home from school the previous week. The one on top, of Emily and Hannah sitting on adjacent swings at the park, had been taken a year earlier, on Hannah's ninth birthday. Emily's conceited smile seemed to mock him. Although the physical distance between the swings was next to nothing, the emotional distance between the two of them appeared far greater.

A few weeks back he'd needed to dig out the photos so Hannah could prove to some of her disbelieving peers that her mother really was the actress, Emily Henrikkson. Not that the other children had heard of her, of course, but Hannah had told them about her all-singing, all-dancing star of a mother, and for reasons he didn't wish to consider, they'd failed to believe her. It tore him apart—the fact that some of them called her a liar. He had waited anxiously for her to come out of class, to see whether providing the evidence had calmed or further provoked the situation.

From what he gathered, one of the girls in her class, who was apparently *kind* but whom, he imagined, was also a bit of a ringleader, had put the doubters in their place by emphasising the fact that Hannah and her mother shared the exact same hair colour.

There were other signs, too, of late to suggest Hannah might be having a few difficulties at school. He hoped it was down to her age. Of course, the prepubescent stage was difficult for any parent, so why should it be different for him?

Stirring the chilli with one hand, he checked his phone. Why the hell hadn't Emily replied? Bloody law unto herself.

He took a few deep breaths. He must try to focus on the positive, and not get wound up. At least Hannah was enjoying drama club. He considered himself fortunate to have found such an inclusive and considerate group of people within their catchment. The research he'd carried out beforehand had proved worthwhile. It had led him to discover the group she attended was well established, highly rated, and that some of its older students had even gone on to do professional acting and dancing roles in theatre and television.

It seemed as if Hannah was destined for the stage. He'd always encouraged her creativity and would continue to do so. He hoped it was what she truly wanted, and she wasn't simply emulating the success of her mother. It was all he could do in any case—encourage, and continue to motivate, while at the same time allow her to make her own discoveries and ultimately her own decisions. He would never give up on her.

***

A week later, he pulled up in front of Emily's apartment, near Covent Garden, at around ten. They'd set off before dawn, and Hannah slept for the first hour. Bleddyn took it as a positive sign, presuming if she was relaxed enough to sleep, she couldn't be feeling too anxious. He was glad he was picking her up again later, and she wouldn't be staying the night, even though she usually slept over on her birthday visit.

"We're here, Missie. Come on, grab your bag."

She pouted as he opened the passenger door. Her face burned hot and little beads of sweat glistened on her top lip.

"You okay? You look a little flustered."

She scowled. "Just hot. What time are you picking me up?"

Her words spoke volumes.

Emily stood at the counter top, sipping a bitter-tasting herbal tea. She was a mere whip of a thing—skinny and fragile as the day they'd met. However, there was a strength and determination in her which belied her appearance. He knew how single-minded she could be. It was good to have ambition, but her behaviour often bordered on narcissism. Hannah had inherited her mother's small stature, her pale-green eyes and dominant Titian locks, but in personality they were chalk and cheese, which wasn't surprising, considering how little influence she'd had over Hannah's life.

"Hannah, go and wash your hands and face, you're all sweaty," Emily said, the moment she set eyes on her.

Was that the best she was capable of? Most mothers, having not seen their child for six months, wouldn't care less about a bit of sweat and grime. She hadn't kissed her yet, either. He watched Hannah as she stood in the kitchen doorway, clenching and unclenching her fists in her habitual manner.

"Come on—we'll go together." He took hold of her sweaty palm and led the way to the bathroom.

One thing was certain—Emily seemed edgier, more flustered, and as he was leaving, she followed him to the door. "I need to talk to you about something," she said, in a voice close to a whisper. "When you collect her later—we'll have a coffee."

His meeting with Tom was scheduled for eleven. Tom's office was just a few miles away, but with the damned traffic in the city Bleddyn knew even the shortest of journeys could be painfully slow. They'd arranged to have lunch together after they'd discussed future work opportunities.

It was 3:30 before he returned to Emily's. Greetings over, she distracted Hannah by producing a trunk of her old theatre costumes, and while Hannah was in the bedroom trying them on, she shot the bullet. So he'd guessed correctly; she was returning home to Sweden, and it would be a permanent move. She was tired of theatre, she said, and there were far more opportunities in television back home. And besides, she'd met someone, or rather reignited a relationship with an old flame and they were moving in together.

He couldn't care less about the relationship—he'd been past jealousy for a long time—but how on earth would he break the news to Hannah? Of course, he'd asked whether or not she'd spoken to Hannah about it, to which she'd replied, "I imagine it might be best coming from you."

Why were narcissists so often cowards? Yet again it would be down to him to deliver the blow.

Trust

Hannah had thought about it a lot these past weeks. The trouble was, the more she thought about it, the more it puzzled her. If the wolf was dangerous—if it really wanted to eat her—why hadn't it done so? Was there a chance it was just curious? Might it even want to be her friend?

April, and the garden was changing. Every day Hannah witnessed something different. She'd not had much of a garden in Peterborough, not compared with this. This new garden was a big slice of nature—all wild and free—with only the bits nearest the house tamed.

Dada had bought her a real camera for her tenth birthday and was teaching her to use it. The days were getting longer too, which meant that after school she was able to spend some time outdoors—at least when it wasn't pouring with rain. It rained more often here in Wales than it did in England.

It was the snowdrops she'd noticed first. They'd popped up some time ago, all around the garden. They looked like ballerinas with their delicate white caps. Sad ballerinas though, because their heads were always drooping. They reminded her of the ballet, *Giselle*, which

Dada had taken her to see at Aberystwyth Theatre after Christmas.

The story was about a poor girl who loved to dance but who had a weak heart. Well, Hannah's heart was a bit weak, but it didn't stop her dancing. She remembered it being a sad story, and she hadn't understood all of it. Still, she wasn't sorry Dada had taken her because the dancers were incredible.

This week her whole garden was covered in daffodils. Spattered dabs of bright yellow everywhere—her favourite colour. She knew daffodils were important in Wales because a few weeks back she'd worn one to school for St. David's Day. Some kids had worn tiny leeks made of felt, and a few kids forgot and hadn't worn anything at all. Miss Morgan had brought spares, so they wouldn't feel left out.

Last week, under the hazel tree, she'd found a stinky plant. Dada had called it wild garlic and had cut some to put in the spaghetti bolognese. The wild garlic had smelled a bit like a leek.

Now, when she watched the sky, she often noticed red kites flying overhead. There were two in particular that flew over the wood and above her garden. Dada said they were a breeding pair, and they probably had a nest site with chicks up in the wood. He told her that in the summer she would see them teaching their young to hunt. She looked forward to it. She loved to listen to the sound of their call as they warned other birds to stay away from their territory. It was a haunting sound, a bit like a scream.

Through the fence in her garden, she'd witnessed the changes in The Lane as it had sprung to life. She stood at the bottom, contemplating the path that climbed ahead. The bed of leaves had disappeared—rotted to nothing, or blown away on the wind, and the floor was littered with dead twigs that made a snapping sound as she walked. Would they give her away? She stole a glance towards the cottage to check.

Either side of the pathway was strewn with daffodils. They must be very clever flowers, because Dada had told Aunty Ffion no one had been in The Lane for years, which meant they couldn't have been planted. Many of the trees in the wood were in full leaf and proudly modelled their new outfits in various shades of green, and the banking to her left was peppered with rabbit holes. She picked up a long twig and poked it deep into one of the burrows, hoping a rabbit might pop out to see what was going on, but she was disappointed when nothing happened. She remembered the story of *Alice in Wonderland* and about how Alice had fallen down a rabbit hole. Hannah didn't think she would be likely to fall down this hole. It was too small.

Before she knew it, she had climbed the path as far as the gap in her fence. She glanced back at her cottage. She knew she should go straight back, but today The Lane didn't seem threatening at all. Perhaps it was the soothing spring sunshine. Maybe the wolf had gone away with the winter, perhaps to snowy Sweden, where Mamma lived. Her shoulders slumped when she thought about Mamma, and Sweden.

She would continue a little further, as far as where she'd spotted the woodpecker, then she would return home.

There they were! The pair of red kites circled overhead, crossing the path where she stood. *Wheeoo, whee, whee, whee, oo,* they cried. Were they warning her away? Did they view her as a predator? She hoped not. She would never harm a bird. Then, carried on the warm breeze, a different sound—a whisper … *Hannah.* It couldn't be

Dada, because it didn't sound like his voice at all. Was she imagining it? It came again. *Hannah*, a breath of wind in the trees.

She stood still and silent, alert as the kites, her eyes searching all around.

A rustle from the branches; two amber nuggets. For a moment, she thought it appeared smaller, then she realized it wore less fur. She knew about dogs shedding their winter coats because she'd seen it happen to Jipp. Except it wasn't a dog—not really. It was a wolf. Why was she not afraid? Tail aloft, it sniffed the air before approaching her, head up and shoulders back, all confident.

The closer it got, the more unsure she felt, and yet something in the pit of her stomach told her she had nothing to fear. It rubbed against her legs, as if it wanted to be stroked. Hannah let the tips of her fingers stroke the warm fur, soft as her blanket straight out the wash. Its scent was musky, dog-like, its breath a gentle puff of warm wind. It licked her fingers, softly, tickling, making her giggle.

"You're not a bad wolf," she heard herself say. "You won't eat me, will you?"

In reply, it nuzzled her arms, requesting more contact.

She stroked its back, noticing the highlights in its fur—umber, mahogany, and ochre, mingled with shades of grey. Warm as toast, its muscles rippled in response to her touch.

"I know a story about a wolf," she said, her voice little more than a whisper. "In fact, I know lots of stories 'bout wolves." The wood had fallen silent, holding its breath in anticipation of what might happen next. She remembered how the birds had suddenly stopped singing all that time ago, the first time she'd heard the rustle from her garden.

And then, to her astonishment, the wolf spoke. "And I'm certain the wolf is evil in every one of those stories."

She hadn't expected that. It threw her off guard, causing her spine to tingle and the fine downy hairs on her arms to stand on end. She slumped down on the stone wall in shock.

"You can talk?"

"Indeed." It sat beside her, panting, its focus not on her, but away into the trees, lost in thought.

She pictured Dada, and a wave of guilt washed over her. He'd drummed it into her not to talk to strangers, and she'd always listened. Now here she was, not just talking to a stranger, but to a strange wolf.

The wolf seemed to sense her unease and so, as she moved to stand, it spoke again, calmly, pleading almost. "Before you go, may I tell you a story, Hannah? Listen carefully, for this story bears an important message."

She didn't know what to say, so instead she nodded, the smallest of nods.

As it told its story, it studied her closely, so she was able to see how its heart felt at the telling. Its amber eyes, flecked with blue, twinkled as it spoke.

"There's a place not far from here called Devil's Bridge," the wolf said.

She gasped and put her hand to her mouth, shocked at the word *devil.* The wolf's voice was calm, yet it wasn't the voice that had whispered her name, because that voice had been smooth as silk. The wolf's voice had a slight husky tone, like crunchy peanut butter, yet something about it suggested it was a female wolf. More butter than peanut, if that made sense.

"Oh, don't worry. The Devil's not there now," it said with a throaty chuckle. "Long, long ago, he came to visit Wales. He'd heard how beautiful it was here and was sorely tempted to see it for himself. Remember, the Devil is always on the lookout for new souls." The wolf fell silent.

Had the wolf finished? If so, it wasn't much of a story because nothing happened.

The wolf yawned, its mouth a pink-and-black cavern, and shook its huge head before continuing. "The Devil came across a little old lady who seemed very upset. He asked her what the matter was, and she told him her cow had wandered across to the other side of the river, and she couldn't get it back."

The wolf glanced at Hannah, to ensure she was listening. "'What you need here is a bridge,' said the Devil. 'Go home, and when you return in the morning, I will have built one for you.' The old lady was thrilled. 'All I ask in return, is that I get to keep the first living thing that crosses the bridge.'"

Hannah nodded. "Fair enough."

The wolf observed her for several moments before continuing. "When the old lady returned the following morning, there stood a fine bridge. Expecting her to thank him before crossing the bridge to bring back her cow, the Devil was excited. However, the old lady was wily as a fox."

"What's wily?"

"Clever, Hannah. It means thinking carefully before doing something that might harm you … Just as the devil was licking his lips at the prospect of claiming another soul, the old woman whipped out a loaf of bread from her apron, and threw it across to the other side of the bridge. Swift as a hare, her little dog ran across to retrieve the bread. So you see, instead of claiming the life of the woman, all the Devil got was a little dog."

The story had ended. Hannah knew because the wolf didn't say any more. She liked the story, though she wasn't sure about the ending. She didn't like the idea of the Devil having the poor little dog's soul just because the dog wanted the bread. After all, it was an easy mistake for the dog to make.

She paused before speaking, her forehead lined with indecision. "Why did the Devil want the dog?" she asked, not sure she wanted to hear the answer.

The wolf stretched its front paws, stuck its bottom in the air, and yawned again. The tail end of its yawn made a piercing whine that hurt her ears. She quickly covered them with her hands. A thin strand of saliva stretched from the roof of the wolf's mouth to its tongue. And those teeth! Why was she not afraid?

"Who knows, Hannah? Sometimes the ability to take the lives of the innocent is enough for those who are evil."

"Suppose," she said, not wanting to show she hadn't understood.

"We must always be on the lookout for those who try to trick us, Hannah. Do you understand? Those who pretend to do us a favour when they actually mean us harm."

She watched its eyes. They still seemed kind. "Thank you, wolf. And I'm not afraid of you anymore. When I come again, will you tell me another story?"

"When you return, Hannah, when you return. Now, you'd best be off or you'll get into trouble. But remember what I told you."

A CONFIDENCE

Deryth Morgan studied Hannah's back as she pretended to choose a book. Hannah seemed on edge this morning, as if she wanted to avoid engaging in anything too close. It wasn't difficult to read the signs—Hannah might think she didn't notice, but experience had taught her well, though how she might get Hannah to open up eluded her at present. She seemed to have pulled away lately. She wanted to help her, but was still unsure of the best plan of action.

During play, Deryth watched from the classroom window to see how Hannah interacted with the other children when she was not on playground duty. Was she being bullied or isolated? If so, she'd do something about it. She knew bullying was often a secretive issue, and children of Hannah's age were less inclined to tell tales for fear of making the situation worse.

Hannah was easy to spot, as she was smaller in stature than most of the other children, which was typical of those with Down syndrome. Fifteen minutes of observation allayed her worries a little, as much to her relief, Hannah seemed engaged in the game of freeze tag. She was neither ignored, nor particularly sought out by the others. There had to be something else worrying her, then. She was timetabled for a one-to-one library session with Hannah after break. Perhaps with the right encouragement she might get to the bottom of it.

***

"Dada! You're late!" Hannah hurled herself at her father and clung to his jacket.

"I'm so sorry. An important phone call came in as I was about to leave, and I—well I had to answer it."

"Don't worry, it happens to everyone once in a while." Deryth was glad of the chance to speak with him without other children or parents around. She had spoken to Mr. Andrews, and he was happy for her to have a word with Hannah's dad.

"Keep the tone light," he'd suggested. "Or, if you prefer, I'll have a word with him myself." Deryth didn't mind doing it, especially since it was she who spent most time with Hannah. Now, instead of having to phone him, which always seemed more official, she could have a word with him in person.

"Hannah, why don't you go and get your laptop from the library to show your dad the wonderful story you've been writing?" she said, with a friendly wink in Bleddyn's direction.

"Ooh, yes! I won't be a sec. Wait there, Dada."

As soon as Hannah was out of sight, Deryth turned to him. "I hope you won't think I'm interfering, Mr. Lewis." His expression darkened. "Today, Hannah told me about her mother emigrating to Sweden." He flinched. "It's just she hasn't been her bubbly self these past few weeks, so I asked if something was troubling her—I hope you don't mind." She noticed him squirm and pitied him.

"Not at all. I've been meaning to tell you myself, but—well, you know how it is." He flushed.

"Don't worry, I understand. We're here to help you know—in any way we can. Would you mind us speaking about it, to Hannah I mean, if she brings it up again?"

"No, no, not at all. It's difficult to know what to say to her sometimes. I mean, what can you say to a child whose mother has practically disowned her?"

Hannah reappeared, carrying her laptop. "Look, Dada. I'm writing a story about a wolf, a *good* wolf."

He grinned. "She has a thing about wolves. I don't know how many times I've told her the story of Gelert—and it has to be the exact same version every time." He took the laptop from Hannah and began to read in earnest. "How much help did she have with this? It's very good."

"Just spelling and punctuation. The ideas and descriptions are all her own."

"This is incredible, Hannah. Could I read it again when it's finished? Tell you what—we'll get it printed and make a book, shall we? You can draw pictures to go with it."

Hannah beamed. "Yes. And we'll make a special cover for it too, with a picture of a wolf on the front—a wolf with blue bits in its eyes."

He laughed, and ruffled her hair. "Come on—we'd best be off. We've kept Miss Morgan too long already."

"Not at all, and remember, we're here to help."

She watched them from the classroom window as they walked towards the car, Hannah's hand swinging in his as she skipped beside him. They were deep in conversation. Wouldn't it be nice if all parents were as caring? The world would be a better place.

***

Bleddyn paid lip service to Hannah's chatter as they walked to the car. His thoughts were on Miss Morgan. As she'd sent Hannah to fetch the laptop she'd winked at him, a teacher-to-parent wink, and the tightness in his gut had eased. Hannah was right—Miss Morgan did have the most incredible blue eyes. He felt the heat rise to his face. What on earth was he thinking? He'd not noticed any woman for the past eight years, and now—Hannah's classroom assistant? It concerned him, the fact that she'd found it necessary to speak with him about Hannah. Yes, he'd noticed she'd seemed a little quiet of late, a little subdued perhaps, but he'd not paid it too much attention. Come to think of it, her behaviour had changed since her birthday visit with Emily. He'd need to keep a closer check on her from now on.

***

During the journey home, Hannah's thoughts returned to the story she was writing. Of course, neither Dada nor Miss Morgan knew the wolf was real. They believed it was all in her imagination, and that was precisely what she wanted them to think. And what was more, after she'd returned home from speaking with the wolf, she'd remembered it calling her by her name. How on earth had it known? The puzzle grew larger and larger, like one of those five-hundred-piece jigsaws she'd never be able to complete.

"What's up, Hannah? You seem a little lost."

She shrugged. "Watching the cars." She didn't want to tell him what was really on her mind. She didn't want to say she went walking in The Lane, and that she'd been many times, ever since they'd moved in. And she certainly didn't want to tell him about the talking wolf.

"Sure you're okay?"

He was waiting for an answer. She'd have to come up with something or he'd worry, and she didn't want that. She'd have to fib.

"Thinking, that's all."

"About what? You seem a little sad."

From the passenger window, her eyes traced the route of the river beyond the fields as it widened and narrowed, snaking into the distance. It seemed so free, as though it were able to do exactly as it pleased, without needing to worry about anything.

"We're learning about the war in school. It's very sad, and lots of people died in it."

"And learning about it is making you feel sad, is it?"

She hesitated. "A bit … I don't understand it much."

"Tell you what, how about we learn a bit more about it at home together. That should help you understand what happened."

"Yes please, Dada. Can we make a book?" That seemed to make Dada happier and got her off the hook—at least for now.

Dada always helped her when she was stuck, and it wasn't a lie—she hadn't fully understood what Mr. Andrews had taught them so far. She knew there'd been a bad man called Hitler, and that he'd wanted to be the king of every country in the whole wide world. She also knew the boss of England at the time was an old man with a fat face who made a rude sign with his fingers. She couldn't remember his name—something about a church—but she didn't think he behaved like he was in charge, more like he was messing about.

However, one of the things she'd learned had made her especially sad. The Hitler man had been cruel to lots of people called Jews, and also other people too, all because they were different. Jack Evans had asked Mr. Andrews what other kinds of people were treated cruelly, and Hannah noticed Mr. Andrews seemed a bit uncomfortable, as if he didn't want to say too much about it. She saw him glance at her, like she might be one of them, except she couldn't have been, because she wasn't even born then.

All the same, his look made her feel especially sad, but she couldn't explain why. It reminded her of when she'd go somewhere with Dada and someone would say something like, "Oh poor thing," or even something like, "Isn't she funny," when she wasn't being funny at all. She knew such people made Dada cross because his body would go all stiff, and his forehead would get two deep lines like the number eleven. Usually, he wouldn't say anything to them, though she sometimes felt it was because she was there, and perhaps he would have said something rude to them if she wasn't. She knew people said strange things because she had Down syndrome, but it wasn't fair, because if she said something rude to someone, Dada always told her off, even in front of them.

Sometimes she wanted to tell Dada everything, but she couldn't. For one, she knew he wouldn't believe her—nobody would—and she knew he'd worry. She also knew he'd stop her from visiting The Lane ever again, and that wouldn't do at all.

Scent

Early May and the top of Hannah's garden—the steepest and wildest part—resembled an oil painting. It filled her with joy to be outdoors. Pale pink blossoms adorned the three apple trees, while red campion, dog violet, and several other species of wildflower blanketed the ground. Enchanting.

Dada warned Hannah not to touch them, as some were poisonous, and others could irritate your skin. She wouldn't have picked them in any case, as it made her feel cruel picking flowers. She preferred to see them in the ground than in a vase.

She knew Mamma loved white lilies. Each time she visited, Mamma would have a bouquet arranged in a plain glass vase. They smelled horrid—like cat's pee, and they'd caused a rash on Hannah's arm by dripping sticky, gooey sap on her. She'd heard Dada tell Aunty Ffion that her mother should have more sense, knowing Hannah had sensitive skin, but Mamma had told her off for touching them in the first place.

The ground layer of the wood wore a dense carpet of bluebells. Dada told her that ringing a bluebell called the fairies, but she knew it was against the law to pick them.

She preferred the other story—the one that named them harebells instead of bluebells. This was because witches were able to turn into hares and hide themselves among the flowers. She would take a little walk, in order to see them up close. Dada wouldn't know because he was too busy working.

As usual, the bottom of The Lane was in shade. The front of the house faced south, casting a shadow behind it for most of the day. Hannah climbed the path until she was adjacent with her garden. She preferred the warmth of the sun to its shade, because it helped her to see things more clearly. Dada had taken her to the optician the previous week, and she was waiting for her new glasses. She'd chosen a pale yellow frame, the same colour as the straw house in her *Three Little Pigs* book. Would the wolf think the glasses suited her? She hoped so. It hadn't appeared the last time she'd come, which was a bit disappointing. If it didn't come today, she'd try not to be disappointed. She'd rather it see her when she was wearing her new glasses, anyway.

She sat on the wall, gazing into the wood beyond. The canopy of trees was in full leaf, so despite the strong sunshine, there was still lots of dark in the wood. The bluebells sat bunched together, whispering secrets in the warm breeze. They reminded her of the nasty girls in the playground, those who always seemed to be whispering things about others. Gently, so as not to hurt it, she shook the stem of a lone bluebell between finger and thumb, and tried to imagine the fairies gathering, but it was no good—she'd not believed in fairies since she was about seven. Magic only worked if you believed in it, but then she'd never have believed she'd have spoken to a wolf, so you never knew.

You needed to be still to experience the best things, that's what she'd learned about nature. And so she sat on the path and watched … and waited … and listened.

Within seconds, a speckled comma butterfly visited to feed on the bluebell nectar, its auburn wings in sharp contrast to the blue flowers. Last week, Miss Morgan had told her about the comma butterfly to help her remember where to add the punctuation mark to her wish list.

"Imagine the butterfly flitting from one flower to the next … and the next, Hannah," she'd said. "It takes a little break each time it stops."

Miss Morgan had shown her a video of the comma butterfly on the internet. How was it possible to know all the stuff Miss Morgan knew? And Dada, too. He knew loads of stuff. And Mr. Andrews did, and Erin. She hoped she'd get more clever as she grew up. Miss Morgan was the most clever at knowing about nature though—well her and Dada. Who would win, if they had a competition?

Mr. Andrews had asked all the children to write a list of five wishes, but only one of them was allowed to be an object, like a new phone or something. The others were things like what you wanted to be when you grew up, a place you'd like to visit, and stuff like that. He'd asked them to make one of their wishes *from the heart,* something to do with a feeling.

Apparently, Millie had come up with a clever one. She wished the people in charge of the world would work together to stop climb-it change. Well, something like that anyway. Mr. Andrews said Mille's wish was thoughtful and for the good of the world, and everyone gave her a clap.

Hannah's list consisted of one—tickets to go and see her favourite singer, Eliza Doolittle, in concert. Two—to be an actor when she grew up. Three—to be able to do good animal impressions. Four—to have Millie and Megan round to tea some time, and five—her *heart* one, was to always be happy. She'd even remembered to put in the commas with the help of a cardboard cutout of the comma butterfly Miss Morgan made for her, and Miss

Morgan drew a smiley face in Hannah's book to show how pleased she was. She knew her last wish was a cop-out. She'd wanted to write that she wished Mamma would come back from Sweden, and maybe even get back with Dada, but she didn't want to say it in front of everyone.

Hannah didn't want to think about sad things. The Lane helped her mind weave a pathway to happier thoughts. She lay curled on the sun-kissed ground, and closed her eyes against the fierce rays above.

Hannah. Just once—the same voice as before. Up she sprang, all ears.

Where had it come from?

And again, *Hannah.* Her name floated down The Lane on the warm breeze, straight into her ears. She was certain it wasn't the wolf's voice because she remembered the difference. Although she wasn't good at making her own voice sound like something else, she was good at playing sound bingo. She'd played games like that since she was little, when Dada had taken her to speech clinic every Friday.

She climbed the path a little further, stopping every few seconds to listen. As she was about to give up and retrace her steps, it came again.

Hannah … Come.

The silent wood made her shiver. Moments earlier, as she'd lain on the path with her eyes closed, she'd heard all kinds of sounds—like the high-pitched *chook* of the blackbird, and the repeated, rhythmic song of the thrush. Now, there was nothing.

Up ahead, the crown of a catkin-laden alder shivered, as though disturbed. Delicate, invisible feet marked a trail through the bed of bluebells, right to the edge of the pathway—the lightest of footsteps, for the flowers recovered instantly. Hannah watched closely, hardly daring to breathe. Whatever it was, it remained at the boundary, separated from her by a length of barbed wire. Then a scent carried on the breeze. Hannah filled her lungs, holding the fragrance inside her. The scent seemed familiar somehow, and yet she couldn't say what it reminded her of.

And then the wolf appeared—swiftly—darting towards her from higher up in the wood. Snarling—its fur all bristled—it bared its teeth, though not at her. The enchantment of the moment vanished in an instant. Startled back to reality, Hannah felt unsteady on her feet. She was pleased to see the wolf, and yet its sudden presence broke the spell.

"Go home, Hannah. It's not safe."

It sounded anxious—angry almost. It hardly glanced at her as it spoke. Instead, it focussed its attention on the wood, ears erect, pacing, listening.

"But—" Hannah began, but the wolf didn't want to talk to her today.

"Now, Hannah. Go now!" It cut her off—rudely—before she even finished her sentence, then, sensing her confusion, it glanced at her, its focus still on the wood. "I will explain when I see you next."

So Hannah did as she was told, though she felt a bit cheated, as if she'd woken from a beautiful dream.

She ran home and went straight to her bedroom, closing the door behind her. She needed to think. She lay on the bed, the comfort of the warm sunshine pouring through her window, cradling her. The wolf had been her friend, but she'd witnessed a different side to its character. Although she knew the wolf's anger was not directed at her, it had spoiled the moment. But what moment? What *had* been there, watching her from the wood?

With a groan, she reached her arm round the side of the bed and slid out the trunk. Dada believed she loved the costumes because she liked dressing up, but the truth went far deeper.

She pulled out the pale cream dress, the one Mamma had worn when she'd been Eliza Doolittle. The silk was almost the exact same shade as Mamma's skin—a cool, creamy white. Holding it close, she breathed in Mamma's scent.

***

The she-wolf, Tarian, crouched low, panting, its steely eyes scanning the trees and its ears pointing skyward, listening. No sign of the witch now. She'd vanished the moment she'd sensed the wolf. So she wasn't yet ready to do battle?

Gradually the woodland birds returned, the courageous kites spearheading the flock. Soon the glass-button eyes of a wood mouse peeped from its hiding place in the roots of an ash, while a thirsty brimstone butterfly suckled nectar from an early purple orchid. They should be careful, especially the weak among them, for she would grant them no mercy.

Tarian knew precisely what the witch, Rhiamon, wanted with Hannah, and what lengths she would go to in order to succeed. She would likely take the child hostage, then bargain for her freedom. But the witch could not cross the boundary, not with the runes protecting it. Therefore she would need to persuade Hannah to come to her. Hannah must not fall under her spell. Tarian must keep Hannah safe, no matter what.

It was true that she did not possess the same skills of trickery as Rhiamon. In comparison, her own strength lay in her physical bravery and sheer determination. Tarian would need to rely on Hannah making the right decisions, which would not be an easy task. She would need to tread carefully, take things one step at a time. If she rushed in, she feared she might forfeit Hannah's trust.

Rhiamon would be in no hurry—of that Tarian was certain, for she knew she enjoyed the thrill of the chase as much as the kill.

For now, the wood resumed its calm. Tarian lay at the foot of an oak, one that had recently burst its spring leaves, considering what to do next. Rhiamon, with her lust for revenge and the ability to manipulate the vulnerable, was not an easy opponent. She never had been. Tarian had already witnessed how she put an end to those she considered weak, but she would not give up on Hannah. With one paw she nudged the roots of the oak, coaxing it awake. It was a wise old tree, perhaps it might help her devise a plan.

MISSING

May tumbled headlong into June, and the weather grew fiercely hot. Tarian had spent the morning in the shade of the oak, drifting in and out of a dream-filled slumber. Through sleepy lids, she observed Hannah in her garden. The child was alone again, technically speaking. But she wasn't really alone, for she sang and performed to an invisible audience, one that sat enthralled below her, in the imaginary auditorium in front of the raised deck. Perhaps Hannah was finally turning a corner and coming to terms with the loss of her mother.

Every now and then the sun caught the gold and copper tones of Hannah's hair as she danced, creating fine, dazzling shards of light. She wore it curled today. The resplendent tresses bounced and swayed in tune to her movements. She danced well, in sync to the rhythm of the tune that resonated from the speaker on the patio table in the corner. Tarian knew the song was one of Hannah's favourites, she'd heard her sing it on several occasions. While the notes she sang jarred at times, she had to award her full marks for effort. So what if she was a little out of tune. The sheer pleasure and determination on Hannah's face was what mattered most.

Tarian yawned and stretched, satisfied in the lazy heat of the day.

***

Hannah hadn't felt as excited as this since Dada had taken her to see Mamma in concert in London. Thursday night's auditions had gone well, and she'd secured the part of Jessica in the play, *Miss Nelson is Missing,* which her drama group were to perform in September.

The play was about a teacher who was so nice she failed to control the class. Carys, Hannah's drama teacher, had tweaked the script, and they were adding in some extra bits.

"Carys, could we sing 'Missing'?" Hannah had asked.

"You mean your favourite Eliza Doolittle song?"

Hannah nodded and held her hands in a prayer-like gesture.

"I don't see why not," Carys had said, then she'd asked if Hannah and the other girls would make up a dance routine to the song, and Hannah wasn't able to contain herself. She had hugged Carys so hard, she'd almost knocked her off her feet.

Jessica was one of the popular, pretty characters in the play, so Hannah couldn't believe her luck at being given the part. Dada said it wasn't luck and reminded her of the hard work she'd put in to prepare for the audition. She knew having Down syndrome meant she needed to work harder than other kids, but she didn't mind. Things like this made it all worthwhile.

Megan was to play a girl called Phoebe. Megan's part meant she had more lines to learn than Hannah, but otherwise all the singing and dancing was the same.

Even more exciting was the fact that today Megan was coming round to her house so they could practise together. It would be the first time she'd had a friend round since moving to Wales, and she thought she might burst with excitement the moment Megan arrived.

Earlier that morning, Hannah had persuaded Dada to curl her hair with the tongs so she looked even more like Eliza Doolittle. All right, so it hadn't turned out perfect, but it wasn't a bad effort … for Dada.

Megan's mum was dropping Megan off at around half one, so Hannah had spent the last hour in the garden with "Missing" on repeat, trying to come up with a routine. It was a bit frustrating at times, trying to fit the movements to the tune, but she hoped Megan would be pleased with what she'd come up with so far. It was hot in the garden, so she'd have to go in soon and get a drink.

***

Bleddyn sat on Hannah's bed, watching from her little window. He was so proud of her. She was a fighter, that much was certain. Despite the many pitfalls that inevitably came her way, she always managed to bounce back.

He'd spent the whole morning making sure the house was spick and span, because the last thing he wanted was Megan's mother thinking their home unsuitable for her daughter to visit. He'd met Megan's mother several times these past months as they'd ferried the girls to and from drama club, so it wasn't as if they didn't know each other. Yes, attitudes had changed over the years, of course they had, but there was still a sense of uncertainty whenever friends of Hannah's were invited round. It was a battle of sorts, for not only were they putting their child in the hands of a single man, but he had to admit, Hannah's Down syndrome could also be an issue. It made some adults wary of encouraging positive friendships with their own children.

The psychologists had been clear from the start, it would be he who would need to take the initiative in Hannah's social development. When she first attended school back in Peterborough, a few of her classmates had assumed she was younger than they were and had treated her like a little doll because of her short stature and the delay in her motor skills, but now she was older his concerns had more to do with the prospect of her feeling isolated.

Lately, he'd thought a lot about Emily and what motivated her behaviour. Ever since they'd met, he'd been aware of her egotistical tendencies. Still, he'd never expected her to abandon Hannah in the way she had. The pregnancy hadn't been planned, and it had taken Emily some time to get used to the fact they were going to be parents. Then, when Hannah's diagnosis was confirmed, it had been the final nail in the coffin. It had come as a shock to both of them and had taken the wind out of their sails, especially as no indicator had shown up in prenatal tests. But then Emily had missed some of those. Buried her head in the sand like an ostrich. The more he considered her behaviour, the more apparent it became that the signs were there from the beginning. How had he been so blind?

At first, he'd hoped her nonacceptance of Hannah was due to the shock of the diagnosis and postnatal depression. However, over the following months, he witnessed so many acts of rejection and selfishness, it poisoned him against her. She'd returned to work when Hannah was six weeks old, and had left much of Hannah's care to him. Yes, he worked from home, so it made more sense for him to look after her, but when she refused to take time off work after Hannah's surgery to close the hole in her heart he had felt as though she didn't care. He remembered with bitterness how he alone had taken

Hannah into hospital, and how Emily had paid a fleeting visit to the ward that evening before returning home.

Afterwards it was all downhill, until they finally agreed to separate once and for all when Hannah turned two. Emily hadn't even wanted to fight for custodial rights, saying she would see her whenever possible, which grew less and less frequent, eventually fading to around twice a year.

However, one thing he couldn't criticise her for was the financial support she voluntarily set up for Hannah. It grated on him, not being in a financial position to hand it back to her, but his income from writing was neither as regular nor as highly paid as hers. What pissed him off most about this was he knew Emily used it as a way of absolving herself for her lack of presence.

Coming back to the present, he resumed watching Hannah dance. She put her heart and soul into it, and that was more than enough reward. Emily had no idea of the joy she was missing.

***

Flamingo pink, evening sun flooded the room as Hannah lay on her bed recalling the wonderful day she'd had—the best in a long time. Between them, they'd worked out a dance routine ready to show Carys on Thursday, and it had been so much fun. Megan loved Hannah's garden and her bedroom. She said it was like something out of the film *The Secret Garden.* Hannah had never seen the film; she'd have to ask Dada to get it for her.

What impressed Megan most were her mother's costumes—especially the Eliza Doolittle dress. She'd let Megan try it on, and she'd paraded around the room, dancing and singing. They'd laughed until tears rolled down Hannah's face. She giggled again, remembering.

Reaching under the bed with one arm, she slid out the trunk. She didn't even need to look with her eyes—she recognized the dress by touch. The silky fabric fell willingly into her grasp. Hannah smoothed out the dress until it lay beside her on the bed in vacant human form, stroking, caressing. "Beautiful Mamma," she whispered.

She gasped. Trembling, she sprang off the bed and searched the room. No use—the precious brooch of seed pearls that sat at the waist of the gown was missing.

***

Much to his disappointment, the Sunday following Megan's visit failed to sustain Bleddyn's optimism regarding Hannah's behaviour. He sensed her thunderous mood the moment she woke. Expecting her to rise with great enthusiasm for the day ahead, he was surprised when he needed to call her three times before she was willing to get out of bed. She failed to eat breakfast and merely stirred her cereal around the bowl.

"What's up, Hannah?" he asked, exasperated.

Instead of answering, she burst into tears. Bleddyn went round to where she sat and put his arm around her. He hated seeing her like this; it made his stomach churn.

"What's the matter, sweetheart? You must tell me."

Between the sobs, she explained about the missing brooch.

Was Megan's honesty to be trusted? She seemed like a nice girl. She was polite during the visit, though high-spirited, but he'd put it down to excitement. He needed to think rationally.

"Well, Missie, how about you and me go do a thorough search of your bedroom. I bet it's fallen off and we'll find it hidden somewhere."

"But it's pre-precious!" she sobbed.

"It wouldn't have been made of real pearls, Hannah. They don't use real gems in stage costumes you know, so it won't be worth more than a few pounds. It's not the end of the world."

"It's pre–precious to m–me," she'd replied. "It be–belonged to M–Mamma."

And his stomach hit the floor. So maybe she wasn't moving on after all.

Despite a thorough search of the room, which included pulling out the bed and even moving the furniture, the brooch was nowhere to be seen. He tried his best to comfort her, but to no avail. He hoped it hadn't crossed her mind that Megan might have taken it. They'd become such good friends, and friendship was so vital for Hannah. The best he could do was suggest they searched for a replacement, perhaps in the antique shop in town, and hope in the meantime it would turn up. Stranger things happened.

***

Clutching the gown to her chest, Hannah watched the sky grow darker and darker. Within minutes, the heat of the summer's day became a gathering storm. Huge, billowing clouds, in hues of grey and lavender, rolled in above the garden, bruising the sky and sending the birds flurrying to safety.

And the wood! She climbed onto the deep windowsill in order to view it more clearly. The trees were silhouetted black against the sullen sky. Fat drops of rain tapped at her window, slowly at first, then, within seconds, they became a torrent that poured down the glass in teary streaks. Her heart leapt as the thunder broke, sending a tremor of fear along her spine.

Under normal circumstances she would have run for Dada, but she didn't want to. His wasn't the kind of comfort she needed at the moment. What did she need? Deep inside her there was a darkness as black as this storm. She'd never felt like it before. She was hollow—like someone had scooped out her insides.

Suddenly, the moody sky flashed silver, the energy of the lightning splitting it in two. Like her, it was consumed with anger, and the relentless rain drummed hard against her window, filling her head with its sobbing rhythm.

She closed her eyes, listening, still as stone. She was the storm—angry and wilful.

Why didn't Mamma want her?

She heard his call. The voice she knew best in all the world. Her bedroom door opened and Dada came close, wrapping her in his strong, warm arms and kissing the top of her head. She knew she was safe because he would never let anything bad happen to her.

But the emptiness remained.

"Hey, how about we do some more of your project book? We can't do much else in this storm."

She frowned. It sounded like work to her, and she didn't feel like concentrating, but at least Dada would be spending time with her if she agreed. "Mmm, suppose."

She'd designed her own propaganda poster the previous week, to encourage people to grow their own food. It sat proudly in her scrapbook. It had a lovely picture of a vegetable garden like the one she and Dada had started in early spring.

"So, what did you learn this week, Hannah?"

She spoke sullenly, her mind still on the brooch. "About children leaving their parents and going to live in safer places. It was called something, but I can't remember the word."

"Do you mean evacuation? The children were called evacuees?"

"Yes, that's it." She waited for him to take the lead.

"Well, Hannah, some parts of the country were in more danger than others during the war—more likely to be bombed by the Germans—so the government thought it best to send the children who lived in those places somewhere safer."

"Without their Dada?"

"Well, some parents went too, especially mums with young babies, but lots of parents needed to continue to work, and lots of dads were soldiers in the war, so they weren't able to go."

"If there's another war, will they make you be a soldier?"

"No, Hannah. Number one—there won't be a war like that again, and number two—even if there was, I'm too old to be a soldier."

She frowned. "You're not old."

"Well perhaps not very old, but soldiers need to be young and fit, not approaching forty with a bit of a tummy from spending too much time sitting at the computer."

She looked him over, top to bottom, considering. "Well, I'm glad you're old—and a bit fat." She allowed the corners of her mouth to twitch. The kitchen was silent for a few moments.

"Dada, when Mr. Andrews told us about the Nasty's, he said they killed people called Jews. It's cruel isn't it?"

"Yes, of course it is, Hannah. The Nazis did many cruel things."

"Mr. Andrews said they killed other people, too." She paused. "What kind of people, Dada?"

"Well … it's complicated, Hannah. A lot of things about that time are difficult to understand, even for me," he said, frowning.

She wasn't going to let him get away with that. "But what kinds of people did they kill, Dada?" She saw him hesitate.

"Well, Hitler and others in his party had this strange idea that only people who looked a certain way, or were able to do certain things, were worthwhile, so if people didn't fit their idea of the perfect German they were targeted by the Nazis."

People often spoke in riddles around her, but she understood more than they realized, and she sensed he was keeping something back. "But no one's perfect, Dada, you always say so."

"You're right. No one's perfect, except you, of course." He winked.

She sat fidgeting with her fingers, ignoring his comment. "So if you weren't perfect, they killed you."

Bleddyn groaned. "The thing is, Hannah, such cruel behaviour has gone on all over the world for a very long time. The Nazis weren't the first, nor will they be the last to behave in such a bad way."

Her bottom lip quivered. "Is that why Mamma left—because I'm not perfect?" This was the question she'd wanted to ask for a long time, but until now she hadn't found the right moment.

He held his head in his hands. "No, Hannah. Mamma didn't leave because of you." He walked over and kissed the top of her head. "Mamma left because of Mamma."

His face was as dark as the storm outside. She knew he was angry with Mamma. "What do you mean?"

He hesitated. "Well, if you really want to know, I'll tell you the truth. At least what I believe to be the truth."

She sensed the tension in him. He was struggling to answer. Before he spoke, he took a deep breath and adjusted his posture.

"It's like this. I knew Mamma for a long time before you came along, Hannah. She could be funny and crazy—a bit wild. Probably like the naughtier children in your class, except in a grown-up kind of way. For a long time, I loved that about her. Perhaps it was because I was more serious, more careful than Mamma. I didn't do things just because they seemed like fun. Instead, I considered whether things were right or wrong first."

She hung on to his every word, intense, green eyes fixed on his face. She felt calmer, glad he was finally talking about Mamma.

"She used to tease me. Her nickname for me was Mr. Red Light. She used to say I saw danger in everything and needed to learn to have fun. Your Mamma never took anything serious, Hannah. She'd try and make a joke out of things that went wrong, and I loved that about her at first. In some ways she was good for me. She helped me to lighten up a bit."

Hannah nodded, eager for more. She loved hearing stories about Mamma. People thought it best not to talk about Mamma in case it upset her, when what actually upset her was *not* talking about Mamma.

"Really, Hannah, she was just a big kid. The life she led as an actor meant she was always pretending to be someone else, and I believe it stopped her from facing up to who she really was." A puzzled expression sat upon his face, as though his understanding of Mamma's actions was registering for the first time. "Maybe she chose acting for that very reason—she didn't want to face reality. The real world scared her, so all the larking about and not taking anything serious meant she was able to avoid responsibility."

She nodded, her eyes keen, though she didn't understand all he said.

"When Mamma found out she was having a baby it came as a big shock. Mamma was so small, a little wisp of a thing, and you were in her tummy for quite some time before she grew a bump. I think that helped her forget she was having a baby. Made her believe nothing would change."

He leaned across the kitchen table and took her hand. "When a baby is born, Hannah, a parent is no longer able to think solely about what they want. They must consider what the baby needs. I don't think Mamma was ready for this. She wasn't grown up enough to accept the responsibility that comes with bringing up a child. She wasn't ready to put herself second. I don't believe she left because you were born with Down syndrome, Hannah, truly I don't. I don't think any baby would have been right for Mamma. Do you understand?"

She sobbed, a big quivering sob that began in her throat and travelled all the way to her feet. She knew he was telling the truth. Dada never lied to her. It helped a little bit, knowing Mamma was just a big kid. After all, she didn't think *she* would cope with a baby either. "But wh–why did she have to go back to S–S–Sweden? I won't get to s–see her at all now."

He swallowed hard, and she saw the lump in his throat move up and down. Adam's apple, but it wasn't Adam's. It was his.

"Because she's still running away, Hannah. Maybe one day she will find herself and stop running."

She screwed up her face; the last bit didn't make sense. Anyway, she felt better, knowing it wasn't her fault, just Mamma's. Perhaps some time in the future, when Mamma found herself, she'd come back and find Hannah. Until then she would wait.

With that, the sun peeped in the window. It had chased the storm clouds away, and the sky was blue and empty again. She'd been so caught up in Dada's story, she hadn't noticed the rain had stopped.

"You see, the sun will eventually chase away the storm. Happens every time. Some storms last a bit longer, that's all," he said.

She knew he wasn't talking about the real storm, the one that had raged outside her bedroom window a short while ago.

REUNITED

Hannah hadn't visited The Lane for several weeks, not since the day the wolf had spoiled the magic. She'd been too scared, and also too busy. From time to time she'd peered over her fence into the wood beyond but hadn't noticed anything strange.

The days seemed to be getting longer and longer, and although evening was approaching, the sky was still light. Hannah found she had more spare time after school than ever before, and there were times when she got a bit bored, especially when she was on her own.

No dawdling or weighing it up this evening, she knew she didn't have long before Dada would call her indoors. Within seconds of climbing The Lane, she reached the gap in the fence. The reigning sun had dipped in the sky. It shone between two tall trees at the top of the wood, transforming them into black shadows that loomed like giants. She closed her eyes. Now everything appeared black, with a jagged circle of light in her vision. The hollow sound of the wood pigeon's song echoed above her head, accompanied by the sleepy chirp of crickets a little in the distance. She sniffed the air. The summer storm of the previous day had tainted the woodland with a damp earthy smell.

Even if she'd wanted to enter the wood she would have been unable to, for apart from the steep climb, several strips of fierce-looking barbed wire separated it from the path. Glancing in the direction of home, she decided to go on a little farther. The bend in The Lane was still a long way in the distance, but it seemed to call her. There was always something tempting about wanting to see what was around any corner. Would she ever be brave enough to go that far?

The incline was steep. Combined with the humidity of the air, Hannah soon found herself puffing and panting. Her chest made the familiar squeaky sound. She hadn't noticed it for quite some time, but she remembered Dada asking the doctor about it ages ago. It hadn't been anything to worry about, though. She paused, hands on hips and turned around, deciding she'd come far enough.

The whole day had been still, the air heavy and laden, so it took her by surprise when a sudden gust of wind blew through the canopy of trees, causing them to bow and bend as though dancing a waltz. She shivered, watching the fine hairs along her arms stand to attention.

Hannah. It came from up ahead. Whoever spoke her name wanted her to go on, not turn back, but it was getting late. She froze, a quiver of curiosity causing her to turn around. The confident June sun had made its way around the top of the wood and sat directly above the bend in The Lane. Hannah squinted into the distance, her heart beating fast. Then came the smallest of movements among the trees to her left, gentle, like a hand caressing silk. Then silence again, any sign of life in the evening wood instantly snuffed out. Complete stillness—peaceful—and yet it felt wrong.

Not daring to move, she stood and waited. Something would happen soon, she knew. At the edge of the wood a hawthorn flourished, proudly displaying its head of delicate, white blooms. Hannah blinked in disbelief, as right before her eyes its trunk took on a human form, transforming into the most delicate of creatures. A spiral of ivy became a twisted braid of hair cascading from shoulder to waist. Almond eyes fixed on Hannah, as the creature glided gracefully towards the edge of the path. The creature wore a simple tunic, its surface textured like slivers of bark, and her feet were bare. Closer now, her lips as crimson as the hawthorn berry in autumn.

She was magnificent!

With a hint of a smile, the creature held out a hand to Hannah, offering her a gift, a crown of blossoms. Entranced, Hannah reached through the barbed wire fence and took it, her eyes never leaving the creature's own. She was good at reading eyes, but although the creature's were clear crystals, there was nothing to read. They were as empty as eyes in a photograph.

"It's yours," the creature said, in a voice as smooth as silk.

"Th–thank you." Hannah held the crown to her nose, expecting a floral aroma. Instead she was greeted with the pungent smell of rotting fish. Her nose wrinkled, but she felt obliged to wear it. As she lifted the crown to her head, a sharp thorn pierced her thumb, leaving in its wake a tiny pool of blood.

Hannah's face burned hot. She turned to leave, instinctively aware something wasn't right, when the creature called her back.

"Wait! I have something else for you."

Hannah hesitated. The creature held something in the closed fist of her left hand. Slowly, she uncurled her fingers, and as she did so, Hannah saw her nails were the claw-like thorns of the hawthorn. Her palm lay open, revealing a cluster of tiny pearls—Hannah's brooch. She gasped. "How—"

The creature put her finger to her lips. "Sh, it's a secret. I'll tell you when next you visit."

With trembling fingers, Hannah took the brooch, noticing how cold the creature's hand was as she brushed against it.

"Hannah!" It was Dada's voice calling from the back garden, and he sounded a bit concerned. Her heart leapt. If she was quick, she might be able to run back to the front of her cottage before he discovered her in The Lane. She was about to say goodbye, but when she looked, instead of the beautiful creature, there stood the hawthorn tree—in full bloom and entwined with ivy.

She sprinted down the path, reaching the bottom just as he appeared at the front of the house. She slung the crown of blossom into the hedge. He would know she hadn't made it herself—it was too perfect. She gripped the brooch tightly, hoping he wouldn't be able to read the deception on her face.

"What are you doing out here? I was getting worried. It's almost dark, and you know I don't like you playing out the front because of the road."

Hannah was grateful for the dusk, perhaps it would disguise her guilt.

"Look what I found, Dada!" She held out a trembling palm. His brow furrowed. "It was in the bush, over there. I must have dropped it."

Was he convinced? She didn't care. It was enough to be reunited with the precious object.

***

Veiled by the fissured, cinereous bark of the old hawthorn, the witch Rhiamon watched the child leave.

So the first encounter had gone well. A wry smirk played about her lips. Why—the girl was even bold enough to take the gift from her hand. She closed her fist tight, holding on to the scrap of human warmth that tingled at the centre of her own frigid palm. If *he* hadn't called her back, she might have been able to persuade her to cross the boundary and enter the wood. Rapacious though she was, she would prefer the game to last a while longer. Devouring the child's spirit would be all the more enjoyable after a little toil to whet the palate, and besides, the child was more use to her alive than dead. She would make an ideal hostage with which to barter her freedom. The old dewin would not risk the life of a child, no matter the cost.

She chuckled as the child tossed the crown into the hedge. Ah, so she did not want her father to see it. All the better, for it proved she kept the fact that she visited here secret. It was bad enough that there were two already intent on keeping the girl safe without having to worry about a third.

"Pfff!" A slender hand, graceful as a dancer's, flicked the air dismissively. Once she had the girl in the palm of her hand she would use it to her advantage, and in doing so would wreak revenge on both the dewin, Emrys, and his granddaughter, Deryth. She would fool them into believing she would exchange the girl for her freedom, but it would mark their downfall. Once free of this wood, she would claim all three of them … what a feast it would make!

Rhiamon climbed to the bough of the hawthorn, allowing its strong arms and delicate blossoms to cradle and soothe her. It had been ten years since the wintry tempest had delivered her to this place, setting her down atop the snow-clad mountain. Adjusting her position in the bough, she leaned back and closed her eyes, remembering …

She had claimed the souls of the newborn lambs first, pure and white as the snow.

Perfect. Untainted, yet vulnerable. The purer her victims were, the more sustenance they provided.

Six unsullied souls had satisfied her appetite for a while, the sound of their tiny bleats as she stole them from their mothers ringing joyfully in her ears … but not for long.

Soon she'd descended with ease down the snow-blanketed mountain and into the fields, hungry for more. The journey on the icy squall had been long, and she was ravenous.

The hawthorn swayed in the breeze, its white blossoms whispering to remind her of what had happened next, but she did not wish to remember. Instead, she wanted to imagine the satisfaction she would feel when the child, the dewin, and his granddaughter succumbed. With fingers cold as icicles, she snapped a twig from the whispering tree, relishing its pain. That would teach it to remind her of *his* magic.

Alighting from the hawthorn, she made her way deeper into the wood, claiming a few morsels of moth and damselfly rendered lethargic by the heat, along the way. A mere appetiser.

In its deepest, darkest heart, Rhiamon lay curled on the fragrant carpet and watched with amusement as a black and orange sexton beetle buried the decaying rib cage of a field mouse among the leaf litter. Her bare foot hovered above it, undecided. Should she crush it? Many considered this beetle the undertaker of the animal world, but it was unfair. Like her, the beetle was willing to defer gratification.

A whole decade she had watched this house. Being confined to the wood as she was, there was little else to do. Until now, not one of its occupants had stimulated her interest like the girl. What was more, the old dewin and his granddaughter had shown no interest in the previous occupants. This time it was different. When she foraged among the girl's soul, she saw it shone brightly, the most transparent shade of citrine. But look deeper—really deep—and dark blemishes of pain and disappointment were visible.

Rhiamon would use those scars to her advantage. With careful handling, this girl would provide the key to her release from this charmed prison. She would tease her first, like a cat does a mouse, and enjoy the game … then she would win her trust over theirs.

Yawning with satisfaction, she drifted to sleep, and dreamed of how best she might accomplish her plan.

Emrys Brown

Hannah missed her name when Mr. Andrews called the register, and he needed to repeat it. After Dada had dropped her off, she'd taken her bag to the cloakroom as usual, but when she returned to class, Miss Morgan was nowhere to be seen. A glance out the classroom window told her Miss Morgan was in deep discussion with Dada. They stood side-on, but Hannah could tell the conversation was serious. Was Dada telling her about the brooch? She hoped not. Although itching to join them, she knew Mr. Andrews would tell her off if she did. She watched them closely, but being unable to see their faces properly was frustrating.

"Guess what, Hannah?"

She wasn't doing very well at the times tables game at the moment—unable to concentrate. She glanced up from the laptop.

"You might be meeting my Granddad soon." Miss Morgan seemed pleased, though Hannah had no idea what she was talking about.

"How come?" she asked, her face screwed in confusion.

"Well … I've been talking to your dad, and he told me he was struggling to keep on top of jobs in your garden."

Eyes narrowed, Hannah searched for signs of betrayal. All morning she'd wanted to ask what Miss Morgan and Dada had talked about, but knew it would be rude to do so, plus she was a little nervous in case it was something to do with her.

"Anyway, my tadcu, Emrys, lives on the farm not far from you. In fact it's at the top of the lane behind your house." She paused, and Hannah had the feeling she was waiting for her to say something, so she pressed her lips together to stop them from spilling the secret. "He loves gardening, so I gave your dad his number."

Ah, so that was what they'd been discussing. Miss Morgan's eyes seemed to be telling the truth, but Hannah wasn't certain because they twinkled.

***

Hannah's dad had recounted the whole episode of the brooch to Deryth and had asked her not to tell Hannah. They'd discussed how she was doing, and he seemed concerned when she admitted there were times when Hannah seemed preoccupied. Deryth noticed how he'd run his hands through his hair and how his jaw clenched with tension.

He'd mentioned how he was so busy he wasn't even able to keep on top of the garden. *Wild* was the term he used to describe it, *with a life of its own.* He obviously wasn't familiar with the way in which a warm spring made things grow exponentially here in rural Wales. That had been when she'd mentioned him—her tadcu Emrys and his love of gardening. He seemed keen, so she'd passed on his number, saying she'd ring her granddad at break time to let him know he should expect a call. If he took her up on the offer, he'd be doing her a favour, too. In fact, it might prove to be the opportunity they needed to get closer.

***

The following Saturday, Miss Morgan's granddad arrived just after breakfast, and Hannah liked him immediately. Miss Morgan called him tadcu, Welsh for granddad, but Hannah was told to call him Emrys. As Dada gave Emrys Brown a tour of the garden, she went, too. Emrys Brown had a way with kids—that was what Dada always said about people like him. His unruly hair was a mop of thick white waves that matched his eyebrows. He didn't have many teeth left, but instead of making him appear scary, it made him seem more fun. His face was ruddy, with lots of cracks that moved when he talked, and he peppered some of his words with Welsh, apologising when he saw neither she nor Dada understood. Welsh was his first language, he said. He'd spoken it since the beginning of time, and he didn't think in English. Dada said perhaps he could teach them a bit of Welsh, too. But her heart stopped when Emrys suddenly pointed in the direction of The Lane.

"My farm's 'bout a mile in that direction," he said, his pale blue eyes squinting into the distance. "'Cept I don't do much farming these days, least not the hard stuff—too old now. My daughter an' her husband look after that side of things. 'It's how I've got time to do gardening, see."

"How come you're Miss Morgan's granddad?" Hannah asked.

"Well, she's my daughter's girl, see. Hope she's being good to you in school." He chuckled, and nudged Hannah with his elbow.

"She's a wonderful help, isn't she, Hannah? You two get on like a house on fire."

"That's a silly thing to say, Dada. A house wouldn't get on with a fire 'cos it'd burn down."

Emrys laughed, and his eyes sparkled like diamonds.

Arrangements were made for Emrys Brown to start work the following Saturday.

"Bye, Emrys," she said, holding out a hand for him to shake.

"We're gonna be good friends, aren't we, Hannah? You can lend a hand when I come if you're not too busy."

The thing about the hand was a silly thing to say, because if you lent someone your hand you'd be left with one and it would make lots of things tricky. As he spoke about lending him a hand, he looked straight at her, and she noticed he had the same dark ring around the blue of his eyes as Miss Morgan.

***

The moment Emrys finished cutting the grass he heard it, a mere whisper on the breeze. Nevertheless, it was enough to let him know the witch was watching. He sniffed the air. Yes, it carried a faint scent of decay. Taking a handkerchief from his trouser pocket he blew his nose to make her aware of his presence.

As if from nowhere Hannah appeared, her porcelain skin freckled around the nose from the sun and her hair shining copper and bronze. Fragile, and yet already he sensed a resilience in the child. If they were able to gain her trust, things would turn out okay.

"Dada made me stay indoors while you used the machine." She pointed to the petrol strimmer. "He said I'd get under your feet."

Emrys grinned.

"Why do people say such things? I mean, how *could* I get under your feet?"

"He meant you'd get in my way—make a nuisance of yourself. But you won't. I don't mind you being out here with me. It's nice to have a bit of company."

Hannah sneezed three times in a row and rubbed her eyes.

"Bless you! Hay fever?" He pulled a clean tissue from his trouser pocket and handed it to her then leaned on the rake. "So, Hannah, what d'you like best 'bout your garden?"

She bit her lip and thought hard. "I love the wild flowers on the bank, and I love all the fish in my pond. I like everything. Dada says it's a crazy garden, but it's not."

"That's because your dad is too busy working to see its real beauty. You an' me have more time, don't we, bach?"

Together, they strolled over to the wild meadow on the steepest part of the garden. "See here, Hannah, most of these wild flowers will have spread from the wood at the back. It would be unlikely anyone would have planted them."

"How can you tell?"

"Well, cos they're native woodland species, like this dog rose here." He bent low and ran his hand over a cluster of pink flowers, beckoning her forward. "Look here—near the stem. See the little hairy ball of prickles?"

"Ooh, yes. That's a funny flower."

"It isn't a flower, it's a gall, also known as robin's pincushion."

She screwed up her face, waiting for him to explain.

"A tiny wasp, called a gall wasp, will have laid hundreds of eggs on this dog rose. Now, the eggs have turned into larvae, an' they'll feed off this plant until fully grown, then they'll fly away."

She bent to study the flower. "Why is it called the robin thingy? I've got a robin living in my garden."

"A robin's pincushion. Do you know what a pincushion is?"

"No."

"It's a little ball for holding pins, like when someone's sewing. The pins stick out from it like those little hairs on the gall, so if your robin lands on this rose it'll have a nasty surprise, I'm afraid."

Her eyes narrowed. "I don't think we should laugh at my robin getting prickled."

He tousled her hair. "Ah, you needn't worry. Robins are clever, Hannah—same as most birds. It'd know better than to land there."

She nodded, satisfied with his answer.

Emrys groaned as he straightened his back. "Did you know a robin symbolizes a new beginning, Hannah? It's in your garden to tell you to leave the past behind an' begin a new life here."

She thought about it for a moment. "That makes sense. Me and Dada moved to Wales to start over again." She frowned. "How do you know so much stuff?"

Emrys Brown laughed. "Because I've lived a very long time, bach. You'll know lots by the time you're my age as well. An' anyway—I bet you could teach me a few things."

She pressed a finger to the corner of her mouth. "Mmm, I know! I can teach you the "Missing" dance. Watch!" She twirled and tapped while singing the song. "Your turn."

***

Rhiamon contemplated the scene from her hiding place behind the oak. The way the old dewin and the girl bonded so effortlessly sickened her to the core. It was obvious the girl was already falling for his charm … she would need to promise the girl so much more if she was going to win this battle. She'd seen enough. As silent as her thoughts, Rhiamon retreated to the dark heart of the wood.

***

Bleddyn stood at the bottom of the path. What a sight they were. Poor old Emrys. He must be seventy-five if he was a day. She had him spinning in circles. They were so caught up in the moment, neither of them noticed his approach. It was wonderful to see her so full of joy, more like the old Hannah.

Emrys and Hannah stopped dancing when they saw him coming.

"Duw, duw! I'm worn out," Emrys said, his face ruddy and sweating.

Bleddyn laughed. "She'll have you running round in circles if you let her, Emrys."

Emrys gathered his breath. "She was teaching me something I didn't know. Had to give it a go, didn't I?" He winked at Bleddyn. "I've left the wild flower meadow for now—best cut later in summer, when the flowers have died back. They spread their seeds better then. That way you'll have an even better show next year."

"You dance, Dada!" Hannah bounced on the spot, enjoying the attention.

"No chance, Missie. I'll put my back out."

Emrys had recovered somewhat. "I'll cut the hedge back a bit, up there," he said, pointing towards the gap in the fence, "then I'll call it a day."

"Like I said, Emrys, do as much or as little as you feel. I'm only too glad of your help."

"Can I stay with Emrys, Dada? Please?"

Bleddyn hesitated. It was difficult to know whether or not she'd be in Emrys's way, and he didn't want her being a nuisance. At the same time, he was glad the two of them were getting along so well. It was one of his biggest regrets, the fact that Hannah had missed out on the love of grandparents, as both his parents had died before she was born, and Emily's were in Sweden and had never shown the slightest interest in her.

Emrys saw him hesitate, so answered for him. "Don't mind me—I'm happy to have her out here as long as it's okay with you. Might take me a bit longer to get things done is all." Arms folded, he grinned at Hannah. "We get a bit distracted don't we, bach?"

***

Hannah kept her distance, reluctant to follow him to the hedge. What if he knew about The Lane? Hadn't he said he lived near the top of it, on a farm? And she was sure Miss Morgan had said so, too. If so, in time, she'd be able to ask him things, like about the wolf … and the tree creature. She wasn't ready yet—she didn't know him well enough. She'd wait a bit longer.

So instead of following him, she sat at the edge of the pond and watched the fish. Within moments, some of the more confident orfes swam to the surface. She'd already fed them that morning, and Dada said she wasn't to give them too much food or she'd kill them with kindness. How might you kill something by being kind? It didn't make sense.

***

Emrys Brown leaned back in his armchair in front of the fire, recalling his earlier conversation with Hannah. Although she'd wanted to remain in the garden with him, as soon as he'd gone over to the hedge she'd backed off. She didn't want him to know she visited the lane, and for now he'd keep her secret, just as he'd keep watch. He needed her to trust him before telling her about the past. The last thing he wanted to do was frighten her.

The coals spat and hissed as they succumbed to the heat of the flame. Reaching for the poker, he stabbed at the dying embers, causing them to reignite momentarily. *Nothing on this earth gives up without a fight*, he thought.

CROWN OF THORNS

Had Hannah imagined it? She couldn't have, because if she had, how come the seed-pearl brooch sat once more in its rightful place at the waist of Mamma's gown? She and Dada had searched high and low, and she'd been so upset. She would find the crown of flowers, that's what she'd do. Then she'd be doubly certain she hadn't imagined the tree creature.

The air was thick and heavy, an invisible blanket wrapped around her chest. Dada called it *humid,* whereas to her it felt like being in a jungle. Long ago, Dada had taken her to visit a house that looked like a palace. In the huge gardens there stood a butterfly house, full of exotic plants from faraway places, and yes, there were many beautiful butterflies, but what Hannah remembered most was the hot, moist air that made her feel light-headed.

Dada had needed to take her outside, and she had to drink lots of cold water before she felt better. It had been such a shame, because butterflies were one of her favourite insects. In her opinion, the way they grew from ugly, fuzzy caterpillars was one of nature's best magic tricks.

She was sure she remembered exactly where she'd tossed the crown when Dada had called her that day.

Searching the hedgerow at the side of the path, she was surprised when she couldn't find it. She remembered how it had caught on a low branch and swung back and forth a few times before coming to rest. She supposed the white blooms would be dead now, having been plucked from the tree, but the wreath of twigs should still be easy to spot.

She was about to give up the search when her eye caught a glint in the hedge. Reaching forward, she grasped the shining object buried in the undergrowth and tugged, attempting to release it from where it lay ensnared in the tangled branches. Reluctantly they gave up their prize, but not before knocking her off balance. Within her hand she held a ring of wire, not a ring of hawthorn. Several loops of it lay in twisted bands, forming a perfect circle. The wire was barbed. What she'd believed were thorns on the day she'd worn it were, in fact, vicious spikes of the sharpest metal. No blooms adorned the hoop. Instead, scraps of plastic and that poly stuff, the stuff used to protect parcels in cardboard boxes, clung to its prongs.

How strange! How hadn't she noticed it was artificial? She'd been certain it was made from the hawthorn tree. Her heart raced. Was she mistaken? Was this the same crown? She fed it through her fingers, examining it full circle, taking care not to touch the barbs. No, it was the same crown, but it had definitely borne blossoms. She remembered how she'd held them to her nose and they'd stunk of dead fish.

She didn't know what to do with it. Not wanting to put it back in the hedge, she held it between finger and thumb and looked about, as though the answer might suddenly present itself. It was ugly—a thing made of litter among nature, and what was more, it was dangerous. If some small animal should get caught in its prongs, it might get hurt. She would have to put it in the bin and hope Dada wouldn't notice.

Hannah climbed The Lane as far as the gap in the fence and sat on the low wall, pondering. Tempted though she was to climb higher, she wasn't sure she was ready to meet the tree creature again should she appear, not after finding the dangerous crown. And what of the wolf? She hadn't seen it for some time, though she sometimes heard its howl at night as she lay in bed.

She'd looked up *wolves* on her laptop, so she knew they preferred the cool of night to the heat of day, and it had been so hot lately. Who did the wolf call to in the dead of night? Did it belong to a pack? She didn't think so, as this was a magic wolf, one that spoke to humans, in English … and maybe even Welsh.

And what of the tree creature? Hannah's feelings towards her were confused. She sure was tempting. In some ways she reminded her of Mamma … and she had given back the brooch. But how on earth had she found it in the first place? Had she stolen it from Hannah's house? None of it made sense. The more she thought about it, the more confused she became.

She remembered the wolf warning her away, telling her to run home. From what? She'd seen no one in the wood the day someone had called her name. She'd smelled Mamma's perfume though; she was certain. It was all so strange. Should she put her trust in the wolf or the tree creature? Perhaps they were both good … or perhaps both were evil. And if that was the case, what on earth was she doing here? It was asking for trouble.

But the wolf had promised to tell her more stories … and the creature had promised to explain how she had come by the brooch … so she simply *had* to return.

***

Tarian lay panting in the shade of the oak. From where she lay, Hannah was in plain view. She seemed to be lost in her own world, as every now and then she would strike up conversation with an imaginary person. She was a dear little thing, so delicate yet brave too, or why else would she dare to return? And she'd kept it all to herself so far, Tarian was certain.

Would this be a good time to talk with her again? It had been several weeks since she'd spotted the witch in the wood—no, not spotted, rather she had sensed her presence. Did she not know that while her own sorcery might well be powerful, Tarian's tracking skills were equally as keen?

From the canopy above her head a gentle rustle caused Tarian's fur to ripple, ever so softly. What was the oak trying to tell her? Re-positioning herself against the base of its trunk, she pondered how she might win Hannah's trust. An exposed root of the old tree nudged her underbelly, as if to say she should make her move. Proceeding slowly down the embankment, with Hannah in plain sight, she drew closer and closer …

***

Lost in thought, Hannah didn't notice its approach, not until the wolf stood almost at the edge of the wood. It paused, not wishing to alarm her. Nevertheless, Hannah jumped. Her head told her to move, but her legs failed to follow the instruction.

Gradually, one pace at a time, it came closer until Hannah was able to feel the warmth of its breath through the fabric of her summer leggings.

"Hello," she heard herself say, shy again after what seemed a long separation.

For a moment she imagined the wolf would say nothing. Hannah met its eyes—intense and wise, not playful and alert like Jipp's.

"You have courage, Hannah." The wolf's voice was soft and smokey. Again, Hannah noticed the flecks of bright blue in its amber eyes. "Bravery is good. It enables us to do things we do not feel comfortable with."

Hannah would need a bit of time in order to consider what it meant. "Why do you have bits of blue in your eyes?" There, she'd said it. Dada would have told her not to be personal, but the words slipped out before she had a chance to stop them.

The wolf didn't seem to mind. If wolves could smile—which of course they couldn't—this wolf would have done so. She knew by the way its mouth opened slightly, and its tail wagged.

"Wolf cubs are born with blue eyes, Hannah. Then, as we grow, they change colour."

"Actually, they're golden, the same colour as honey … but they have blue bits too. Beautiful!"

"I appreciate you saying so, though beautiful things cannot always be trusted."

Hannah frowned, uncertain of its meaning. "You promised to tell me more stories … if I came again."

The wolf relaxed and settled at her side. It smelled of the wood—the soft, creamy scent of elderflower mingled with sweeter, woody fern. Hannah enjoyed the soothing warmth of its fur as its back snuggled close to her leg. It sat beside her, facing the wood, so that she couldn't see its face.

"Before we begin, I think I should introduce myself properly," the wolf said. "My name is Tarian. Tarian of the Wood."

Hannah gave a little gasp. "That's a nice name. My name is Hannah … the favour." She shrugged. "But you already know about the Hannah bit, cos you called me it." Had she told the wolf her name when they'd met before? She couldn't remember doing so, and yet she was certain it had called her Hannah.

"Favour indeed," it said, wriggling closer still, until its soft fur tickled her bare ankle.

"I like your name. Is it Welsh?"

"Indeed it is. Tarian means shield. I am the guardian of these woods."

Hannah nodded. She knew what a shield was because Captain America carried one. So Tarian protected the wood, then. What an important job to have. Perhaps this would be the right moment for her to ask about the tree creature. After all, if Tarian protected the wood, it should know whether the tree creature was good or bad. She opened her mouth to speak, but the wolf interrupted.

"There is much in this world that needs protecting, Hannah. You'd be surprised if you knew the whole truth."

Tarian's eyes scanned the trees, and its ears pointed skyward, listening, even as it spoke. She'd better not ask just yet.

AN UNEXPECTED VISITOR

Miss Morgan must have asked her a question. Hannah could tell by the way she looked at her. The trouble was, Hannah didn't have the faintest idea what she'd been asked. Her head was still in The Lane, still trying to make sense of all Tarian had told her.

"Pardon? Sorry … Didn't hear you."

Miss Morgan repeated the question with a twinkle in her eye. "I asked whether or not my tadcu worked on your garden over the weekend."

"Ah, sorry, I was daydreaming." Hannah grinned. "No, next Saturday."

"Oh, that'll be nice. You two have become good friends by all accounts."

"He tells good stories—from long ago. And he knows loads about nature."

"Well, if he's due on Saturday, I might have to bring him. He rang Mam last night to say his van is off the road."

Hannah frowned. "Why doesn't he drive it back on?"

"Sorry, Hannah, *off the road* means it isn't working properly."

"So it's broken?"

"Exactly. So I might have to give him a lift to your house."

"Cool! When you come I can show you my bedroom and my things."

"Hey, better speed up, bach, it's almost break time," Miss Morgan said, tapping Hannah's exercise book with her finger.

"That's what Emrys calls me—bach," Hannah said, smoothing Miss Morgan's newly polished midnight-blue nail. "Nice! Will you do mine?"

Miss Morgan laughed. "And it's what he called me when I was young, too. In Welsh it means little one."

***

Megan was absent because she was sick, so rather than seek out someone else to play with, Hannah decided to find a quiet corner of the playground where she could be alone. The tree stump at the back of the mound would suit. From there, she would be able to hide away from the others and tell herself a story.

When they'd last met, Tarian had told her the story of Leto. It was an ancient story about a goddess who was able to turn herself into other creatures, one of which was a wolf. Leto was the goddess of mothers and children and as such protected them. Hannah didn't understand all of the story. It seemed complicated, but Tarian told it well. Her voice was soothing, like cough syrup, and as she'd spoken Hannah had found herself drifting to sleep.

"Things are not always what they seem, Hannah," Tarian had said, jolting her awake.

What was Tarian trying to tell her? Leto was a woman who could also be a wolf, and the tree creature was a woman who could also be a tree. It was so confusing.

Before saying goodbye, Tarian had told her something important. She'd nodded towards a broken bit of barbed wire fence, further along the path—further than Hannah had ever walked before—and warned her never to enter the wood, even though that part of the fence would make it easier for her to do so. "No matter who or what may try to lure you in, Hannah, you must resist, even if the person or thing makes you promises and appears to be kind, you must not enter the wood."

Hannah had asked why—what was so dangerous there? Tarian hadn't said exactly what it was, only that she must promise, no matter what.

So she'd promised. But what about the tree creature and the gifts she had given her? She felt a bit guilty about those. Dada had taught her not to accept things offered by strangers. But the crown had seemed so tempting … and the brooch, well, it was irresistible. And so she'd decided against mentioning the tree creature for the time being.

***

Deryth was a little uncomfortable at Hannah suggesting she should see her bedroom, so she'd changed the subject. It was sometimes difficult to remain professional, especially when working so closely with one particular pupil. She'd check with Mr Andrews and ask his opinion.

"Confidentiality is what matters, Deryth. Several staff are friends of pupils' parents in school. The thing is, in this kind of community, everyone knows everyone else. I mean, I went to school with some of the parents myself, so it's difficult at times to be seen in a different light."

"Yes, I appreciate that, Gareth, but I only intended to drop Tadcu off. I wasn't planning on going in. I probably shouldn't have mentioned it to her, I suppose."

"Look, Deryth, Meryl does private maths tuition for a couple of the pupils, and Sioned gives piano lessons. You shouldn't worry so much. As long as you steer clear of discussing any other pupil, I can't see any harm in it. The two of you are already close. It might be nice for Hannah to show you her surroundings, and might help her to open up a bit. She's still not back to her bubbly self, is she?"

Deryth nodded. "No, she isn't. I suppose you're right. I'll let you know how it goes on Monday."

***

The first inclination that something was up was when Bleddyn heard Hannah's squeal of delight. "Dada! Miss Morgan's here—with Emrys!"

"Miss Morgan? What do you mean?" She shot off without answering. His stomach churned. By the time he caught up with her, Miss Morgan and Emrys were busy unloading the tools from the boot of the car.

"My van's off the road," Emrys said, his ruddy face fixed on Bleddyn who'd suddenly appeared at Hannah's side, "so Deryth's dropping me off."

Miss Morgan straightened and smiled. She wore a floral knee-length dress that showed off her curves to perfection. Sun-kissed skin made her blue eyes vibrant.

"Can Miss Morgan come in, Dada? I want to show her my bedroom and my trunk."

His face reddened, and he ran his hands through his messy hair in an attempt to put it in some kind of order.

"Yes, of course! Welcome—or should I say croeso?" He pointed at his stained T-shirt and flushed. "Excuse the state of me. It's been a busy morning." He wished he'd done the usual weekend clean instead of procrastinating, but he'd been writing an article and had decided to put it off until Sunday instead.

"Oh no … I don't want to intrude, doing Tadcu a favour, that's all."

"You're not intruding—you're most welcome. Just make sure you don't allow her to dominate your free time," he nodded at Hannah who beamed at his side. Embarrassed, he turned away and lifted Emrys's hedge cutter. When next he glanced up, Hannah was leading Miss Morgan by the hand around to the back, where Bleddyn assumed she would take her straight to her room. He hoped she'd kept it tidy, but to be fair, she usually did. She liked things in their place.

He put the kettle on and watched from the window as Emrys clipped the hedge. From upstairs, Hannah's excited chatter was incessant. He was able to make out the *ooh's* and *ahh's* of Miss Morgan's affirmations to whatever it was Hannah was showing her. Emily's gowns were currently being pulled out of the trunk, no doubt. With a dish sponge, he scrubbed at the stain on his T-shirt, inflicting a huge wet patch. "Bloody hell, Hannah! Why didn't you warn me?" he muttered through clenched teeth.

***

Hannah was saying something about Eliza Doolittle, but Deryth wasn't paying attention. Bleddyn's embarrassment at her unexpected appearance was blatant. It made her feel awkward. Hannah had obviously forgotten to mention she'd be dropping Tadcu off. Should she have declined his offer to come inside? Made up some excuse, perhaps? Hannah was so excited, and he'd encouraged her with words of welcome. Still, the moment had been embarrassing to say the least.

The view from Hannah's bedroom window was enchanting. From where she sat at the edge of Hannah's bed, she was able to see Tadcu clipping the hedge, and it also afforded her a clear view of the lane.

The garden gradually climbed away from the side of the house, the length of its back bordered by a tangle of bramble and ivy that she knew disguised the stone wall from its perimeter. They'd walked the lane so many times, her and Tadcu. It led all the way to Mynydd Lleuad Farm—Moon Mountain Farm, the place that would always own a little piece of her heart. She hoped one day it would be hers, that Mam and Dad would pass it down and she might live there forever. The little flat in town would do for now. It was closer to work and afforded her some independence, but her heart remained at the farm.

"What are you doing?" Hannah's abrupt question brought her swiftly back to the present.

"Sorry, Hannah—I was admiring your garden. It's huge. Do you love it? I bet there are a few good hiding places out there."

"Yes—come on, let's go outside. I'll show you my favourite bits," she said, pulling Deryth from the bed by her arm.

As she stood, Deryth noticed the pale cream gown draped on the bed. The centre of the highwaisted band of silk wore a brooch of pearls, like the one Hannah's dad had described some weeks back, the brooch that was lost and found again and had caused Hannah so much upset. Would Hannah tell her what had happened if she mentioned it? It was worth a shot.

"Oh, what a gorgeous dress! And this brooch—" she lifted the gown and studied it closely. "How glamorous. You'll need to look after it, won't you?"

"I lost it once," Hannah said, her face turning pink.

"Did you? I bet it gave you a scare. Where did you find it?"

Hannah flinched, seemingly undecided whether or not to answer. Deryth knew how truthful she was. Unlike most other children, she was usually brutally honest.

"In The Lane … at the back of the house."

"How on earth did it find its way out there, Hannah?"

"No idea," she said, with a dismissive shrug. "Never mind. It's back now. Come on, let's go see the garden."

Deryth concealed a smile. Hannah hadn't lied, but she hadn't been willing to reveal the whole story either. Maybe she would at some point in time. Perhaps she would learn to trust her enough to tell her everything. It would be easier to help her then.

***

After Miss Morgan left, Hannah hung around Emrys as usual. He seemed a bit quieter today. Perhaps he was worried about his van.

"You okay, Emrys?" Her face held a look of concern.

"Iawn, bach, never better. Remembering the past, is all. Deryth being here today brought it all back."

"Why? Has she been here before?"

"Not here—not in this garden—but the lane … yes."

Funny how Miss Morgan hadn't mentioned it when they'd been in her bedroom. "Tell me about when Miss Morgan was a kid."

"Your eyes are twinkling." He laughed. "Why do children love to hear tales about their teachers?"

"Tell me, tell me!" she said, bouncing on the spot.

"Aye, all right. You can give me a hand to deadhead these primroses at the same time. Here, let me show you."

Hannah squatted beside him and watched closely as he held the stem and pinched off the wilted flower with a finger and thumb.

"Why do we need to do this job?" she asked, puzzled.

"Well, bach, lots of things like to imagine they're still young see, like me an' your Dad." He winked. "If you remove the dead flower head, you trick the plant into thinking it's still young. That way it will most likely produce another flower, whereas if you let it go to seed it will think it's done its job an' it won't bother."

"Ah, I see." She knelt among the flowers, picking off the heads, just as he'd shown her. "So, tell me the stories about Miss Morgan." She had no intention of letting him get away with it.

"Well … let me see—" He straightened and rubbed the small of his back with his fists. "You see the lane there?" He pointed. "It leads all the way to my farm. Now, many years ago, before milk came in those plastic cartons, the farmer would store the cows' milk in great big metal containers called churns. He'd load them onto a horse-drawn cart an' take them from the farm down to the road where they'd be collected by the dairy. So the lane once served a purpose, you see."

She studied him closely, her chest a rattle because of the hay fever.

"When Deryth was young, she an' I'd often walk the lane. She was just like you. She loved to hear stories about the olden days, an' she loved to learn about the magic of nature." He paused and stole a glance. "From time to time we'd wander into the wood"—again he gestured in its direction—"I'd teach her to identify the different trees an' woodland plants. In winter, we'd keep watch for the first hazel catkins an' signs of snowdrops to show us spring was around the corner. Mind you, a walk through the wood in snow can't be beat," he said, shaking his head. "There was always something to do. We'd build dens an' sit inside listening to the drumming o' rain showers. Sometimes we'd take a picnic an' go scavenging for mushrooms an' edible berries … all sorts o' things."

"Will you take me?"

She'd resisted interrupting so far, but couldn't help herself. She loved picnics. Emrys didn't answer. Instead, he continued his story.

"Her favourite thing of all was to make crowns out o' twigs an' bits of moss an' flowers."

Hannah gasped as he said the *crown* word, and turned her attention back to the primroses. Did he know about the crowns of twigs? she wondered, remembering back to the one the tree creature had gifted her.

A few moments of silence followed.

"Years later, when Deryth was a teenager, things changed."

She studied his face, her emerald eyes alert. He scratched his head. He seemed a little worried. Perhaps he knew about the wolf and the tree creature. But how could he? She patted the grass where she kneeled, inviting him to sit.

"It was after one particularly hard winter. It'd been biting cold for weeks. The water troughs on the farm were continuously frozen over an' I had to try to keep my sheep away from Top Field as it was so exposed to the wind up there. Whip your skin raw it would. Anyway, one night it began to snow …"

Hannah huddled closer, enjoying the tension.

"A blizzard, it was. When I got up as usual before dawn an' opened the farmhouse door, the snow had drifted half way up. It was impossible to get out without first digging it away."

With her index finger, she stroked the rough, weather-beaten skin on the back of his hand as he spoke.

"A whiteout, they called it. Hardly see a thing in front of you, an' the snow continued to fall for the rest o' the day an' the following night." He nodded, remembering.

"Dada said it snowed a lot when I was born, but I can't remember."

"It would have been the same winter, Hannah—ten years ago. You wouldn't remember if you were a baby. Anyway, I lost a few lambs that year—ewes delivering up on the mountain cos they couldn't get down in time. Sad sight." He shook his head. "As I was saying, something changed after the blizzard. There was something in the air, so to speak."

Hannah shuddered, anticipating what was to come.

"The wood seemed different. When the thaw finally arrived, you'd have expected things to reawaken, wouldn't you? By then it was almost April. However, in this wood, it still seemed like winter. The blizzard had come an' gone, but it had stripped the life from the wood; put it in mourning so to speak, or at least I believed so at the time."

"So the spring things didn't grow?"

He shook his head. "Not that year, no. But it was more than that." He fidgeted where he sat. "The blizzard brought something with it. Something evil."

She waited, breath baited and eyes wide. He seemed to be taking a long time to get to the best bit. It crossed her mind as to whether or not he was telling her a true story, or another tale. It had seemed to start off true but now … well? She wasn't so sure.

"Hannah!" It was Dada calling. "Lunch is ready."

Not now, she thought, horrified. Not as Emrys was about to tell her something important.

"Dada, can I—"

"Now please, Missie. Aunty Ffion and Evan will be here soon, and I want to get cleaned up before they arrive."

She pouted and folded her arms across her middle.

"Go on, better do as Dad says," Emrys said. "I'll finish my story next week, okay? I'll rely on you to remember where we got to."

"But—" She huffed, lost for words.

He ruffled her hair. "Do one thing for me, Hannah. Stay away from there." He nodded towards the lane and the wood, his expression solemn. "Stay away until you've heard the whole story—promise me."

She hesitated momentarily. "I promise," she said, though she knew her words didn't sound very convincing, even to herself.

Emrys was raking the cuttings when Ffion and Evan arrived. Hannah loved playing with Jipp, but she preferred it when he stayed at the farm. After his escape on the day they'd moved in, she felt anxious whenever Evan brought him to visit in case he ran off again.

"Don't play out the back until Emrys has finished clearing up. Jipp'll get under his feet," Dada said.

Hannah was glad. They'd have to stay indoors in that case. Dada didn't allow her to play out the front, as he worried about the road.

"Come on, we'll play out the front for a bit," said Evan, already heading for the door.

No, she mouthed. Jipp would be bound to take off up The Lane if they played out there.

She saw her father hesitate and, for a moment, thought he was going to give permission.

"The road's too dangerous, Evan—Jipp might run out. Stay indoors for a bit. I'm sure Emrys won't be much longer, he's already tidying up and Miss Morgan's picking him up at two."

"Her real name's Deryth," Hannah said, grinning. "Emrys told me."

"Now, Missie, just because she's visited doesn't mean you can get personal. She's still Miss Morgan to you."

She noticed him wink at Aunty Ffion, and giggled. She liked to push her luck, given half a chance.

By the time they'd eaten Aunty Ffion's carrot cake, Miss Morgan was back to collect Emrys. As there was no space on the drive, she remained in her car and beeped the horn. Hannah ran to greet her, with Jipp close at heel. Within seconds Dada joined them, seemingly eager to help Emrys load the tools into the boot.

"See you next Saturday." Emrys gave Hannah a knowing wink as he spoke, which she did her best to return.

How did people do that? How was it possible to keep just one eye open? She'd have to practise in front of the mirror. Dada was leaning into the passenger window of the car, chatting to Miss Morgan, and he'd changed his clothes and combed his hair. As he turned, she saw that he'd shaved. She was sure he wasn't going anywhere later. She glanced at Miss Morgan who seemed a bit giggly. Was she blushing? The fine down on Hannah's arms tingled. Surely Dada and Miss Morgan didn't fancy each other? She laughed out loud. Gross! She'd ask him later, once Aunty Ffion left.

"Let's play hide-and-seek," Evan shouted, already running around to the back garden. 'I'll hide first.'

Where were they hiding? How on earth would Evan manage to keep Jipp quiet and stop him from giving the game away? She loved hide-and-seek—it made her tummy tingle with excitement.

She seemed to be searching for ages. She'd discounted all the obvious places. He couldn't have gone indoors—it was against the rules. And he wouldn't have gone around to the front because they'd agreed you were only allowed to hide somewhere in the back garden. After several minutes she was beginning to feel a bit apprehensive. She sat on the bench and listened. Nothing.

She was about ready to shout *give in* when she heard it, the smallest of yaps, quickly stifled, coming from behind the log pile. But she'd already searched there. Evan must have moved when she'd been looking elsewhere. Sneaky! Stealthy as a fox, she crept towards it.

"Boo!" Evan jumped out before she managed to sneak a peek.

"Scared the life out of me!" she said, doubling over in a fit of giggles. Jipp circled round and round, yapping with excitement.

Now it was her turn to hide. She'd already thought of a good place, one where Evan wasn't likely to find her. Earlier, as she'd been showing Miss Morgan her bedroom, she'd noticed Emrys trimming the hedge at the furthest corner of the garden. He'd stacked the cuttings in a dense pile ready for burning, but the pile was difficult to see from the rest of the garden as it was in shade, and well camouflaged.

She considered herself rather cunning, as she was wearing a dark green T-shirt. She'd be able to curl up nice and small behind it, then Evan wouldn't find her for ages. She hoped Jipp was hiding his eyes for the countdown, because otherwise it would be cheating.

Evan was searching at the other end of the garden, close to the house. She heard Jipp's excited yap somewhere in the distance. She hummed to herself, smug. She was a hedgehog, curled in a ball, all safe. From the freshly cut pile of laurel a warm scent wafted—like mint and honey. She picked a leaf and studied it. Glossy green, strong—like a winner in the Olympic Games.

Mr. Andrews had explained about the crown of laurel last week when they'd been practising for sport's day. She remembered how she'd looked away as he said the *crown* word, so her face wouldn't give her away.

And Emrys had told her something else about the laurel too. He explained that a Greek god, called something like *Apple*—she couldn't remember—had fallen madly in love with a nymph named Daphne. She remembered the name, because she watched *Scooby Doo* on Cartoon Network. Anyway, Daphne didn't want to marry the *Apple* guy, so she ran away.

When he caught up with her, she asked her father to help, so he turned her into a laurel tree so the *Apple* guy wouldn't want to marry her. Emrys said the *Apple* guy promised to take care of her and make sure she would live forever, and that was why laurel was evergreen. He also said the laurel was a symbol of fame. Perhaps she would ask him to make her a crown of laurel when he came next week, then she might become famous like Mamma. Wouldn't it be cool? After all, the crown of thorns, given to her by the tree creature, had been *so* disappointing.

Evan was getting closer. She held her breath. Would Jipp catch her scent? She hoped the fragrance from the laurel would disguise it and keep her from discovery.

Perhaps, if she wished hard enough, she might turn into a laurel like Daphne. He would never find her then. Squeezing her eyes shut tight, she wished hard.

***

"Are you keeping a secret from me, Dada?" Hannah said later, when they were curled up on the sofa, Bleddyn with his Saturday night glass of wine and her with hot chocolate topped with whipped cream.

"No, whatever gave you that idea?"

"Do you think Miss Morgan's pretty?" She giggled and put her hand over her mouth because the words had spilled out without permission.

Bleddyn stiffened. Then, pausing for a second or two, he answered. "Well of course she's pretty. But lots of people are pretty—you're pretty, Tess Daly's pretty—"

He tickled her playfully, but she knew he was a bit mortified. So he did fancy her then. She grinned, then held her breath, before biting the bullet … "And Mamma? Do you think she's pretty?"

His expression turned solemn. He seemed to struggle to find the right words. "Yes … I always considered Mamma pretty, but beauty isn't just on the outside, Hannah. What's far more important is inner beauty. Even the most beautiful or handsome of people can be unattractive if they are not nice on the inside."

She frowned, puzzled. "How can you see what someone's like inside? Do you mean give them an x-ray?"

"No … when we talk about what someone's like on the inside what we mean is their personality—what kind of person they are. So if someone's mean, and does nasty things to others, it's difficult to find them attractive. Does that make sense?"

She nodded, deep in thought. "So you think Mamma was mean to go back to live in Sweden?"

Bleddyn groaned. "I don't know, Hannah. All right, if I'm honest I do think it was mean of her to go back to Sweden while you're still young."

"So you don't find her pretty anymore?"

"Good grief, Hannah! She's pretty to look at, but I'm not attracted to her as a person any longer because she's been hurtful to you, and anyone who hurts you is unattractive to me. End of!"

She knew she was pushing her luck, but she had him talking about Mamma and Miss Morgan, so she wasn't ready to let go yet. "So you think Miss Morgan is pretty on the outside *and* on the inside because she's kind to me?"

He slapped his forehead. "Now don't start having any fancy ideas about my thoughts on Miss Morgan. She's your special helper, and I'm glad the two of you get on well—and that's it. Discussion over!"

She slurped the creamy remnants of hot chocolate, swiping a finger round the last of the froth before turning to him. "But you don't want to marry her." It was a statement, not a question.

He stood. "Right. Bedtime. You have rehearsals at nine in the morning, and you know what you're like when I have to get you up early on Sundays. Off you go." Pulling her from the sofa, he pinched her cheek playfully and laughed. "You're a wicked little devil at times."

She lay in bed, unable to sleep. What if Dada got married again? To Miss Morgan, or to anyone else? How would she feel? Thinking about it made her tummy feel a bit sick. It would be nice to be a bridesmaid, though. But she didn't want another Mamma.

***

Bleddyn drained the remnants of the bottle of merlot into the glass. Switching off the TV, the contents of which since she'd gone to bed had merely washed over him, he leaned back on the sofa and folded his arms behind his head. How would she cope if he found someone else? Still, he supposed there was little chance of it ever happening. He knew without a shadow of doubt, it would be difficult to find someone willing to commit to a man in his situation. Hannah was his responsibility, and his alone. He would never even consider a relationship with another woman if it might in any way adversely affect Hannah's wellbeing.

He must admit though, Deryth Morgan was special. He hadn't felt this way about a woman in a very long time.

Talent

"Well done!' Carys clapped as the girls ended their dance routine. 'You've obviously been working hard. I'm so proud of you, and I know September seems like a lifetime away, but it's only eight weeks, and I tell you, those weeks will fly."

Hannah's insides bubbled like a glass of champagne. On the one hand she was thrilled she'd finally managed not to make a single mistake throughout the whole routine, but the thought of performing in front of a real audience within a matter of weeks was something else.

"Come." Carys beckoned the children to sit on the floor in front of her. "I have something special to tell you." The excited chatter stopped instantly. "I didn't mention it before as I needed to be certain." Her gaze swept over the group. "I have a friend who works for the National Youth Theatre, and I've persuaded her to come and see the show." All eyes fixed on her, expectantly. "And this friend of mine is what's called a talent spotter, which means it's her job to look out for young people with exceptional talent."

A gasp of surprise spread throughout the class.

"Megan's sorted, then," one of the boys crowed.

"Don't be stupid!" Megan said, embarrassed because everyone's attention had turned on her.

Carys raised a hand. "We won't be singling anyone out. It's not kind to put individuals under pressure. It's a special opportunity for all of you, that's all. Nothing more, nothing less. All I'm saying is practise hard over the next eight weeks, so at least you can feel you gave it your best shot."

"Miss—what will it mean if you get spotted?" Jasmine asked.

"Well, it means she might take your details and add you to her directory, then, if and when a suitable role comes up, she might contact you for an audition."

"For the TV?"

"TV, film, theatre—you name it."

Animated chatter filled the room, and Carys wondered if she'd done the right thing by telling them. Perhaps it would have been better to have said nothing and let Ife do her thing. But shouldn't they have the opportunity to give a hundred per cent?

She clapped her hands. "Come on, guys—back to it. Chloe, Jack—we need to go over The Crime and Punishment Tango."

As they drove home, Hannah watched the cars whizz by on the other side of the road. Dada seemed in a hurry. She watched him out of the corner of her eye. His eyebrows met in the middle when he was stressed, so he must be stressed right now. She hadn't told him about Carys's friend, the talent spotter, yet. When he picked her up from drama club, he seemed to want to hurry her, and besides, she wanted to think about it a bit first. Had Carys's friend, Ife, been the one who'd spotted Mamma's talent? It couldn't have been her, because Mamma had been an actor for a very long time … unless of course Carys's friend was very old. Hannah thought it unlikely.

***

Bleddyn caught a glimpse of his frown in the rear-view mirror and tried to relax his face. The conversation last night about Emily and Deryth had unnerved him. For some reason he'd been unable to get it off his mind ever since. He'd hoped to make a stab at completing his final round of edits while Hannah was in drama club so they might do something nice with the afternoon, but he'd been unable to focus. He'd have to try harder.

"Fancy a walk after lunch?" He glanced across at her.

"Ooh, yes! Where to, Dada?"

"Well, how about we walk the lane as far as Emrys's farm? Be interesting, wouldn't it? Perhaps even have a wander through the wood."

"No!"

The decisiveness in her voice unnerved him. "Why not? I thought you'd enjoy it."

"I—I think it would be rude."

"Rude? How so?"

"Well—it doesn't belong to us, does it? So we'd be tresping. What if Emrys sees us and thinks we've turned up for tea without being asked?"

He grinned. "You mean trespassing. Emrys owns the track and woodland, and he's a friend, so I'm sure he wouldn't mind. Anyway, it's up to you. Do you have a better idea?"

"Yes. The beach."

He groaned. "It will mean another drive, Hannah. I meant a walk from the house."

"Please, Dada? I love the beach … and I have something important to tell you."

"Oh all right. You win—as usual." He laughed as she fist-pumped the air. "I'll have to remember to ask Emrys about the wood. It'll be nice to have a walk up there some time. So what's this important news you have for me?"

"You'll have to wait." She tapped the side of her nose. "I'll tell you when we're at the beach, eating chocolate ice cream."

"Ooh, you canny devil! You can raid your piggy bank—the treats on you."

She giggled. She knew he didn't mean it.

***

When he'd picked her up, Dada's face seemed serious, all frowny, but after they decided to go to the beach his face looked okay again, as if a dark cloud had blown away. She was worried for a minute, when he suggested a walk in The Lane. She'd needed to think fast. She'd promised Emrys to stay away until she'd heard the whole story. And there was another reason—what if Dada saw Tarian or the tree creature? She'd managed to convince him to go to the beach, which wasn't surprising. She usually managed to get her own way. When Emrys came next, she'd need to prepare him in case Dada asked again. She'd get Emrys to make up some excuse.

Her feet, still hot from dancing, were instantly soothed by the cool sea. She stood still for as long as possible, enjoying the challenge as the strength of the waves sucked the sand from beneath her feet, until it made her so wobbly, she had to take a step.

She grasped Dada's hand to steady herself as the next wave pulled back out to sea.

"So, what's this important news then?"

"Ah, nearly forgot! Well, Carys has a friend called a talent spotter, and she's coming to see the show." Hannah shrieked as the next wave broke, wilder than the previous few.

"And what has Carys said about this?"

"She'll be looking for kids who have special talent. Then she might get them a job on TV."

"Well, that sounds nice, doesn't it? Does anyone in your drama group have special talent?"

Hannah paused. She knew *she* didn't, and she also knew lots of the other kids were nothing special, even though they did their best. "Mmm … Megan."

"Megan who came to visit?"

Dada didn't sound convinced, but he hadn't seen Megan on stage, had he? "Yes. She's the only one who can do a handstand with one arm and she"—she shrugged—"don't know … she's just better than us," she said without envy.

They were headed away from the sea, back towards the rocks. "Perhaps she's more confident, Hannah, you know—truly believes in herself. Sometimes people are able to let their inhibitions go so they seem more capable than others, when, in fact, they aren't necessarily."

"What's in–ib—?"

"Inhibitions? It means shyness, so if someone isn't at all shy, they don't care what others think when they perform."

"Like a show-off?"

He laughed. "I suppose. The thing is, in the world of acting and dancing, you could be accused of showing off if you do well, which isn't really fair, as if you weren't able to let go of your shyness you wouldn't be any good at it, would you?"

"Suppose." She shrugged. "Come on, let's go get ice cream." She sprang off the rocks. "Last one there gets to pay!"

Hannah stole a few glances over her shoulder as she ran. Dada was struggling to run in the sand. She was bound to beat him.

DEATH OF THE LAMBS

A persistent drizzle threatened to spoil the whole weekend. Emrys rang at nine to see if Bleddyn still wanted him to come. Hannah stood listening at the kitchen doorway, her fingers gripping the frame tightly.

"I'm happy as long as you are," Bleddys said.

Hannah fist-pumped the air. "Is Emrys still coming?" she asked, the second he put down the phone.

"Yes. He's going to tackle the junk in the old shed at the bottom of the garden as it's too wet to mow the lawn. You'd best keep out of his way. It's dangerous in there."

Her face fell. "I'll help him. I won't get in the way."

"No, Hannah, when we moved in, I threw all the stuff we didn't want, and what was left around the garden, in the shed. It's dangerous. There are things you might cut yourself on—bits of wire and stuff. Stay indoors."

She pouted and folded her arms across her chest. "But I'm bored. I want to help Emrys."

"If you're bored, spend some time learning your lines. You don't have much time left before the show."

"Know them already!"

"Do you indeed?" He raised an eyebrow.

She stuck out her chin. "Yes—all of them."

He picked up the copy of her script. "Come on then. I'll play the other parts."

Hannah grinned, knowing she had him beat.

Bleddyn was flabbergasted. To his knowledge, her script had remained unopened on the kitchen shelf where she'd left it. She was word perfect, she even had the gestures off to pat. And what thrilled him most was the hint of expression in her tone of voice, something he knew she found especially difficult. Granted, she didn't have many lines, but he was astonished at how well she'd learned those she did have.

"Well done, Missie! Tell me how you managed that when the script's been in the envelope this past month? I was beginning to think you didn't care."

"Ha, ha! Fooled you. I had another copy in my bag." She beamed with pleasure. "So—can I help Emrys now?"

How could he refuse her? "We'll see what he says when he gets here, okay?"

"Deal!" She raised her hand for him to strike the bargain.

***

"Now, where were we?" Emrys handed Hannah another half-used tin of paint to add to the stack already threatening to topple off the wooden pallet.

"Something evil came with the snow." She hadn't forgotten—his story had even crept into her dreams.

"Ah yes, that's right. Thing is, in my head I've gone over and over what happened so many times I forget where I got to." He chuckled and ruffled her hair, as he often did.

She squinted at him, waiting for the next bit.

"Well … remember I told you 'bout how we lost a few lambs cos of the snow?"

She nodded.

"I didn't see it at the time, but later on, after the other bad things, I realized it wasn't right."

She frowned.

"You see, all the dead lambs appeared perfect. They'd been cleaned off by the ewes which meant they could breathe freely, an' each one was found a little distance from its mother, as though something had dragged it away. You see, Hannah, if a lamb is already dead inside its mother, she usually has trouble bringing it into the world, but it wasn't the case. Once they're up on their feet they stick together, lamb and ewe."

She stopped stacking cans and watched him closely.

"A ewe doesn't leave its lamb like that, Hannah. It sticks close. The lambs we found were all separated. Like I said, I didn't pay too much attention at the time. I put it down to the snow an' the ewes being too exhausted to allow them to suckle." He paused, lost in the past. "Some'ut wasn't right." He shook his head. "It didn't add up. There was nowt wrong with those lambs when they were born. No—something killed them afterwards."

"Like a wolf?" Hannah asked, eyes round as pennies.

"Not a wolf—they'd have borne the marks if it was a wolf. These were perfect—not a scratch on them. So whatever killed them did it out of spite, not for the want of a meal."

Hannah gasped.

"You rarely find that kind of behaviour outside of the human world, Hannah. Animals hardly ever kill out of spite, an' if they do, you'll see marks from the attack."

Hannah thought hard. "Perhaps they died because of the snow."

"That's what we all believed … for a while. But later on, we discovered the true reason."

***

Hannah couldn't sleep. She wasn't in the least bit tired, but it was ten o'clock and Dada insisted she went to bed. She lay awake, going over and over what Emrys had told her that afternoon. She hadn't been frightened so much as— How did she feel about his story? Confused, perhaps.

The death of the lambs was one thing, but the rest of it? She wasn't so sure. And yet lots of the things Emrys talked about she'd witnessed herself, such as the birds suddenly taking flight, the small creatures hiding in their dens, and even the leaves falling still, all of which resulted in a strange silence in the wood.

And he'd spoken about the smell, too, only whereas she'd smelled Mamma's perfume, he'd smelled decay and rot. "Death," he'd said. "When you live on a farm you can spot the stench of death a mile away." He hadn't wanted to scare her, but it was important she knew about the wood so she would be safe.

"There are dangers we know about," he'd said, his face all serious, "then there are dangers we aren't prepared for, which can surprise even the hardiest of folk, like me."

"Dangers like wolves?" she'd asked, hoping he would say no. Tarian's face had sprung to mind. Such a kind face.

"Nah, bach. We've done more harm to wolves than ever they've done to us," he'd said, and his face had seemed sad. The creases at the corners of his mouth travelled all the way to the end of his chin, and his pale blue eyes, with their little red veins, glistened like glass. "Hunted them out of lands we could have happily shared with them—an' that's coming from a farmer."

At first his face had been a bit angry, but soon he'd cheered up a bit, more like his usual self. "Together we can beat her, Hannah."

Who did he mean?

"We need to stick together an' do what's good an' right. Mustn't let her tempt us with her trickery. As long as we stay on the path, she can't harm us … Do you understand what I'm trying to tell you?"

She hadn't, so she asked him if he meant the path in The Lane, and he said yes. Then she asked him who *she* was, and he answered with such confusing words, she still hadn't understood. "The witch who comes to us in disguise," he'd said. "She who lets us see what we want to see; hear what we want to hear; smell what we want to smell. She who arrived on the blizzard an' whom we've kept captive for a decade." His voice was little more than a sore whisper, and his eyes penetrated the wood as he spoke.

He'd forgotten Hannah, or he wouldn't have said such confusing things. Before she had a chance to press him for more information, Dada appeared with two mugs of tea, one for Emrys and one for himself, and from his pocket handed her a finger of chocolate. She hadn't felt like eating it because her mind was all churned about like the inside of a washing machine. And to top it all Dada had said, "Oh, by the way Emrys, would you mind if me and Hannah walk the lane sometime—maybe have a wander in the wood?"

She'd forgotten to warn Emrys about Dada being likely to ask that stupid question, and she'd kicked herself in the shin for forgetting. She reached under the quilt and rubbed the sore part. It still hurt … she'd probably have a bruise in the morning.

She'd been horrified, but Emrys had remained calm. "The wood is fenced off with barbed wire, Bleddyn," he said. "Did it a couple of years back cos there was evidence of people messing with nest sites an' such. Steep under foot in there, too. Don't know if Hannah'd manage it. Tell you what, why don't you drive up to the farm one day an' I'll walk you around the tracks?" He'd seemed so genuine that Dada had fallen for it without being in the least bit suspicious or offended. Emrys had winked at Hannah behind Dada's back.

Who was this witch that could make you see things? She'd wanted to ask Emrys more about her, and yet again Dada had spoiled it. She was glad he'd stuck up for wolves, because her heart told her Tarian seemed trustworthy. Instinct, Dada called it, like knowing you shouldn't jump off a bridge.

Was it possible the witch he talked about was the tree creature? Yes, she was beautiful, but beautiful people weren't always good. She'd learned that much. She closed her eyes and asked her instinct for help, and it told her what she didn't want to hear. *The tree creature is the witch*, it said, and her heart fluttered like a butterfly.

But the tree creature had given her back the brooch … and more than that, she reminded her of Mamma. A lump formed in her throat. Ugh! If only she'd had time to ask Emrys more questions. Why did Dada always seem to arrive at the best bits? She beat the pillow with her fists.

And deep in the wood, a thwarted fox screamed in kindred empathy.

***

One might consider it a mercy killing, Rhiamon mused, as she snapped the fox's neck with one swift twist. Clearly it was already injured. She'd watched it drag its hind leg for several nights but had been too disinterested to end its suffering … until now. She would not take its soul. It was sullied by surplus killing, and therefore of no value.

As to her real motive? Didn't she have every right to be angry? The old dewin and the girl had spent several hours together in the garden, gossiping and whispering while pretending to work. The mizzle in the wood had helped cloud her appearance as she spied from the canopy of hawthorn.

He was already warning the child, spinning his tales and lies to fill the girl with fear. She must entice Hannah to return soon, and tempt her with the promise of granting her anything she wanted by means of her magic. Perhaps she would enchant her with music, then make her an offer too good to refuse. She crowed at the thought and kicked the useless carcass of the fox into the hedge, its sightless, yellow eye judging her all the while.

Perched within the boundary, she watched the girl's window, the ripening moon a guiding orb in the secretive night sky. The girl lay disturbed; unable to sleep. So he had told her things that caused her mind to become restless.

From inside a small bag, hewn from the plucked carcass of a rook, she withdrew a single, white hair and twirled it between forefinger and thumb. One silver thread, spinning in the moonlight. How much suffering might she inflict were she to use it against the dewin? She'd taken it from the coat he'd carelessly discarded in the yard before—

The screaming bark of the badger, deep in the black wood, resonated with her frustration. Rhiamon lay her head on the cool, mossy ground, remembering.

***

The long, summer evening finally succumbed to dusk. As she waited for the milk to boil, Deryth gazed beyond the kitchen window towards the constellation, Scorpius. How apt, considering she'd been remembering what had happened all those years back. It had been a sting in the tail, and they were still having to endure its repercussions.

She remembered as if it were yesterday …

She and Tadcu had spent most of the morning unfreezing the water troughs and laying fresh beds of straw in the byre for the cows in an attempt to save their teats from frostbite. It was hard work, especially with the snow still falling and the temperature remaining close to zero.

During the previous week, several calves had been born at the farm. They'd made sure all were cleaned off, and that each and every one of them received the cow's colostrum shortly after birth to give them the best possible start.

Deryth shook her head, remembering the lull before the storm. A few days earlier it had seemed as though spring was about to arrive early, like an eagerly anticipated visitor. Without warning, the temperature plummeted, swiftly followed by the blizzard, the likes of which she'd never seen. How old had she been? Seventeen, in the first year of sixth form.

Warm milk with a sprinkle of cinnamon in hand, she returned to the comfort of the sofa. Glancing at the clock, she saw it was well past midnight, but she wasn't in the least bit tired. There was too much on her mind. The comfort of warm milk always reminded her of childhood, when Tadcu would let her drink a glass straight from the cow.

"Good for your immunity," he'd say. "Got to have your peck of dirt—makes you strong."

He believed in the old ways. She wouldn't dream of drinking it unpasteurized these days. He still drank it though, and it had done him no harm. Then again, it would take more than a few bacteria to see him off, as he was made of iron. *Emrys* … named for the great Merlin. She'd have to remember to tell Hannah the story of Dinas Emrys, the place of legend, where two mighty dragons had fought.

The pages of her magazine remained invisible as she flicked through, her mind returning to the first day and night of the blizzard all those years earlier …

It was she who'd spotted the first dead lamb, its frozen body stiff and silent in the snow. As a farmer's daughter, she was familiar with death—already on speaking terms. As she lifted it by its middle, its little woolly head had hung limp, its eyes were closed, peaceful. She'd called out to Tadcu. No sign of injury, no blood, and the lamb had been licked clean by its mother. She recoiled, recalling the traces of caked milk around its tiny black nose, its lips already blue. As she held it aloft to Tadcu, its mother, sheltering behind a rock a little way off, had bleated pitifully.

"We'll take them both down," he'd said, freeing her of the lamb. "Find her a surrogate. She'll be all right."

That was before they'd found the others.

***

Emrys tossed and turned, unable to sleep. The events may well have happened almost a decade ago, but the memories were as fresh as today's bread. It hadn't made sense at the time and still didn't to some degree. Six newborn souls lost, and he could only surrogate two. It had been a conundrum all right, then to have lost the calf too. Closing his eyes, he summoned the memory.

They'd waded knee-deep down from the mountain, cheeks two rosy apples, and each breath a cloud of grey to match their sadness. Two sacks of feed on the way up bore six dead lambs on the way down. Neither spoke on the return journey, each bearing the mental and physical burden of the carcasses as the sacks bounced against their backs.

He'd deposited them in the bin used especially for fallen stock. "It's a tough old life at times, bach," he'd said when Deryth had asked how they died. "Might be the cold, who knows? I'll ring the knacker to arrange a collection. It'll be a few days before he'll get through this snow I reckon." Even then he'd known deep down that something more sinister was afoot, though he hadn't wanted to tell her, not until he was certain.

Deryth had said nothing, but the ring of indigo that ran around her irises had turned a shade deeper.

They'd entered the barn next, where the calves were being kept in pens to protect them from the snow. 'Let's get the thermal jackets on those young 'uns,' he'd said. But as soon as they slid open the door, they knew something was wrong. The calves seemed skittish, their heads and ears lowered, and their tails tucked between their legs. Something had frightened them. And the smell … The familiar aroma of warm hay and manure was tinged with another scent—death. Emrys recognized it immediately. The third pen revealed the victim, a black-and-white belted Galloway, its snub nose dry as cinders and its huge, black eyes open—pleading for help that never arrived.

Deryth had stomped off in fury, the deep snow in the yard silencing her wellington-clad footsteps. Minutes later the barn door slid open and she stood there calmer, anticipating his reaction. Slipping something from the righthand pocket of her coat, she held it out to him—an offering of peace. He took from her hand the Rowan stick, bearing the Ogham symbol, Luis, a symbol of protection against enchantment and magic. Like him, she'd also known what they must do. "It's not just the snow is it, Tadcu?" she'd said, her mournful eyes as sombre as those of the dead calf.

They'd stood in the shelter of the barn door, gazing into the magenta twilight sky beyond the farm into the snowy hills, both deep in thought. The snow had finally relented, but the howling wind was bitter, venomous with anger.

He'd witnessed it all before down through time, whereas for her it was new. One's first experience of death at the hands of evil was always the hardest, and he hadn't wanted to acknowledge its presence in her company. "We need to be certain," he'd said. "Wait 'til the thaw an' see what happens."

He was buying time; denying the truth; wanting to protect her from what was to come. But deep down, he'd already known it was witchcraft.

Temptation

One more week of school remained before the summer holidays. Hannah was looking forward to all the things she and Dada had planned, but she also felt a bit sad, as school holidays meant she wouldn't get to see Miss Morgan or her friends for six whole weeks. And there would be times when she'd be bored because Dada would have work to do. Still, at least she had drama club, and Carys was fitting in extra classes during the school holidays so they could prepare for September's production.

Her stomach did a jig, then it did an encore, as she realized that when she went back to school in September, she would be in Year Six with one more year before High School.

On Friday, after she'd finished her work in the library, Miss Morgan told her the legend of Dinas Emrys, a mountain near Beddgelert. Hannah had heard of the wizard Merlin because she'd watched *Shrek the Third.* The funniest bit was when Shrek said he trusted Merlin, even though his cloak didn't cover his butt. She laughed out loud, remembering. However, the story Miss Morgan told her about the real Merlin was far more serious.

Apparently, Myrrdin Emrys, Merlin's real name, had told the king the reason his castle on the mountain kept falling down was because the two dragons who lived beneath it were constantly fighting. The red dragon beat the white dragon, and the king was able to build his castle. As a reward the king named the mountain after him.

Miss Morgan also reckoned Merlin had hidden treasure in a cave in the mountain, and whoever found it would be fair-haired and blue-eyed. Hannah wanted to know what kind of treasure, but Miss Morgan said she wasn't sure. Hannah closed her eyes and pictured a heap of gold coins spilling from an old trunk, and jewels too. Yes, there must have been jewels. She'd love to find some emeralds. She'd have them made into earrings, when she was old enough to have her ears pierced. Dada insisted she'd have to wait until she was sixteen … such a long time! The emerald earrings would match her eyes, and at a glance, someone might even think she had four eyes—that would be weird! Like some kind of alien.

She wished she'd known about the treasure when Dada had taken her to Beddgelert, then they might have gone looking for it. However, there wouldn't have been much point, as her hair wasn't fair, and she didn't have blue eyes. Her face lit up. Ah, but Miss Morgan did. Maybe they'd go again in the summer holidays and take Miss Morgan with them. Perhaps they'd find the treasure, plus she wouldn't have to wait six whole weeks before seeing her again … and perhaps Dada'd get to kiss her! Her stomach did a somersault at the thought.

Aunty Ffion and Evan had already left, and Dada was working in his office, so she was all alone in the garden. She'd heard a strange sound in The Lane the night before—a mixture of a scream and a bark that seemed to go on and on for ages. In fact, she was surprised Dada hadn't heard it. It had sounded like a bad-tempered child having a tantrum, except the voice was deeper than a child's. She'd wanted to ask Dada what it might have been, but she didn't want him asking too many questions, so she'd kept the sound to herself and throughout the day replayed it over and over in her head.

She was *so* tempted to walk The Lane. It was like trying to resist a second jam doughnut. It was right there, willing you to reach out and take it. However, she'd promised Emrys she wouldn't, at least not until he'd finished telling her the story right to the end without Dada interrupting. Or had she promised to stay on the path? Yes, come to think of it, she'd promised to stick to the path.

Elongated shadows criss-crossed the path ahead as she climbed. Walking beneath the shadow's limbs reminded her of the playground game, *Oranges and Lemons.* What was the last line? Oh yes, *and here comes a chopper to chop off your head!* That bit always made her nervous.

Would Tarian or the tree creature come this evening? Her heart gave a little stab at the thought of the tree creature, reminding her that she might be the witch Emrys tried to warn her about. Meeting her again was tempting. Not only was she very beautiful, but Hannah still needed to ask how she'd got hold of the brooch. She sat on the wall and waited to see what, if anything, might happen.

***

Perched high in the oak, Rhiamon smirked. She hadn't even needed to call her. The girl had come of her own free will. She'd need to keep the conversation jovial today, as she was certain he'd tried to warn the girl off.

Light as a feather, she dropped to the ground and edged nearer and nearer, watching. Drawing close to the vicinity of the boundary, she stopped. The girl neither saw nor heard her approach. She took another step, her expression innocent as a lamb's.

"'It's a beautiful evening," she said.

Hannah did not reply, nor did she make eye contact. Unsurprising, considering the dewin had got to her.

"You have not lived here long. From where have you come?"

"England." Hannah sniffed the air, detecting a hint of her mother's scent.

Rhiamon suppressed the smirk that played around her lips. The child remained seated on the wall, her fingers gripping the edge. Rhiamon noticed the whites of her knuckles and knew it had taken courage to return.

"Where did you find my brooch?" Hannah asked, her voice as small as a field mouse.

Rhiamon paused. "Do you believe in the truth? Even if it hurts?"

"Y—"

She raised an eyebrow and studied Hannah's face. "You won't like what I'm about to tell you."

Hannah remained seated, waiting.

"Come closer, so I might whisper." She beckoned a graceful finger at Hannah, who did as she was bid.

Keeping her distance from the boundary, Rhiamon leaned forward and placed her ruby lips close to Hannah's ear—so close it tickled. "The girl who came to visit that day, the day the brooch went missing."

Hannah remembered. "You mean Megan, my friend."

"Huh! Believe me, child, she is no friend of yours. A wolf in sheep's clothing, that's what she is."

Hannah stepped back and looked deeper into the woods, half expecting to see the wolf dressed as a sheep. The sun lit Rhiamon from behind, projecting her in a goddess-like aura.

"I'm afraid it was she who stole your brooch. I saw her slip it inside her coat pocket as she left the house."

Hannah gasped in disbelief. "She wouldn't—"

"Ah, but she did."

Hannah's eyes brimmed with tears and her bottom lip trembled.

Rhiamon pouted. "There, there. I told you the truth would hurt. Don't be sad. I got it back, didn't I?"

"Yes, but how?"

Rhiamon shook her head. "Let's just say a little magic goes a long way."

Hannah felt sick. Surely Megan wouldn't do such a thing? But she had fallen in love with the dress … and the brooch. Perhaps the creature was telling the truth. She'd heard enough. "I have to go. Dada'll be worried."

Rhiamon watched her leave, a smirk upon her pernicious lips. The child had taken the blow hard. Her head was bowed, and her shoulders sagged. Such fun!

***

Hannah sat on the garden bench, considering what she'd been told. She wouldn't go indoors yet, not unless Dada called her. She needed time to think things through, otherwise her face might give her away. More and more the tree creature disturbed her. Yes, she was like something out of a fairy tale—a beautiful woodland creature. And yet … Emrys's words sprung to mind, especially his warning about her making you see what she wanted you to see.

Might it be true? Was Megan a thief? Hannah knew Megan was used to getting her own way, but until now it hadn't bothered her in the slightest. Also, she was great fun to be with, and wasn't she one of the few children who always set out to make sure Hannah wasn't alone in the playground, as well as in drama club? On the other hand, she had paraded around the bedroom in the dress. Hannah knew she'd fallen in love with it.

Should she talk to Dada about it? But she couldn't. Not unless she was prepared to tell him about the tree creature, too, and she didn't want to.

At times like this she felt so alone.

A PLANNED VISIT

Miss Morgan was going to Kos for the first two weeks of the holidays. Hannah didn't think the place sounded very nice. In fact it sounded a bit rude, like when you asked someone a question and they couldn't be bothered to answer so would shrug their shoulders and say, *cos*. People often did it to her. Still, she wished her happy holidays as she said goodbye on the last day of term.

It had been a pretty tough week at school. Although Megan had seemed the same as usual, Hannah felt distant. She wanted to trust Megan, but she was all confused. And to top it all, Megan was involved in an argument with Millie over who the red Sharpie belonged to. As usual, Megan ended up the winner and told Hannah not to speak to Millie. It made her wonder about the missing brooch again.

***

The second he saw her, Bleddyn knew something was wrong. Her downcast eyes spoke volumes. "What's up, Hannah? I thought you'd be happy at the thought of six whole weeks off school."

She shook her head. "Nothing. Just a silly argument."

"It's not like you to argue."

"Wasn't me—it was Megan and Millie. They argued over a stupid Sharpie. I don't want to be on one person's side. I want to be friends with them both."

"And you can be. You don't need to pick a side, Hannah."

"You're old. You don't get it." She nibbled a hangnail and spat the skin onto the ground.

He decided against reprimanding her. Sometimes it was easier to let things lie.

"Bet Miss Morgan was happy today," he said, glancing at her in the rear view. She always chose to sit in the back when she didn't want to talk. He knew her of old. "Six whole weeks without kids." She ignored him and continued to watch the passing cars.

"Did she say if she was going anywhere nice?"

"Yes, Kos."

"Oh, lucky thing, it's beautiful there. She'll probably come back with a nice tan."

"Where is Kos?"

"It's a Greek island, Hannah … Did she say who she was going with?"

"Friends."

And that was the end of the conversation. He knew she didn't wish to say any more on the subject. He'd wait until they got home and try another tack.

***

As Dada was dishing out dinner, Hannah busied herself with laying the table, so she didn't have to look at him. She didn't know why she took her anger out on him because he'd done nothing to annoy her. She just couldn't help it.

"Emrys is coming around tomorrow," he said.

She wasn't sure whether or not she was pleased to be seeing Emrys the following day. She felt a bit of a traitor having walked The Lane again and having talked to the tree creature, which reminded her, she still hadn't told Hannah her name. She'd have to remember to ask next time.

Perhaps she should talk to Dada. She knew he was concerned, and it wasn't fair to upset him. She'd begin by asking about something that the tree creature had said and take it from there. "Dada … what's a wolf in sheep's clothing?"

He frowned. "Where did you hear that?"

She hesitated. "In school." It was a lie, so she turned her back and pretended to hunt for something in her school bag.

"It means someone is pretending to be nice when in actual fact they are nasty. It's called an idiom."

"An idiot?"

"No Hannah, idiom—when the spoken words have nothing to do with their actual meaning."

She screwed up her face. "Don't get it."

"Well, let me give you another example. Let's take the argument in school today, the one between Megan and Millie."

She nodded.

"Imagine that instead of arguing about who the Sharpie belonged to, Megan pretended to be nice to Millie, then behind her back, she told the other children Millie had stolen it from her."

Did he know the tree creature had said it about Megan? She felt herself blush.

"That would suggest she was a wolf in sheep's clothing because she was pretending to be nice, when in actual fact she was being mean. Do you understand?"

Hannah wished she hadn't mentioned it, so she turned her attention back to laying the table.

***

So her sullen mood hadn't lifted. Since they'd arrived home, she'd hardly spoken—and he'd expected her to come out of school bouncing, what with the holidays ahead. Then again, she needed routine, thrived on it, even. Perhaps this was the reason for her sullenness; maybe she was anxious about the prospect of change.

"Right, Missie, let's make some plans for these coming weeks." They'd cleared away the dishes and were in the process of clearing out her school bag. "Give ourselves something to look forward to, hey?" He desperately wanted to cheer her up.

She pouted. "You have to work."

"True, but I don't intend to work every day. I've been pushing the boat out these past few weeks, so I'll have plenty of time to spend with you."

"You got a boat?"

He slapped his forehead, instantly regretting his mistake. "No Hannah, it's another idiom, it means I've been working extra hard. We can go on a boat ride this summer if you like. How about a trip to Skomer Island? If we're lucky we might even get to see seals—dolphins even." At last a smile.

"That'd be nice, Dada—and don't forget we have to go see Dinas Emrys too. You promised."

"Don't worry—I haven't forgotten. Hey, how about we ask Emrys to come with us? I don't think he has many fun days out, he's always so busy."

The suggestion hit the spot. Grabbing his face in both hands, she kissed him hard on the nose—so hard it hurt.

"I'll ring him!" She skipped towards the living-room to get the phone.

The knot in his stomach loosened a little. "Hey, slow down a minute! He'll be here tomorrow to do the garden. We'll ask him, then we'll be able to arrange a specific day, if he agrees."

"Next week—yes! We'll go next week. Emrys is bound to want to see his own mountain." She held the phone in her hand. "Can we take Miss Morgan too? Please, Dada?"

He hesitated.

"Please?"

"She won't be back from Kos until the following week, so you'll have to be patient if you want her to come."

"“She'll come, I know it. How many sleeps is two weeks Dada?"

He needed to prepare her for possible disappointment, in case Deryth said no. "Listen, Hannah, we can ask her, but you must be prepared for her to say no. You must remember teachers look forward to their summer holidays without kids. She might not want to come—and you mustn't pressure her if she doesn't want to. I know how you can be."

"She'll come. I know she will. Dinas Emrys is her favourite story."

***

Hannah was tucked in bed, reading by what remained of twilight. The book was called *The Snow Queen*, by Hans Christian Andersen, and she'd spotted it in a charity shop a few weeks back. The words were difficult to read, but the pictures were amazing, and she knew the story because Dada had read it to her a couple of times.

One of the reasons she liked it was because Dada had told her the author had been born in Denmark, which wasn't far from Sweden, where Mamma lived. Her favourite picture was the one of the Snow Queen in the wood, the one where Kay is snuggled beneath her icy cloak with the queen kissing the top of his head. It reminded her of when she'd touched the tree creature's hand and it had been freezing. She wouldn't mind betting Kay's lips were turning blue. Never mind, it was summer now, not winter like in the picture, and she had the trip to Dinas Emrys to look forward to. She closed the book and lay it on the windowsill, the one with the lace curtain.

Lifting the corner of lace, she peered into the garden. Dusk—that's what Dada called this time of day, and it was one of her favourite words. It felt nice on her tongue—and it rhymed with tusk, and elephants were her favourite animal … apart from wolves.

Quietly, so as not to alert Dada, she slid the window half open. The trees appeared black against the creeping darkness of the sky. Little hand-shaped silhouettes of summer leaves waved at her in the warm night air. And the fairy lights that led all the way up the path to the top of the garden were beginning to glow. Dada had strung them for her a week or so earlier. He'd told her to imagine they led to another world—one where all the best fairy tales were real. She closed her eyes, delighting in the sweet smell of jasmine that wafted from the climber beneath her window.

Getting back into bed, she pulled the sheet all the way up to her nose and watched as the sky took on hues of mauve and midnight blue.

In the distance, sheep bleated as they were rounded into pens for the night. She would try to enjoy the break from school, for Dada's sake.

Hannah was so focussed on the changing night sky, she failed to notice the beady eye of the tatty old crow, perched atop the blackthorn.

DINAS EMRYS

After her talk with Dada, Hannah resisted speaking to Emrys about the proposed trip to Dinas Emrys when he came to help in the garden the following day. It wasn't easy, and there were a few moments when she needed to physically bite her tongue.

By the time another two weeks had passed, she imagined she might burst. Never before had she needed to keep a secret for such a long time. Dada said he was proud of her, and it was another sign she was growing up. However, when Emrys arrived, she was temporarily distracted when he handed her a small parcel wrapped in pale blue tissue.

"Deryth asked me to give you this—she brought it back from Kos for you."

"Ooh, look Dada, a present."

She tore the gold sticker that secured the folds of tissue in one swift rent, and the wrapping gave, spilling its contents to the floor. It was a small purse, made of turquoise leather, with a long strap. "Wow!" She passed the strap through one arm and wore it cross-body, examining the illustration printed on its front.

"What do you say to Emrys?"

"Thank you, Emrys. I love it!"

Emrys chuckled. "Deryth will be pleased. She's put something inside, too. It's unlucky to give an empty purse—asking for trouble."

Hannah was too busy tracing her finger along the outline of the magnificent bird engraved on the front to acknowledge his comment. Its wings were huge and brightly coloured in shades of peacock blue.

"It's a phoenix, Hannah, the mythical Greek bird of rebirth," Bleddyn said.

She frowned. "Felix is a cat!"

"No, I said phoenix—a bird. Emrys said there's something extra inside for you, too."

She heard that time. With a twist of the catch, she opened the purse and groped about. "Ooh, what's this?" Between thumb and forefinger she held a dark stone, attached to a leather cord.

Emrys winked at her, and his eyes glinted in the sunshine. "A necklace—black tourmaline. Used to belong to Deryth. She wants you to have it—keep you safe from harm."

She passed the cord of the necklace over her head and tucked the stone beneath her T-shirt. She wasn't keen on black jewellery but didn't want to appear rude. She bounced on the spot. "Can I ask now, Dada?"

He laughed. "Go on then, but remember what I said about not putting on the pressure."

"What's all this, then?" Emrys said, giving her his full attention.

"Me and Dada are going to North Wales to visit your mountain, and I really, really, REALLY want you and Miss Morgan to come with us." She tilted her head, eyes pleading.

"We'd both love you to come, Emrys—if you can spare a day away from the farm of course. A treat on us, and a way of saying thank you for all you've done. Thought we might take a picnic and have a pub meal on the way back and—" He stopped himself and shook his head. "I've spent the last two weeks telling Hannah not to pressure you, and here I am doing the same thing. Sorry, Emrys."

"Not at all! Sounds grand. Can't speak for Deryth, but I'll give her a ring tonight and let you know." He ruffled Hannah's hair. "Right, Missie, you gonna give us a hand today?"

"Yes! Yes! But do you think she'll come?"

"Patience, Hannah," Bleddyn warned. "Emrys has said he'll ring and ask. Don't nag."

She pouted.

"What day did you say you're going?" Emrys asked.

"I didn't. We're pretty much free all of next week, so we'll be happy to fit in with you and Deryth … and the weather of course."

Later that evening, and to Hannah's delight, Emrys rang to confirm Deryth would accompany them, so the visit was planned for the following Wednesday. Hannah fist-pumped the air. 'Yes!' Reaching inside her T-shirt, she produced the black stone. It was warm to the touch, and felt as if Miss Morgan was sending her a hug from wherever she was right now. This time she left it on show.

"Can we google this, Dada?" She held the stone between thumb and forefinger.

"Google what, Hannah?"

"This stone. Emrys called it a black something. I can't remember."

"Black tourmaline … all right, give me a minute to boot the computer."

She sort of knew how to search for simple words on the internet, but one—she didn't have a clue how to spell the *torma* word, and two—whenever she tried to find out things by herself, so many words and adverts popped up, she ended up learning nothing, so it was always best when Dada helped.

Dada did this thing with his eyes when he was looking for information on the internet—they seemed to flick over the words, and she knew he wasn't reading properly. Sometimes he made a funny noise at the same time, a sort of hum, until he discovered what he was looking for, then he read the words out loud.

"Why do you do that? It's annoying."

"Do what, Hannah?"

"The noise. It makes me feel left out—like I don't know what's going on inside your head."

"Sorry. I'm skimming the text—you know, trying to find the bits of information I need rather than read the whole thing. Some of it's a load of rubbish, see."

"Like skimming a stone?"

"Kind of. In fact it's a good way to think about it. Remember when we went to the beach and I taught you how to skim stones on the water?"

"Mmm."

"Well, think of the stones as my eyes bouncing over the page."

"Right … and?"

"Well, when they find what they're looking for, they read it properly. That's called *scanning*, like the machine that scans the barcode on the things we buy at the supermarket."

She paused, considering his explanation. "Will I be able to do it when I'm older?"

"With practise you will. Like every skill, it takes practise. As your reading improves, it'll get easier."

"I'll be on Stage Nine books when I go back to school."

"I know, you clever thing. Which reminds me, Miss Morgan gave you an extra three books for the holidays, and we haven't read any of them yet."

She ignored his remark. "So what does it say about the stone?"

Bleddyn interpreted the information on the screen in a way she would understand. "Black tourmaline is the best crystal to use against harmful spirits. It creates a kind of force field around a person to stop anything evil hurting them."

"Ooh, I like!" She spotted a ghost-like image on the screen and knew it was a YouTube video. "Play the ghost, Dada!"

"No, Hannah, it's not for children. It's too scary."

"But—"

"No buts. Now, go and get one of those reading books."

She giggled as he flipped her across the bottom, and ran off to find her school bag.

After tea she sat in the garden for a while. She still wore the necklace outside her T-shirt. Taking it in her right hand, she studied it closely. It was highly polished and, in the sunshine, reflected the fish pond behind her. The lilies were beginning to die back now August had arrived. They seemed a bit sad.

When Emrys said about the stone keeping her from harm it hadn't made sense, but remembering what Dada found out on the internet made her think a bit more about it. *A force field,* he'd said, *from evil.* Perhaps when she wore it, she would become the Invisible Woman from *Fantastic Four.* That'd be cool. Turning to the fish, she yelled, "This is our chance to make a difference!"

Why had Miss Morgan chosen it? Did she know about Tarian and the tree creature? She doubted it. More than likely Emrys had told her what the two of them spoke about when they had their little chats in the garden. Yes, that would explain it.

***

Bleddyn considered the climb to the top of Dinas Emrys pretty taxing, but despite the steep climb, Hannah did not stop talking. He often needed to hold her hand or give her a bit of a push as she tired easily. He guessed she was so caught up in the moment that she didn't even register the effort it took. And besides, Emrys struggled a little, so they took their time. He wouldn't mind betting she'd be exhausted later.

They picnicked beside Merlin's Pool, and after they ate, Hannah insisted on Deryth retelling the story of the two dragons.

Emrys grew quiet as Deryth spoke of the warlord Vortigen's plans to kill Myrddin in order to appease the supernatural powers he believed were preventing him from building his fortress. He sat at a little distance from the rest of them, hypnotized by the unceasing torrent of water cascading down the mountain. There was something almost spiritual about him, and yet at the same time down to earth. He was a man who gained pleasure from the simple things in life—totally unpretentious.

Hannah insisted they search for the cave where the purported treasure lay hidden, all to no avail, of course. Still, she made a lucky find in a small piece of iron pyrite close to the water's edge which satisfied her. Deryth explained it symbolized the return of light to one's life and impressed Bleddyn with the way she followed this up with a sound explanation of what such *light* might signify. She certainly understood Hannah's needs.

Having passed through the town of Machynlleth, they were approximately halfway home. Bleddyn glanced at the sat nav—four miles or so to go until they would reach the Llew Coch Inn, their intended dinner destination.

During the journey home, Bleddyn glanced in the rearview mirror to where Hannah lay with her head in Deryth's lap. He'd not seen her so at peace for some time. Her cheeks flushed pink, and her dark eyelashes appeared moist against the delicate, pale skin beneath her eyelids. Deryth's eyes were closed, too. In the passenger seat beside him, the lulling rhythm of Emrys's gentle snores suggested he, too, was exhausted.

What was most comforting was how relaxed they'd all been in each other's company. Dare he consider a future where Deryth might become more than a friend to Hannah? More than an acquaintance to himself, even? And Emrys a surrogate grandparent? He knew he was jumping the gun, but recently he'd been feeling lonely for the first time since Emily had left. Eight years had passed by, and this was the first time the possibility of beginning a new relationship had entered his head. His stomach lurched at the thought.

He stole further glances. Deryth was a real beauty. Her left arm cradled Hannah's head, her hand occasionally stroking her sweat-damp hair, even while her own eyes remained closed.

The bond between Deryth and Emrys had been evident throughout the day—a comfortable ease in each other's company, peppered with seemingly insignificant gestures—nods and glances—had reaffirmed the strength of their relationship. Yet he was sure there was something else, too, something he couldn't get a hold on.

While Hannah had been absorbed in examining her piece of pyrite the two of them had stepped away and had shared a few softly spoken words, which reinforced the sense that this grandparent and grandchild kept their own secrets.

***

Deryth sensed him watching her in the mirror. Though her eyes remained closed, her sixth sense was pretty reliable. She was beginning to love this child cradled in her arms. She knew it, and did not intend to fight it. Why should she? Didn't Hannah deserve a mother figure in her life?

But how did she feel about Bleddyn? He was at least a decade older than her, but she held little regard for such matters. He wasn't handsome in the conventional sense, and yet he had a certain rugged charm, and of course there was his dedication to Hannah which was unconditional and proved his sense of commitment. At the age of almost thirty she regarded men differently, less superficially she supposed, than she had a decade earlier.

Was it the natural ease with which today had passed that enabled her to see things in this light? There had been no tension; no awkward silences, partly due to Hannah's incessant chatter, and spending time with her outside of the school environment had helped Deryth feel more relaxed about the growing affection she had for her. A ready-made family? It certainly had its benefits, as she'd never wanted children of her own, given the secrets in the family. *Wait and see, Deryth*, she told herself. Don't go rushing into anything.

She tuned into Emrys's breathing, relaxed, sleepy. She hoped today might afford him some rejuvenation. Over the past few months, since he'd got to know Hannah, she'd noticed how the child's vibrancy had reignited his old self. He'd always been good with children, and Hannah would provide companionship in his old age. However, she also needed protecting, and this sense of responsibility seemed to burden him of late.

Of course he wouldn't admit it, but Deryth had noticed the worry lines across his forehead and his tendency to suddenly drift from the present. For ten years they'd been safe in the comfort of knowing the witch was held safely bound. Now, with one as vulnerable as Hannah close by, they would need to work doubly hard to ensure she would not pose a threat.

As they'd sat beside the waterfall, she'd slipped him the Cohl ogham. It was August—the month of the hazel moon—and an opportunity to refuel one's inner life force. What better place was there than the magical spring of the very place he was named for? Together they'd whispered the chant, their strange words drowned by the sound of the water as it cascaded in a torrent over the mountain's edge.

Bleddyn and Hannah hadn't even noticed. She'd been too busy examining her fool's gold and Bleddyn insistent on explaining its common occurrence throughout this part of Wales. She'd found it amusing. Why couldn't he let her believe that what she'd found was rare and precious? Logic and man! Still, Hannah had taken little notice of his scientific explanation and had squirrelled it away in the safety of her little carry pouch—the one bearing a picture of a phoenix that she'd bought her as a present from Kos.

Butterfly Gown

Rhiamon had not caught sight of her own reflection in over a decade. The absence of any water pool in the wood denied her the privilege, yet she had no doubt other than her appearance remained magnificent. Evidently the ravages of time could not touch her kind.

With a gossamer touch, she stroked the breast of her newly crafted gown. A thousand butterfly wings it had taken to fashion the garment, each one collected with a whisper of whimsy. Those whose colours were already fading, or whose wings were torn, she crushed in the palm of her hand, thrilling as the bright pigments transferred to her skin. But those which were unspoiled … now they were what she sought.

Each wing ripped from the butterfly's thorax in one, swift rent—far less damaging to the wing. She placed a few redundant, succulent heads and abdomens into the heart of the spider's web, watching with amusement as it pounced from its lair to suck upon the sweet juices. Others she discarded on the ground, before granting herself a few moments pleasure in watching their futile attempt to fly before giving up the ghost.

From the bodice of the gown, the azure eyes of the peacock butterfly judged her actions, its blood-red daubs reminding her of the pain she'd inflicted. She sniffed, dismissively. The red and blue contrasted beautifully with the old gold of the gatekeepers' wings—regal, almost. And for good measure, she'd even acquired a few purple emperors—rare in these parts. Those she'd meticulously sewn along the décolleté with the silken thread of the orb-weaver and a needle fashioned from a wren's rib. Oh, how she longed to look upon the majestic image she must cast! If only she were able to free herself of this woodland prison, then she might travel far and wide and admire her image freely. Why, she might even find herself a beau, someone to toy with for a while, until the inevitable boredom would set in. Then she would break his heart and watch it bleed.

The blizzard was the one thing she feared, and this it knew all too well. With each passing winter it would visit, tormenting her with the threat of being scooped into its mighty arms and whisked away. Yet, at the same time, it waltzed just out of reach, teasing her like the diafol himself. Occasionally it would lick at her shins, pull at her hair, whip up her tunic, but thus far it had failed to return her from whence she came. And for that she was grateful, for she knew there were those who would not have forgotten her deeds and who would have her punished even after so much time had elapsed.

What she desired most was to be free of this wood. Free to roam this land and have others do her will at her behest. However, the wilful wind knew what she wanted. It did not spare her out of the kindness of its heart. No, it was merely biding its time before it would inevitably whisk her into its arms and carry her off again.

For this reason, she dreaded each coming winter. Perhaps this year might be different, for having the girl within her grasp provided a possible means of escape—a life for a life, so to speak. Surely, they'd be willing to trade her freedom rather than put the girl's life at stake. Then she might go where she pleased, taunt whomever she chose, and above all, hide from the wretched wind!

Perched upon the fallen trunk of an alder, a pair of stag beetles—their antler-like jaws locked in a fight to the death over an elusive female—caught her attention. How entertaining! It brought to mind an event which had taken place a short distance from here some two hundred years previous, one she was immensely pleased to have initiated.

It had been during the year 1814. The previous winter, Borrum, god of the wind, had summoned a wicked blizzard to deliver her to a place a few miles from here. She had angered him with her boasting, and hence he punished her. She'd hated it then, almost as much as now, only then she was not enslaved.

To pass the time, she'd found work as a barmaid in a nearby hostelry known as The Old Salutation, a place where wealthy gentlemen sought refuge in liquor and a little harmless flirtation. Her ample beauty caught the attention of one such gentleman who went by the name of Samuel Brown. Although of West Indian descent, Brown happened at the time to be staying locally.

Weaving her charms, she played him off against another gentleman, a lawyer named Harold Snipe, resulting in the throwing down of the gauntlet. A duel was held at a nearby field some two days later. As the men took up position, one either side of a stream and back-to-back, she watched with amusement from her hiding place high in the bough of the alder.

Of course, she knew a duel should be fought according to rules, with each opponent bearing similar pistols and instructed to take their best shot upon the count of ten.

One, two, three … the count reached five. With no more than a nod in Snipe's direction, she summoned him to turn and shoot his opponent in the back, thus killing

Brown instantly. That would teach him to lust after someone beyond his reach!

As those witnessing the duel carried away the sagging corpse, she slept, cradled in the bough, satisfied with her work.

Her thoughts returned to the present. The larger of the stag beetles had wrestled its opponent to the ground and was off to claim its prize who was no doubt waiting in the wings beneath some sliver of decaying bark. She adored the fact that these particular insects thrived on rot. Its defeated rival limped off, head hung in shame. Stone in hand, she put paid to its misery with one swift strike, the crunch of its armoured shell a joy to her ears. A spatter of flaxen liquid spurted from the insect, threatening to stain the carefully crafted butterfly gown. She'd need to be careful wandering the wood in this—it was so fragile. Perhaps she'd hide it away and wear it when she met with the girl. She was certain to fall in love with it—she liked pretty things.

Removing the delicate garment, she folded it carefully, wrapped it in a fleece of sheep wool gathered from the barbed wire fence, and tucked it into the hollow of a nearby birch. For now, her old tunic, woven from fine slivers of silver birch, would have to do. Vanity! She'd been accused of said sin so many times. *Pfff!* What did they know? Human lust for pretty things made her work easier on so many occasions. Take, for example, the girl's obsession with the brooch …

Rhiamon sat beneath the birch, remembering. The two girls had been in the garden. She'd been woken from a sweet slumber by the sound of singing and loud music—an appalling din. Not at all like the soothing sound of the harp, or better still, the haunting call of the carnyx.

She'd tiptoed to the boundary of the wood to get a better look, and there they'd been—the girl with the long

Titian hair and the girl with golden curls. They were not responsible for the singing, nor were they playing any instruments. Instead, the sound emitted from a small, cylindrical object the girl had placed on the table. Huh! The modern world. If this was the sort of thing it produced, she was glad not to have been born into it.

After a while the girls had retreated indoors and soon the sound of raucous laughter could be heard coming from the room in which the girl slept.

"It's precious," she heard the child say. "It belonged to Mamma. She wore it on this dress when she was on stage."

Rhiamon had become all ears at the word, *precious*.

Shortly after, the fair-haired girl left. Swift as gossip, Rhiamon sent the rook in through the open window to take possession of the object … and that was how she'd come by it. The rook was rewarded for its diligence with a fat, juicy grub.

She'd held the brooch to her chest, wielding the power of the object's memory in order to learn more about this so-called *Mamma.* Ah … so the woman was a narcissist! Beautiful in appearance, though not in thought—one who liked to create an impression of fragility. She fondled the brooch some more, caressing, smoothing, enticing it to reveal its secrets. Well, the woman most certainly wasn't fragile.

The brooch had served its purpose well. Not only had it revealed the woman's personality, it had also revealed her scent. All it had taken was a little magic to extract the aroma and use it to her advantage.

A SLIP OF THE TONGUE

With just one week of the summer holidays remaining, Hannah grew more and more agitated. She liked school, but the thought of going into Year Six worried her. A new teacher, a new classroom. She hoped Miss Morgan would still be her helper because sometimes the school switched helpers around.

To be honest, it was more than the prospect of being in Year Six that made her anxious. There were at least two other things bothering her right now. One of them she was able to talk to Dada about. The other? Well that was not so easy.

The show was three weeks away, and while she continued to attend rehearsals, there was still one bit of the dance she always seemed to mess up. Until a week ago she'd been getting it right, but once she'd made the mistake, she kept making it over and over again. It was as if her brain was sending her feet the wrong message. She told Dada about it as soon as she came out of drama club, and he told her not to worry and promised they would go over it at home.

Thomas—the tall boy with the mean eyes, the one who was able to bend his thumb right back until it touched his wrist—had shouted at her. He'd said she was messing it up for everyone else, and it made her cry. Even when Megan put her arm around her, and Carys told him off and made him apologise, she'd still cried.

She'd wanted to practise the dance again as soon as she'd got home, but Dada said she'd be better off leaving it until the following day, then she could look at it with fresh eyes. What on earth did that mean?

By the morning she'd forgotten about it, because she was going to visit Emrys at his farm for the first time that afternoon, which was exciting. However, when they were having breakfast, Dada said, "Shall I phone Megan's mum and arrange for her to come over one day this week before you go back to school? I'm sure Megan will help you practise the bit of the dance you're struggling with." And it made her remember all over again.

She hadn't known how to answer because one part of her wanted Megan to visit, but the other part kept thinking about the brooch. She still didn't know whether or not to believe Megan had stolen it.

In any case, when Dada phoned, Megan's dad answered and told him Megan and her mum had gone away for a little break. Hannah found it strange because Megan hadn't mentioned anything about going on holiday in drama club on Thursday. Was it an excuse? Perhaps Megan never wanted to come to Hannah's house ever again.

If that was the case, why was she still kind to her? It was all so confusing and made her feel worse about the whole thing. If they weren't going to visit Emrys today she would feel like crying again.

Wanting to look nice for her visit to the farm, she dressed in pale blue leggings, a white T-shirt, and a denim jacket with embroidered flowers on the pocket. She opened her jewellery box—the red one with a popup, clockwork ballerina—and lifted out the Pandora bracelet. After four attempts at putting it on, she gave up. It was almost impossible to hold back the tiny catch with her thumb nail while getting the loop over it at the same time. On the fifth attempt it fell to the floor where it lay in a lifeless heap of silver. Urgh! She'd have to take it downstairs and ask Dada to do it up for her.

She hadn't worn the bracelet for some time. Seeing the charm of the little cottage reminded her of Mamma all over again. Mamma was the problem she didn't feel able to talk to Dada about because one, she didn't want to upset him, and she knew that even though he tried to hide it he did get upset whenever she spoke about Mamma, and two, she didn't think she'd be able to talk about it without crying, and she'd cried enough yesterday when she'd got the dance wrong.

She replaced the bracelet in the jewellery box. She wouldn't bother wearing it, in case anyone at the farm asked her about it because then she might cry in public, and she was trying her best to grow up since she would soon be in Year Six.

***

"Are your wellies in the boot of the car?" Bleddyn asked.

"Yes"

"Sure?"

She huffed. "Sure."

"Did I tell you how beautiful you look? Good enough to eat, so you'll have to watch out for Emrys's bulls."

Hannah twirled to give him a better look. "Will Miss Morgan be there?"

"I doubt it. She doesn't live on the farm—only her parents and Emrys live there."

"She knows we're coming, so perhaps she'll be there, too."

Bleddyn hoped Hannah was right. Ridiculous as it seemed, he'd dressed in his newest jeans and a plain, black T-shirt having decided against the one emblazoned with Pink Floyd. This was crazy, he was behaving like a teenager.

As they crawled their way along the rutted track to the farmhouse, his heart pounded in his chest—and it wasn't because of the potholes, but in anticipation of Deryth's car being there.

It wasn't. He wiped his clammy hands on the front of his jeans and swallowed his disappointment.

Emrys stepped out of a barn a little to the right of the house. "Croeso, croeso!" he said, beckoning them over.

At his heels, a black-and-white collie pleaded with solemn eyes to be allowed to greet its guests. As Hannah and Bleddyn drew closer, it whined in anticipation. "Come an' meet Bronwen—she won't hurt you—right old softy she is." He ruffled the plume of white fur on the dog's chest. "Named because of this she is. *Bronwen* means white-breasted in Welsh."

The dog took its master's demeanour as permission to launch itself at Hannah and Bleddyn, almost knocking her over.

Hannah bent down to stroke her. "Hello, Bronwen. I'm not afraid of dogs. Evan's got one like you called Jipp."

"I'll show you around, then we'll have some tea. Deryth should be joining us around three—she had to catch the bank before it closed."

Bleddyn's stomach lurched. Apprehension? Anticipation? He wasn't sure, but Emrys's comment turned his mouth to sand.

***

"Son-in-law's silaging up top field, and my Anwen's gone to the bank with Deryth—farm business. She made a heap of fresh Welsh cakes this morning, a treat for when we get back."

They'd lapped the farmyard and were heading toward an empty field that Hannah noticed backed on to woodland. "Is that the same wood as behind my house?

"Aye, bach. Wanted to show you why it wouldn't be safe for you to wander the wood. Remember me telling you?" He gave her a wink.

As they drew closer to the boundary of the wood, Bronwen yapped—a high pitched, piercing yelp, forcing Hannah to cover her ears with both hands.

"Stay, Bron!" Emrys's command silenced the dog momentarily. "She doesn't like the wood. Nervous old thing she is. Stop fretting girl! We're not going in."

The collie's tail was tucked in tight as she cowered, and her attention did not stray from the wood. It was as if she saw something that none of the others did. Hannah wanted to comfort her, but the dog didn't seem to want to be fussed. In fact, she growled a little when Hannah reached down to pat her.

As the three of them continued towards the corner of the field, Bronwen remained where she was, occasionally emitting a little yelp and spinning in a circle before once again lying flat with her ears pointing skyward.

"Haven't been able to graze my sheep in this field for years." Emrys gestured towards the empty field. "Too boggy an' rutted. The sheep get foot rot in there. I've plenty of land, so it doesn't matter." This time, he avoided catching Hannah's eye altogether, which somehow made his words more suspicious.

"Damn shame that, Emrys. How come it's so wet?" Bleddyn asked, reaching beyond the fence and tugging at a handful of cotton grass. He handed a blade to Hannah. "Pretty, isn't it, Hannah?"

"Natural spring at the top there." Emrys pointed away into the distance. "When the rain's heavy it comes gushing down from there an' floods this field. Like I said, doesn't matter."

Hannah smoothed the fine tuft of white that sprouted from the top of the blade of grass. It reminded her of Emrys's hair, but she didn't like to say so because she was beginning to understand what Dada called *being personal.* It wasn't always easy. Sometimes the words would be on the tip of her tongue, about to tumble out, then she'd remember just in time and suck them back in. She always made a little *slurp* sound when she did it.

"Anyway," Emrys began, pointing away into the distance. "See where the back of the wood meets the field?"

Hannah and Bleddyn followed his finger.

"Well, there's barbed wire fencing all around, see. Dangerous it is. Wouldn't want young Hannah to go cutting herself on the stuff now, would we? An' as you can see, it's all boggy. Even the wood gets boggy where the stream runs into it, slippery under foot. That's why I'd prefer you to visit us by car, see. Wouldn't want you to go falling now, would we?"

"So the lane behind our cottage, Emrys—it climbs all the way to where it meets the bottom of this field, does it?"

"Aye. About a quarter of a mile walk. As I said when you asked about it before, it's not been used for decades, so it's overgrown. Perhaps one day I'll get round to doing something 'bout it."

He winked at Hannah again, and she tried to return the gesture, which, even though she'd practised in front of the mirror time and time again, still managed to elude her. At least it should shut Dada up about walking The Lane, she hoped.

As they retraced their steps towards the farmyard, Emrys said, "If ever you want to bring Hannah to us for a few hours, Bleddyn, all you need do is ask. There must be times when you could do with a bit of a break, an' we'd love to have her. My Anwen'd teach her how to cook Welsh cakes, I'm sure."

"Ooh, yes Dada! Can I come again?"

Bleddyn smiled. "Most kind of you, Emrys. I might take you up on your offer some time in the future. In fact, you might be sorry you asked."

***

Bleddyn was glad of the time they'd spent holidaying at Ffion's farm over the years. It had done Hannah the world of good. Nothing about the tour of Emrys's farm fazed her, in fact she beamed the whole time.

Anwen's kitchen was warm and welcoming, the way he'd imagined it would be, with a big old cooking range set into the chimney breast. A heap of Welsh cakes perched on a red and white china plate, and a matching teapot, the size of which Bleddyn had never seen before, sat beside it. If he didn't know better, he'd have sworn he'd been transported back to the 1950's.

"Come in, come in." Anwen stood at the table, oven glove resting on her shoulder like an extra helping hand. "Now, do you like currants, Hannah? Because if you don't, I've made a few plain ones and split them with homemade raspberry jam."

"Ooh, yummy!" She ran her tongue around her lips. "I like currants and jam."

They all laughed and the tension in Bleddyn's stomach eased. As they'd clambered back down from top field, he'd noticed Deryth's car pull up in front of the farmhouse. She'd spotted them, too, and had waved briefly before disappearing inside.

"Deryth's popped out to check on one of the cows in the hospital pen—been poorly with a foot abscess. She won't be a minute."

Had Anwen read his mind? Surely not. Perhaps she'd seen the look of disappointment as he entered the kitchen … but that would mean she already knew he had a *thing* for Deryth. He felt himself flush.

"Emrys says I can come again, and you'll show me how to make Welsh cakes." Hannah was already tucking into her third as Deryth entered the kitchen.

"Of course you can. It'll be fun, won't it? And how about I show you how real bara brith is made, too?"

"Good at fattening people up is my Mam," Deryth said, patting her own middle before sitting down to join them.

Bleddyn fanned his face with a coaster. "Warm in here, Anwen. Bet it's great having that monster of a range in winter, though."

"Aye, 't is, bach. Can't beat it. Too hot for it today probably, but I couldn't have new visitors around without providing some goodies, could I?"

What was it about Emrys's family that made Bleddyn feel as if he'd known them his whole life? Was it the renowned Welsh welcome, or was it because they reminded him so much of his childhood?

"Deryth tells me you have a part in a play soon, Hannah," Anwen said, topping up her glass of milk.

Hannah had been enjoying her fourth Welsh cake until then. She replaced the half-eaten cake on the plate and scowled.

"What's up, Miss?" Deryth asked, reading her like a book. "Thought you were looking forward to it."

"She's been—" Bleddyn was about to answer but stopped himself. He'd always made a point of not speaking for her—encouraging her to respond in her own words was important.

Hannah bowed her head, chin to chest. "I'm stuck. On one bit of the dance." She seemed so crestfallen that he wanted to hug her, but Deryth came to the rescue.

"Well, you didn't seem stuck when I watched you in the playground with Megan a few weeks ago. You had it off to pat."

Deryth's words had no effect. Hannah's bottom lip pouted, and the Welsh cake remained untouched.

"Want to show me? I'll see if I can spot where you're going wrong." Deryth stood and beckoned for Hannah to join her.

Hannah cast her eyes around the table and flushed pink. She folded her arms across her chest. "No! Embarrassing!"

"Teach it to me. Perhaps it will help," Anwen said, getting up and moving towards the space behind the table. "Come on, bach—show old Anwen how it's done."

Hannah smiled, despite herself. "Haven't got my music."

'Ah, lame old excuse! Deryth—find it on your phone. What's the song called, Hannah?"

That evening, Hannah lay on a floor cushion pretending to read, though Bleddyn sensed she wasn't concentrating. Since they'd returned from the farm, she'd seemed preoccupied—pensive almost. He clicked *Send* on the email he was writing.

"Need to talk?"

She nodded.

He held out his hand and pulled her from the floor. "Is the dance still bothering you? You did brilliantly with Anwen. Slowing it down in order to teach her the steps made you think about it more. Not one mistake."

The corners of her mouth twitched—the smallest hint of a smile—she didn't want to give him the impression she was happy. "Can we do Google Earth?"

He guessed what was coming. So that was behind her sullen mood of late. He should have known. Or had he? Perhaps he'd merely been skirting around the real issue these past few weeks. "Is this about Mamma?" He saw her eyes mist, and it hurt. With his free hand he dragged the spare chair towards the desk and gestured for her to sit.

"Mamma hasn't phoned in ages."

The tears threatened. He saw her swallow hard.

"I know, Hannah. It's been three months, and do you know what? I'm not going to make excuses for her any longer." He held her hand in his, aware of its smallness. "Sometimes I tell you what I believe you want to hear and perhaps it doesn't help."

She nodded, afraid to speak in case she cried.

He loaded the map and pointed. "See, Hannah, Sweden is far away, but it's no excuse for Mamma not ringing you. Would you like me to ring her and see what's going on?"

Again, she nodded. "It doesn't look far on the map, Dada." Her voice was small, a mere whisper.

"See … here we are—and here's Beddgelert." He enlarged the map a bit and pointed. "Now, Beddgelert doesn't look far away at all, does it?"

She shook her head.

"But remember how long it took to get there when we went with Deryth and Emrys?"

She smirked. "Miss Morgan, you mean!"

He ignored the comment and pointed at Sweden. "See how much further away Sweden is? Imagine how long it would take to get there."

She studied the map. "We could fly."

He was lost for words.

"When you ring Mamma, will you ask her if she wants to come and see me in my play?"

He ran his hands through his hair. "Yes, but I have to warn you, I don't think she'll come." The look of disappointment on her face killed him. "But I'm coming, and Deryth. We'll always support you, Hannah."

He'd done it again, called Miss Morgan by her Christian name. Not only that, but in context of her being there instead of Emily. He'd need to watch his words. She was hurt enough already.

"Fancy a bit of supper? Cheese on toast?"

She nodded. "And then can we watch *The Hobbit*?"

"We can watch some of it—you know how long it is—you always end up falling asleep."

"You know my favourite bit, Dada?"

"Let me guess … Is it when Smaug wakes up in the mountain of gold?"

"No. It's when Bilbo puts on the ring and turns invisible. If I had the magic ring, I'd fly to Sweden without paying, cos they wouldn't see me, then I'd peep on Mamma to see if she looks happy."

Blackberry Stain

Plastic tub in hand, Hannah was halfway out the back door when Dada called her.

"Where are you going, Hannah?"

She raised her eyes to the heavens and returned to the foot of the stairs in order to shout her answer. "Good grief," she muttered. "Ears like a shit-house rat." It made her giggle, the naughty word, though she wouldn't dare say it out loud. Dylan had, though—in drama club last night, when Carys had told him off for saying that Jack looked like an idiot doing the tango. She giggled again—the *shit* word. It sounded like it might be Welsh, but she didn't think it was. "Out the garden to collect some blackberries," she said. "Remember you said we were going to make a crumble?"

"Oh, all right. Be careful with the thorns, they're not easy to pick, you know."

"I know, I know!"

"Hey! Watch the attitude, Missie." he called, though she was sure she heard him laugh.

The best blackberries were right up close to the fence. Long, arching stems protruded through the wire from

The Lane, determined to get in. Lots of the berries were shrivelled, which was a bit disappointing, but then it was the last week of August and Emrys had told her the best time for picking blackberries was the end of July.

Still, at least it wasn't the end of September. If it had been, she wouldn't have picked them at all, because Emrys had told her a story about how the Devil spits on blackberries at the end of September because it was the month he got kicked out of heaven—or was it October? She wasn't sure. In any case, she wouldn't take the risk.

A paltry layer sat at the bottom of the tub. Perhaps she'd wander over to the other side of the garden to where the Bramley's grew in abundance, then they could have apple and blackberry crumble. She traced the long stem of bramble with her eyes. On the other side of the fence, right there in The Lane, it held plenty of blackberries, fat, juicy ones too. Perhaps she'd nip around and pick a few more before collecting an apple or two.

The tub was half full, and her fingers were suitably stained, dark purple. She'd acquired a fair few scratches in the process, but then no pain, no gain, as Connor would say when he twisted her arm. She hated him. She'd love to feed him blackberries in October.

Her stomach twisted at the thought of seeing him again on Monday. Two days remained before the inevitable return to school, and the play loomed large, which reminded her—Dada hadn't said whether he'd managed to get hold of Mamma yet to ask her if she might be able to come. She must remember to ask him when she went back indoors.

Why did she always end up thinking about Mamma when she was in The Lane? Was it because of the time she'd smelled her perfume? She sniffed the air. It smelled of dying fern—damp, sweet, woody—a bit like the stuff called hummus that Dada had got her to try on her toast. Yuck! She spat into the hedge.

***

Rhiamon knew she dare not approach the girl today. However hard she tried, she knew she would be unable to conceal her anger.

That day, when they'd visited the farm. She'd seen the way he'd gestured towards the boundary with the wood when he'd spoken to the girl and her father. Trying his best to warn her away he was, of that she had no doubt. And the hound! It had barked like a mad thing. So what if she'd killed its mother? It wouldn't have remembered the incident. She smirked as she recalled the satisfying snap of the dog's neck as she'd given it one sharp twist. Self-defence—it would have bitten her otherwise.

No, now was not the best time. There would be other opportunities. For now, she'd settle for a little meddling with the girl's dreams.

***

What a sight! The bathroom mirror reflected Hannah's pale face, stained purple around the mouth. She poked out her tongue—black. Dada always warned her not to eat blackberries unless they'd been washed, but she hadn't listened because Emrys always said, *you gotta have your peck o' dirt.* She'd listen to Emrys because when it came to nature, he was wiser than Dada.

Filling the sink with warm, soapy water she reached for a flannel and scrubbed at the stain. It took some doing, and her face was suitably pink from scrubbing. Dada would guess she'd eaten some. So what!

She studied her tongue in the mirror, curious as to why it always seemed a bit larger than everyone else's. It looked quite scary—big and black—almost like she had some zombie disease. She remembered asking Dada about it some time ago, and he'd reckoned it was no different to any other tongue, except it was cheekier. She took her toothbrush and tried to scrub away the stain. It helped a bit, but the stain was still there, reminding her of her disobedience.

***

Bleddyn said nothing. He'd given her the job of washing the berries while he peeled and chopped the apples, and he bit his tongue with regards to the stain on hers. So what if she hadn't listened? What harm might a few unwashed berries do?

And besides, he didn't want to cause a fuss over something so inconsequential when he had worse news to deliver later. He'd promised himself he'd tell her that evening, before their usual Saturday night TV stint. She was usually in a good mood then, so the blow might land softer.

Why spoil the best evening of the week? Perhaps he'd tell her in the morning. No—he was procrastinating again. The final day of the school holidays would not be an appropriate time to tell her Emily was not going to attend the concert.

"Try and sprinkle it evenly, Hannah, not in one dollop." The crumble topping was straight from a packet, but it didn't matter—at least he was trying. He was no Anwen when it came to baking, but he attempted to teach her new skills. "I hope you scrubbed those hands."

Hannah grinned and pressed her nails into her palms. They were caked with crumble mix and the cuticles were still tainted purple, even though she had washed them.

"Cor! You're a bit of a nag today," she said, rolling her eyes.

They both laughed.

"Will you be wanting custard or ice cream with this?"

"Custard!" She rubbed her tummy in a circular motion, dribbling slightly from the corner of her mouth as she did so.

"We'll have it later, shall we? When we watch our film."

She nodded, then said, "Dada, did you phone Mamma like you promised?"

Her question knocked him sideways. He glanced over to where she stood spreading the crumble topping on top of the fruit, her eyes and focus on the task in hand. He swallowed hard. "She's not coming, Hannah."

The air of disappointment that settled in the kitchen was palpable. Neither of them spoke, though Hannah's hand momentarily froze above the baking dish. If he hadn't been watching her closely, he wouldn't have even noticed the hesitation. Not so long ago his words would have incited the tears to flow. She was trying so hard to grow up.

"Open the oven, Dada, it's ready."

Still she avoided eye contact. Should he say more? The conversation with Emily had been short, but not sweet. He'd caught her off guard, and, as usual, all she tried to do was excuse her actions, or rather her inaction. While her words implied pleasure at Hannah's success, her tone of voice sounded insincere—bored almost—and he'd hung up before his tongue got the better of him. Jesus Christ, couldn't she have made an effort for once?

"Ah well, there we go," Hannah said, swiping her hands together, abandoning a smattering of crumbs to the floor in doing so.

Was she referring to Emily, or the crumble going in the oven? He wasn't sure. Although he desperately wanted to avoid hurting her, he was no longer willing to lie for Emily.

***

Hannah was standing in The Lane, searching for something. The sun beat down, making her sweaty, and the air was still as still could be. The only sound came from inside her ears—a high-pitched, constant whine. Hannah wasn't sure what she was looking for, only that it was of huge importance. Where should she begin? On the ground? In the foliage? Among the shade of the trees? All she knew was if she didn't find the thing soon it would be lost to her forever.

The sense of panic became overwhelming. She was running out of time, yet all she was able to do was spin slowly in a circle, casting her eyes here, there, everywhere, unable to focus her attention on any one thing.

She heard a murmuring sound, a sound of desperation, and realized it was coming from her. If she could make it louder, make the cry carry through the air, someone might come to her rescue.

She opened her mouth to scream, but no sound came out. She tried again, swallowing huge gulps of air before forcing the sound from her lungs. Nothing. Just a pathetic little moan.

She tried to run, but her feet were rooted to the ground, bound by the knotted roots of the hawthorn. She kicked and struggled, but it was pointless—she'd never get free, and she'd never find what she so desperately searched for. She fell to the ground, anchored by the tree's powerful limbs.

Hands flailing, she grabbed at a low branch of the hawthorn and bit down hard. Her mouth flooded with a bitter, metallic taste as its thorns gouged her tongue and inner cheeks. Again she tried to scream, but her lungs seemed empty, and the only sound she emitted was a choking, bloody gurgle.

Then, from behind the hawthorn, stepped … Mamma. She smiled, and held out a delicate, pale hand for Hannah to take.

Hannah reached out. *Mamma!* She tried to call out, but failed.

With ease, Mamma lifted Hannah to her feet, and the tree relinquished its grip, retracting in shame. Mamma had saved her!

But she let go of Hannah's hand, as quickly as she had taken it, as though scorched by its touch.

Confusion. Overwhelming disappointment. Despair. Surely Mamma wouldn't let her down like this?

Hannah reached out to her, attempting to retake her hand.

For a moment she imagined Mamma might embrace her, for she took a step closer. So that was why she'd let go—she wanted to hold her close. It wasn't enough to hold her hand; Mamma needed to embrace her wholly.

She stood right before her, their eyes locked, a quartet of emeralds set in gold. Hannah moaned faintly with relief. She lay her head against Mamma's chest, aware of its unfamiliarity—her lean frame, her meagre bosom. But Mamma wasn't smiling. The fire of emerald was extinguished. Mamma opened her mouth, as if to speak. Her lips were damson—not pink, and her tongue was black as cherries—not pale red as it ought to be. And her complexion! Deathly white, the veiny structure visible beneath the surface. And she was cold. So cold!

Hannah pulled away, but Mamma held on tight, clawing at the bare flesh of her arms with long nails, drawing blood.

Hannah screamed.

"It's just a dream." Dada stood over her, but she fought him off.

"Mamma!"

"You're dreaming, Hannah. It's all right."

He sat on the edge of the bed, cradling her in his arms, his voice cooing and soothing, like he had when she was a baby. Her body was rigid with fear.

The room was dark, so he reached over and switched on her lamp, and as he did so, there came a sharp tap at the window, followed by a flutter of wings.

She was out of sorts. It had taken ages for her to get back to sleep. Dada had needed to lie beside her for what seemed like hours. She wouldn't tell him about the dream, for she still avoided the subject of The Lane in his company.

Even now, in the light of day, and sat at the kitchen table with the cereal bowl in front of her, she didn't feel right.

She summoned to mind Mamma's face—the one in the dream, since she could recall no other. The dream had seemed so real. Even though Mamma wasn't coming to her play, and even though she hadn't phoned for ages, she still didn't believe Mamma would ever hurt her—at least, not like when she had clawed at her arm in the dream. The toast popped, making her jump.

"Want to talk about it?"

"The toast made me jump, that's all."

Bleddyn sighed. "About the dream, I mean. It must have been scary." He waited. "If you tell me about it, I might be able to explain its meaning, tell you why you dreamed it."

She shook her head. "Can't remember."

Part of her wanted to beg him to phone Mamma again to check she was all right, because in the dream she'd seemed—well sort of dead, like a zombie. Those lips; her skin. The hair on Hannah's arms stood on end. The other part of her knew it was a dream and besides, she didn't want to speak to Mamma anyway because yet again she'd let her down.

"Shall we go to the beach? Take your mind off school tomorrow."

"It's raining." She couldn't even muster the enthusiasm for her favourite place.

"So. We have coats, don't we? It's only water." Dada watched her, his eyebrows furrowed with concern. "Tell you what, we'll go after lunch. I'll treat you to ice cream. What d'you say?"

She hesitated, but didn't have the heart to say no. The effort he was making to cheer her up shone in his eyes.

"Okay." She'd try to cheer up, for his sake. It wasn't his fault. It was Mamma's. She was angry with Mamma; she was sad about Mamma; she still loved Mamma, so it was no use pretending she didn't care.

A Few Curls

Hannah came out of school full of beans. "Miss Morgan's still my helper, Dada!"

Bleddyn's face fell. "You never said she might not be."

Hannah shrugged. "Well, sometimes the school switches helpers around, so, you know."

He knew this sometimes happened, but no one had told him they were considering switching. Had it been another thing on her mind these past six weeks? Why hadn't she mentioned it? He breathed a sigh of relief. "So come on then, how did your first day in Year Six go?"

"Bye, Hannah, see you tomorrow." Her friend Megan interrupted their conversation, but he didn't mind. In fact he was relieved to see they were still friends, as he was sure Hannah had said something about being involved in an argument with her before the summer holidays.

"Bye, Meg." She turned her attention back to him "It was great. And the best thing of all is Connor's not in my class anymore."

"Never heard you mention him before. What's this Connor done to you?"

Hannah screwed up her nose. "Nah … nothing. Doesn't matter."

He thought it best to change the subject. It was pretty obvious that as far as she was concerned, whatever this boy had said or done was a thing of the past, though he was glad to have a few answers as to why she'd seemed preoccupied during the holidays. He mustn't let it get to him, because all kids of her age struggled at times socially. It was part of growing up. He'd have to learn to take it on the chin like any other parent.

She didn't stop talking during the journey home, nor while he prepared tea. His sense of relief was immense. A cloud had finally lifted. Her next hurdle was going to be the forthcoming concert, but if she wanted to realize her dreams of being on stage, this was something else she'd need to conquer. And why not? He'd recently noticed more and more actors with learning disabilities appearing in films and TV series. Finally, the world of media was beginning to wake up to the fact that society consisted of all kinds of folk and was beginning to represent them.

With three days to go before the night of the concert, he stood at the theatre door, waiting for her to come out of dress rehearsal.

She bounded towards him, gazelle-like. "I need to curl my hair for the show, Dada."

He groaned. "Oh, Hannah, you know I'm not good with hair. So tell me, what was it like being in a real theatre instead of in the drama hall?"

It was the first time they'd practised at the theatre where the concert was to take place, and he knew from the years spent with Emily it was a whole new experience. This particular theatre was the traditional kind, with tiered rows, boxes above the stage, and furnishings in deep red and gold—the way all theatres ought to be, in his opinion.

"Brill! Brill! Brill!" She clapped her hands with excitement. "Except when the lights went out and the other lights came on, you know—them big round ones at the front, I couldn't see any of the seats, and it made me think, Dada … remember when we went to see Mamma as Eliza Doolittle?"

He waited, but it was obvious she wanted a response before she would share whatever was in her mind.

"I remember."

"Well … perhaps Mamma couldn't see us. Like perhaps we were invisible, and that's why she didn't wave to us or anything."

Good grief! She was still prepared to find excuses for Emily's behaviour. While it angered him, he understood her logic.

"Perhaps, though I don't think it would have been very professional either, Hannah, if Mamma had suddenly waved to us, do you? Imagine her entering the stage and shouting, "Yoo hoo! Hannah! Bleddyn! Nice to see you!" This last line, delivered in Emily's voice, caused her to double over with laughter. It was so good to see her happy.

She swung her hand in his as they walked to the car. "Anyway … like I was saying, I need my hair curled."

"Well, I'll have to make an appointment for you at the salon then, otherwise my pathetic attempt will let you down. I wish you'd given me more notice. What if they don't have a spare appointment for Saturday?"

"Stop fretting, man!" She giggled.

Although her attitude was a bit cheeky of late, he couldn't help finding it amusing. He wasn't going to spoil her happiness by stressing over a few curls.

The following day, when Bleddyn picked Hannah up from school, he found Deryth waiting at the classroom door. He swallowed hard and tried not to think about blushing.

"Hannah told me she needs her hair curled on Saturday. I'd be happy to do it for her, if it's any help."

His head spun and his heart raced. "Would you mind? It would be a great help. I phoned the salon this afternoon and they're fully booked." Was she blushing? He wasn't sure, but it made him feel better—more on an even keel.

"Do you want to bring her to the farm, or shall I—" She failed to finish the sentence. It seemed a bit presumptuous to suggest she call at his house.

Hannah was engrossed in conversation with another girl, one he hadn't noticed before. At the mention of the salon, she stopped talking.

"Whichever is best for you. She has one of those curl things—what d'you call them?"

"Tongs." Deryth laughed, and he relaxed a bit.

"We could travel to the theatre together. If you want to, I mean." Had he really suggested such a thing? He felt himself redden again.

Deryth's coy smile revealed cute dimples. "That'll be great. Might as well take one car I suppose. Thank you."

"No, thank *you*, Deryth—for offering to do her hair, I mean."

"Thank God!" It was the first time Hannah had involved herself in the conversation. "At least I won't end up looking like the end of a mop."

They all laughed, and the tension eased.

Bleddyn had lost count of the number of times he'd heard her sing, "Pack Up," over the last week, and if she danced the steps once, she danced them a thousand times. Still, he had no complaints. He was glad to see her so determined to succeed. He would be glad for both their sakes when the concert was over, perhaps then life might return to something resembling normality, at least for a little while.

But was it what he wanted? A normal life? Not really, he'd always been a bit of a misfit. And besides, weren't all creative types also a bit eccentric?

***

At six o'clock, the night before the concert, the phone rang. Expecting it to be Ffion, calling to wish Hannah good luck, he answered with a yawn. "Hi, Ffi." There was a pause.

"It's me … Emily."

He was taken aback. Was she ringing to wish Hannah good luck? If so, he was shocked. He hadn't expected her to remember the date.

Hannah sensed his hesitation.

"Who is it, Dada?" she mouthed.

"Oh—Emily." He addressed the telephone receiver, in order to give Hannah time to prepare. His face was ashen. He ran his spare hand through his hair, as was his habit when nervous or embarrassed. Hannah knew the signs. She froze, pencil poised in midair, like an artist in a self-portrait.

"I'm calling to wish Hannah good luck … for tomorrow. Is she there?"

He hesitated. Would it be easier to pretend she was somewhere else? The last thing she needed was to be upset by a phone call from Emily. He pointed at the phone and watched her nod in agreement, but she wasn't smiling. "Yes. Hold on—I'll pass you over."

She put down the pencil and flapped her hands, nervously.

Having taken the phone, Hannah surprised him by walking off into the living room with it, her face pinched. She left the kitchen door open, so hopefully he'd be able to hear what was said. He fought the temptation to follow her.

"'S okay," he heard her say. "Dada's coming, and Aunty Ffion, and Uncle Aled, and Evan, so there'll be plenty of people to watch me."

Her next words startled him beyond belief. "Oh, and I nearly forgot, Deryth's coming too. She's Dada's girlfriend."

The wily little fox. He put his hand over his mouth to suppress a chuckle. No doubt she was attempting to score points against Emily. Clever thing.

The phone call ended seconds later. Hannah returned to the kitchen and handed him the phone. Her face was flushed, and her mouth twitched.

"So, what did she have to say?" He'd decided against mentioning the *girlfriend* thing. She'd tell him herself if she wanted to.

She shrugged. "Not much—just wished me good luck."

With a sigh, she took up her pencil, and pretended to focus on her drawing.

"Hey, I reckon we could both do with an early night, don't you? How about you jump in the bath, get into a nice clean pair of pyjamas and I'll make some toast and hot chocolate."

She groaned. "I know, Dada, but I'm so excited, I won't be able to sleep. I'm fizzing inside, like a firework." She stood and propelled herself around the room, hissing and spinning as she went.

He had to laugh. At least Emily's phone call hadn't depressed her—or was she becoming more skilled at disguising it?

BUTTERFLY WINGS

Hannah slept well despite herself, but having to wait until Miss Morgan's arrival at 3:30 was killing her. How on earth would she pass the time? She knew she was getting on Dada's nerves, but she couldn't help it. She was wound as a top.

Her costume had hung on her wardrobe door since 8:30 that morning, and she'd already had Dada tick off the checklist of items she needed to take with her. In fact, she'd made him check it three times.

"For goodness' sake, Hannah, find something to do. You're driving me nuts! It's only half ten. I can't take another five hours of you twirling around the house. Go and have an hour in the garden. Take your sketchpad and colours and see what wonders you can come up with. There's plenty to draw at this time of year."

She folded her arms across her middle and pouted. "Don't feel like. Can't concentrate."

"That's precisely why you need to do something to help you focus, Hannah, otherwise you're going to wear yourself out before the show."

She eyed him, slyly. "Wish it was Emrys's week for gardening. Wouldn't be bored then."

"Well it isn't, so tough luck. I want to get this house cleaned before Deryth arrives. I don't want her thinking we live in a hovel."

Not so long ago, he'd refused to refer to her as Deryth. "Miss Morgan, you mean. She's still my teacher, remember." Her face was straight as a die.

He ran his hands through his hair. "Miss Morgan, Deryth, it's all the same, Hannah. She's coming here as a friend. That's why I called her by her Christian name. If I'd been talking about her at school I'd have said Miss Morgan, so stop being a smart ass."

Eyes narrowed and mouth twisted to one side, she watched him rant. "Just saying." With a smug look, she picked up her sketchbook and pencil case from the table, where she'd left them the previous evening, and stomped off.

It had been wet for a few days, windy too. Hannah made her way over to the far end of the garden where the apple trees grew, following their sweet aroma as it grew stronger and stronger. There were many windfalls, which was a bit of a waste. Last week, Emrys had reminded her they wouldn't go to waste, as they could be gathered and composted, plus those on the ground also served as a hearty meal for insects such as wasps, and even birds during winter, when there were fewer insects for them to eat. She'd helped him gather a basketful for the compost bin and made sure to leave some behind.

She sat on the grassy bank, watching a few late-summer wasps indulge in the sugary treat. Keeping her distance, she began to draw. Emrys had taught her that as long as she didn't flap her hands about in panic, the wasps would pretty much keep to themselves, and with him beside her to give her confidence she'd discovered it was true.

She hadn't even known how to tell the difference between a bee and a wasp until Emrys taught her. She knew now—wasps were slimmer and less hairy, and their colours were more vibrant. Also, when a wasp came close to you, it flew like an out-of-control helicopter, whereas a bee flew more like an aeroplane.

One wasp in particular busied itself within the heart of the decaying apple. Hannah studied it closely. Its yellow bottom bobbed up and down as it fed, and it seemed oblivious to her presence. She pouted, remembering Dada's earlier frustration with her. So she was less interesting than a rotten apple today. She hoped her performance on stage tonight would change his mind.

She must have been outdoors for at least half an hour, and still Dada hadn't checked on her. Ah well, he must be busy cleaning. She'd offered to help, but he hadn't taken her up on it. She wandered away from the apple trees, and soon found herself standing at the bottom of The Lane.

Hands on hips, she focussed into the distance, towards the point where The Lane veered round the bend and disappeared out of sight. Would she ever be brave enough to climb all the way? One day, perhaps.

The windows of her house were all open. Dada was giving the place a good airing in preparation for Miss Morgan's visit. The faint hum of the vacuum cleaner droned in the distance, sometimes closer, sometimes further away, depending on which room happened to be under attack. An image of Dada as a giant wasp sprung to mind, making her giggle. She put her hand over her mouth to suppress the sound. Why did she always feel the need to be quiet in The Lane? Was it because she didn't want Dada to know she was here? No—it was more than that, but she couldn't put her finger on it.

With guilty footsteps, she climbed. Jeez! How many times would Emrys need to warn her away from here before she'd listen? It was out of character for her. All right, she was a bit wicked at times, but she was rarely defiant. No way would she enter the wood, though. She'd promised him, but today she felt daring. "Hannah the Invincible!" She filled her lungs. "I'm as fearless as Frodo!" She almost expected to see Frodo and Sam come tumbling out of the wood towards her, and was surprised when they didn't.

The effort exhausted her. She stood, half bent with exertion, and, as she straightened, not a hairsbreadth away, there she stood—the tree creature. Hannah gasped. Why, she was even more magnificent than Hannah remembered.

The creature held out a long, slender arm. Surprised by her sudden presence, Hannah instinctively recoiled, putting a little distance between them. How had she managed to get so close without her noticing? It was then she realized she'd climbed as far as the gap in the boundary fence, which meant there was no physical barrier between the two of them, other than a bit of broken wire fence. Hannah's heart raced.

"Don't be startled, child. You should know by now, I wish you no harm."

Her voice was smooth as silk, and Hannah softened inside. "I'm not scared. I just didn't expect—" She felt her face redden and didn't know what to say.

"So … today is a big day for you."

The creature took a step back, and as she did so, Hannah noticed her gown. Deep shades of red, dotted with what looked like crystal blue beads, danced before her eyes. And the neckline! Iridescent shades of purple rippled as the cloth moved against her pale and ample bosom.

"Beautiful," she whispered. She reached out her hand and touched the gown. Fragile, soft as feathers and ever so slightly warm. "Dance!" she said, smiling up at the tree creature, and the creature obliged, twirling and pirouetting where she stood at the edge of the wood, her bare feet seeming to glide.

Hannah watched entranced as a kaleidoscope of colour paraded before her eyes. Why, the gown almost had a life of its own.

The tree creature's display came to a halt. Her figure poised midair, while the gossamer gown took a few seconds longer to settle.

Hannah stood transfixed, bewitched, unable to look anywhere else.

The creature raised an eyebrow. "I could make one for you if you wish, but you'd have to wait until next summer."

"Next summer? That's a long time to wait."

"That's because its source material will soon be unavailable."

What on earth was she talking about? Hannah frowned.

The creature tutted with a smile, as in jest. "Don't all the best things require patience?"

Hannah nodded. "Suppose."

"What do you want, child? Tell me," the creature said, her voice a warm caress.

Hannah stood perplexed, unsure of what she meant. "Like—"

"Out of life, what is it you want?"

Hannah pursed her lips. "Well, I want the concert to go well tonight, for one."

The creature did not answer. Instead she continued to watch her, waiting. Hannah felt obliged to offer more. "And I want to grow up to be beautiful, like Mamma … like you." She flushed, a little embarrassed at having been *personal.*

"And?"

What more did this creature want? "And I wish Mamma was coming to my concert, but only if she wants to—not because I want her to … it's not the same." Her heart did a somersault in her chest.

The creature nodded knowingly. "Patience, child. Good things come to those who wait."

She was smiling, though not with her eyes this time, which made Hannah a little uncomfortable.

"I'd better go. Miss Morgan's coming to do my hair soon." Was she mistaken, or did she detect a flash of red in the creature's eyes at the mention of Miss Morgan?

"Good luck, child—for tonight I mean."

Hannah made to leave, but the creature called her back.

"Before you go—" She beckoned to Hannah and lowered her lips to her ear, tickling the skin. "Beware of those with a sting in their tail," she whispered.

Hannah frowned. "What do you—" She shook her head. "Never mind." This creature had spoken in riddles before. She'd work it out for herself.

Hurrying down The Lane, Hannah pondered her words. Of course! She must mean the wasps. She must have been spying on her as she'd drawn them earlier. The thought of having been watched made her cringe.

Even though Miss Morgan wasn't due to arrive at Hannah's until half three, she'd not left the window since three o'clock. Her breath kept making circular clouds of condensation on the glass, which she wiped away with the palm of her hand until Dada told her off. Finally, and on the dot, Miss Morgan arrived. It did not escape Hannah's notice that Dada's face reddened as he greeted her on the drive.

"Miss Morgan … how much do you like my Dada?"

Deryth stood behind her, about to wrap another section of hair around the tongs. "Ouch!" Instinctively she put her burnt thumb to her mouth, which bought her a few seconds. "Listen, Hannah, do you think you are grown up enough to remember to call me Miss Morgan at school and Deryth outside of school?"

Hannah frowned. "Course!"

"Well, let's switch to doing that, shall we?"

Hannah studied her reflection in the mirror. Her face was flushed.

"Does it hurt?"

"Does what hurt?"

"Your thumb, of course."

"A little. These tongs get extremely hot. You must promise not to try and use them by yourself."

Hannah scowled at her in the mirror. "You haven't answered my question."

Deryth winced. "I did, I said, a little."

"That was when I asked you if it hurt, not about how much you like my Dada."

Deryth paused. "I like the both of you a good deal—you make a great team."

Hannah knew she wasn't answering the question. Never mind, at least she'd planted the seed. There'd be plenty more opportunities for it to grow.

"Miss Morgan? I mean Deryth?" She suppressed a giggle, it didn't feel right yet.

"Yes?"

"What does it mean when someone tells you to watch out for someone with a sting in their tail? Does it mean someone who's like a wasp?" She bobbed her head, enthralled by the splendid coils of hair as they danced of their own accord in the mirror.

"Well, it means that someone who seems kind may hurt you in some way, particularly later on, hence the *tail* bit."

Hannah watched her in the mirror, considering her answer. The silence in the room was tangible. "The thing is, Hannah, wasps have a reputation for stinging people when in actual fact they're hardworking creatures that rarely sting unless provoked or frightened."

Still she said nothing.

"There's a legend about wasps you know. Well … not so much a legend, more an explanation of what they symbolize." Still nothing. She watched Hannah's reflection, waiting for a reaction. "Well? Would you like to hear it?"

Hannah nodded.

"The wasp symbolizes having to work hard for what you want out of life. That simply wishing it isn't enough. Instead, each person has to take responsibility for his or her own actions, like you are doing today by being brave enough to get up on stage and perform in front of hundreds of people."

Hannah thought about the wasp meaning as she dressed. She was brave, she supposed. And to be able to act was what she wanted out of life, though she had to admit, right now her nerves were in tatters. With a whirr of last-minute panic, her costume was folded into her bag and they were off.

"Jump in the back, Missie."

"But—"

Dada gave her the eye, and she did as she was told. She knew how far to push. The air inside the car seemed agitated, like it did before a thunderstorm. Perhaps it was her—a ball of nerves and excitement.

***

"Well, the adrenaline's certainly kicked in!"

It was Carys, addressing the crowd of children in the green room as they awaited the curtain call. Why was it called the green room? Hannah scanned the room, noticing the complete lack of green—anywhere. And what did the *drena* word mean? She sat taking a few deep breaths in an attempt to calm her nerves. Dada had taught her how to do it when she was young and used to get in a tizz over almost anything and everything. Then, before she knew it, she was being called. Her insides hit the floor.

What struck her first was how dark the theatre looked. Hannah found her spot on the stage and tapped her foot to the beat of the music. A rabbit in the headlights, that was how she felt, and she even knew what it meant. For a few seconds, the enormous lights at the front of the stage blinded her. She shielded the glare with one hand and attempted to locate Dada in the audience. She knew he'd got there early enough to be able to get seats near the front, so why couldn't she see him? Come to think of it, she couldn't see anyone.

But wait! Her stomach did a flip. Mamma? There in the front row? She blinked. No, silly. The tree creature? Impossible!

She felt herself prodded sharply in the ribs. It was Megan. Something kicked in and she found her feet.

***

She flung herself at him, arms encircling his waist. "Dada!"

He beamed, and his eyes were glassy with tears. "Ooh, I'm so proud! You were incredible." He took both her arms and swung her around before coming to a stop. He hugged her again, smothering her cheeks with kisses.

"You were amazing, Hannah!" Deryth said. "You didn't put a foot wrong. In my opinion, you stole the show."

Bleddyn released Hannah from his grasp, so she could hug Deryth.

"Wasn't she incredible?" Carys appeared as if by magic and hugged her too. Never before had she felt so special. She had to admit, it was a wonderful feeling, like she'd conquered the world.

***

Removing the stage makeup was a chore, but Dada insisted she wash before eating. Her cheeks glowed pink, like blushing, except she wasn't.

"I wonder if Carys's friend, Ife, spotted me, Dada?"

The corners of her mouth were smeared in tomato sauce and a long string of melted cheese dangled from the slice of pizza in her hand, as though undecided whether or not to attach itself to her pyjama top.

"Whether she did or whether she didn't, I'm proud of you. Put it out of your mind—you'll have plenty of opportunities to be spotted. You're still very young."

She couldn't answer as she was still battling the cheese, so instead, she nodded.

***

Bleddyn tucked her in. It was almost eleven o'clock, but it had taken until then for her to start yawning. Never mind, it was Sunday tomorrow, so she didn't have school. Pouring himself a large bourbon, he retreated to the sofa. He shuddered. The kick from the whiskey or her outstanding performance? He wasn't sure. All he knew was he'd not had a better evening in a long time. And to think he'd spent the whole morning with his nerves in tatters.

He felt guilty for the way he'd spoken to her earlier in the day, when she'd been twirling around the house like a mad thing. The prospect of sitting beside Deryth for the duration of the performance had made him jittery. Plus he'd had to get Hannah to the theatre an hour before the show so she'd have plenty of time to change and have her makeup done. He'd wondered how he and Deryth would pass the time, but he needn't have worried. They'd sat in the little cafe bar attached to the theatre. He'd ordered coffee, not daring to have an alcoholic drink, even though he could have murdered one.

Despite the age difference, they had lots in common, including a love of theatre. Neither enjoyed socialising in large gatherings and preferred intimate restaurants to wild parties. What was more, he'd arranged to see Deryth again the following Saturday. They'd decided to keep it a secret from Hannah for the time being in order to give her time to adjust gradually.

***

Hannah was drifting off to sleep when something rattled against her window. She bolted upright, scaring the rook into flight.

It came to her in a flash. "Butterflies!" The creature's gown was made of butterfly wings! She felt sick to the stomach. And she'd told her it was beautiful. Next time they met, she'd tell her in no uncertain terms not to make one like it for her.

The Lie

It had been a great week, one of the best in a long time. Everyone at school had made a fuss of her after her teacher, Miss Collins, played a video clip of the concert to the whole class. Megan's dad had filmed it, and because Hannah and Megan were in most of the same scenes, Hannah was fortunate enough to have been captured several times. During the first showing she was embarrassed and covered her face with her hands, peeping between fingers every now and then. But the children nagged Miss Collins to play it again, which she did before home time. Hannah was brave enough to watch the second showing without hiding her face. Of course, they all fussed over Megan, too, but they seemed especially proud of Hannah. She didn't know why, because in her opinion Megan was amazing.

She felt as though she'd turned a corner, that her achievements in the concert, and the relief of it being over, meant she was able to go forward with newfound confidence. She was doing well with her schoolwork too. In fact Miss Morgan was astonished at the progress she'd made in reading these last few weeks.

This coming Saturday, after working in the garden, Emrys would be taking her to the farm for a few hours to give Dada a break. She didn't understand why he needed a break because it wasn't like he was busy, he had all day to himself while she was in school. However, she didn't mind, because she was excited about visiting the farm again. Emrys promised Anwen would teach her how to make Welsh cakes, so she was looking forward to it.

"Come and have a quick wash and change." Dada called her from the kitchen door, but she was busy helping Emrys plant crocus bulbs in the patch behind the shed—all colours from bumblebee yellow to royal purple, or so the packet would have her believe. How did they know which colour to grow into? All the bulbs looked the same to her—like baby onions.

"I'm busy!" She grinned at Emrys, hoping he'd back her.

He gestured towards the house. "Off you go, bach, I'll finish this myself. Got the whole afternoon at the farm to look forward to yet haven't we, an' Anwen won't let you in her kitchen covered in dirt."

Why did grown-ups always stick together?

On entering the kitchen she paused, surprised to see Dada all dressed up in a new pair of black jeans and a pale grey shirt. The skin on his cheeks shone, which meant he'd shaved. Her mouth fell open. "Where you going?"

"Nosy Parker. Meeting an old friend, that's all."

She eyed him suspiciously. "You haven't got any old friends in Wales. They're all in Peterborough."

"Hey, I did have a life before Peterborough you know. Now, get a move on, and go and wash."

She remained where she stood and continued to look him up and down, taking in every detail. "Is it a girl?"

He cleared his throat. "Is who a girl?"

"The friend."

"No. Get up those stairs!" He laughed, nervously, and flipped a tea-towel at her, making her giggle. She ran off.

Anwen gave her a big hug as soon as she entered the farmhouse kitchen. Her warm arms felt like she imagined a grandma's would, though Hannah had never had a grandma, not really. Somehow she just knew.

"Is Deryth coming?"

"No, bach, she's out … with a friend. So, come on then, tell me all about it."

Hannah frowned. "'bout what?"

Anwen danced a few steps—at least those she remembered—which made Hannah laugh. "The concert, of course!"

"It was great!"

"So I heard," Anwen said. "Bet you stole the show."

"That's what Deryth said—what does it mean, Anwen?"

"Ah, bach, it means you stood out from the rest, that everyone's eyes were on you."

Hannah wasn't sure whether or not to be pleased about that.

"Now then, let's get cracking on our dough, cos I know Emrys has something to show you outside later."

She helped Hannah to roll up her sleeves before filling the sink with soapy water.

"We've been planting crocus bulbs this morning, Anwen," Hannah said, attacking her nails with a little brush. "They're my favourite cos when they flower, it means spring's on the way."

"Well isn't that queer. They're my favourite, too, and for the same reason. Did you plant any saffron crocus, Emrys?"

Emrys stood at the kitchen door, removing his boots at the door. "What did you say?"

"I said, did you plant any saffron crocus?"

"Don't think we did—blame her," he said, nodding at Hannah and grinning. "She chose them."

Hannah wrinkled her nose. "Saffron crocus?"

"They're a special type of crocus, Hannah, a pale lilac colour. In the autumn they produce little stigma that gives you a spice called saffron. It's expensive to buy—so expensive in fact, it's sometimes called red gold."

"Ooh! Wish me and Dada'd known when we chose them."

"Nice in a paella," Anwen said.

"What's paella?"

"A sort of rice dish, made with meat or seafood. Delicious!"

"Oh … me and Dada are vegetarian."

"Ah well, good job you didn't plant it then," Anwen winked at Emrys. "Now, let me show you how to sieve the flour."

The Welsh cakes were cooling on the dresser. Anwen told her she'd have to let them cool or else they'd burn her tongue, so she put on her coat and went outside with Emrys. At the sound of his whistle Bronwen joined them, fussing around Hannah like an old friend.

"She remembers you from last time, bach—no doubt about it."

Hannah was pleased. She patted the dog's head. "How come dogs have good memories, Emrys? I don't."

"Aye, but that's cos you just use your eyes, bach. Now, she uses eyes, ears, nose, the lot. An' she even has a sixth sense—one us humans have forgotten how to use." He ruffled Bronwen's white plume. "Clever, aren't you, girl?"

Bronwen whined to show she was pleased with Emrys's compliment.

It was funny, because she'd been so excited to visit the farm again, and while she'd been busy baking with Anwen she'd felt fine, but in the last few minutes she'd begun to miss Dada. In fact, she felt a little homesick. "What time is Dada picking me up, Emrys?" Her bottom lip quivered as she asked the question.

"Around seven, bach—long before it gets dark, so don't you worry. Missing him a bit, are you?"

She nodded, not trusting herself to speak. They'd almost climbed to top field, and her heart was pumping hard from exertion.

"It's natural, bach, you an' him are always together, see. Bound to miss him, aren't you?"

"I'm not with him when I'm at school, and I don't miss him then. And I'm not with him in drama club either, but—"

"Ah, but 'tis different, see—you've only been here once before. When you get used to us, you'll be all right."

"I am used to you, and Anwen, but—" She shrugged. "Can't explain."

"It's all right, bach, I understand. I remember when Deryth was a young snip of a thing like you, she pleaded with us to allow her to stay the night at her friend's house."

Hannah watched him through moist eyes, waiting for his story to unfold.

"In the end we gave in, but we knew what a homebird she was." He chuckled. "Didn't surprise us when we received a phone call from her friend's mother asking us to pick her up at one in the morning. Inconsolable, she was."

"What's in—con—"

"Inconsolable—it means they couldn't stop her crying. Babi mawr!"

She laughed. "That means big baby."

"You're picking up the Welsh, I see," Emrys said, and he sounded pleased.

They'd reached the top of the field. Emrys stopped and sat on the grass, patting the area next to him to indicate she should do the same. Hannah could see for miles and miles.

"Now then, if you want to talk about missing someone, I'll tell you the tale of poor Bronwen here." Bronwen pricked up her ears at the mention of her name and tilted her head to one side, ready to listen.

"She likes this story, Emrys." Hannah was beginning to feel a bit better, knowing Bronwen also knew what it was like to miss someone.

"Old softy, she is." He ruffled her white fur again. Bronwen lay on the grass next to Hannah, facing the farm, ready to listen to the story.

"Now then," he settled on one elbow and looked at Hannah. "D'you remember me telling you 'bout the lambs that winter? About how they died in the snow?"

She nodded, eager for him to continue.

"Well, as I told you, me an' Deryth carried them all the way back to the farm an' put them to rest. The wind was whipping up a storm, an' the snow was as high as the top of my wellies."

He explained how he and Deryth had discovered the baby calf, dead in its manger, and how they'd believed it might have something to do with dark magic. She felt a little bit scared, but Bronwen snuggled up close, warming her legs, which made her feel better.

He told her how the snowstorm had been relentless, how he'd not seen snow like it since—well, as long back as he could remember. And then came the saddest part.

"This old girl was a pup at the time, barely a month old an' still nursing off her mother."

Hannah screwed up her nose. "Nursing?"

"Aye—taking her mother's milk."

"Oh." She nodded.

"Grand old girl too, my Morfydd was—that was Bronwen's mother's name. Best sheepdog I ever owned."

Hannah watched his blue eyes glaze over.

"You seen the film, *Babe*?"

"The one about the pig sheep?"

"Aye."

Hannah nodded.

"Well, as good a sheepdog as Babe she was, talk about sixth sense. After we'd seen to the calf, me an' Deryth went to the barn with the pups next. We knew something was wrong, soon as we went inside."

Bronwen whined and snuggled in closer to Hannah, anticipating what was to come.

Emrys lowered his voice, almost to a whisper. Hannah stroked the dog's ears, so his words would be even more muffled.

"All five pups were crying the rain, so distressed they were." He paused, his eyes two murky clouds. "Dead she was—neck snapped clean as a whistle."

Hannah gasped and put her hand to her mouth, causing Bronwen to stir.

"How?"

He shook his head. "Her it was—the witch who's trapped in the wood. Sure as damn it. That's why she's a bit skittish, see." He nodded towards Bronwen. "Pups shouldn't be taken from their mother at such a young age—causes all sorts of problems, it does."

So many thoughts ran around her head. She knew how Bronwen felt because she'd lost her mother too—except hers wasn't dead. When he said the witch, did he mean the tree creature? She wouldn't be surprised if he did. Would this be the best time to tell him she'd spoken to her? She bit her tongue. She didn't want to make him cross with her. Perhaps it would be better if she kept away from The Lane from now on. She buried her face in Bronwen's fur, offering whispered words of comfort.

They sat in silence for a minute or so.

When Hannah finally spoke, she did not make eye contact, instead she fussed over Bronwen.

"How is she trapped in the wood, Emrys?"

"She hid there, bach—after what she'd done."

"Why can't she get out?"

"Ah, it's a long story. One for another day. Suffice it to say, she's not wanted back where she came from. 'Twas the storm that brought her, an' it'll be the storm that takes her away, when it's good and ready, an' nothing we can do will make it 'appen any quicker."

She shivered, the air blowing over the ridge behind her had suddenly cooled. "Bet she's cold in winter."

Emrys tugged the collar of his coat. "Aye, but she survives. She deserves no sympathy, that one. You be sure to keep well away, Hannah, if you catch sight of her. You hear me?"

She nodded.

"And tell old Emrys if she tries to speak to you. She's a sly old fox, that one. Crafty as they come, but don't you worry. Long as you keep well away, she won't harm you. Me and Deryth will see to it."

Her head hung low and her shoulders sagged. If only he knew.

"Come on, let's go sample those Welsh cakes of yours. See if they're good as Anwen's."

***

After Emrys had told her about what happened to Morfydd he remained silent, waiting to see if she'd ask any more questions, but she hadn't.

Sometimes it's the things left unspoken that say the most, he thought, as they tramped back to the farm. She hadn't asked him who the witch was, which suggested she already knew, just as he suspected. He'd not badger her about staying on the path. He'd given her plenty of warnings in the past. Nope, at the end of the day, child or not, it was all about trust.

***

Having devoured so many Welsh cakes, Hannah's stomach ached, but she washed it down with milky tea and soon felt better. She and Anwen sat at the big kitchen table drawing pictures of the animals on the farm. She was better at drawing dogs than Anwen, but they both agreed, Anwen was better at drawing sheep. Then, before she knew it, there was a knock at the door, and Dada was standing there.

"Dada!" She leapt from the chair and ran straight into his arms. He looked happy, and he smelled nice, a bit like a pub. "I missed you!"

He laughed. "I missed you too, Hannah. Has she behaved herself?" He grinned at Anwen.

"She's been an angel. She can come again any time, just give me fair warning so I can make some more jam first." Anwen winked, and raised an eyebrow. "Everything go okay?"

That was a bit of a funny question to ask, Hannah thought, noticing the wink that followed.

"Wonderful, we had a fabulous time, and I'll take you up on your offer if I may, Anwen. It was nice to have some adult company."

"Hey!" Hannah flipped his arm. "Don't say that!"

He laughed and ruffled her hair. "Come on, Missie, best be getting you home. What do you say to Anwen and Emrys?"

"Thanks, Anwen. Thanks, Emrys." She squealed with delight and flapped her hands. She was so happy.

***

"Jump in," Bleddyn said, opening the passenger door. They said their goodbyes through the open window of the car, then he closed it and drove off.

Hannah sniffed the air, suspiciously. She turned around to check the back, half expecting to see someone there, before sniffing again.

His stomach twisted.

"Miss Morgan's been in here."

Bleddyn was speechless. How had he been dumb enough to expect her not to notice? She'd already been suspicious when she noticed him dressed up earlier. He should have given her more credit.

"It's her perfume."

"We'll talk about it when we get home, all right." He heard the tremble in his voice.

He'd lied. He hadn't wanted to, but he simply wasn't ready to tell her yet. Nevertheless, the guilt stabbed like a knife in his guts. He leaned across to touch her hand, but she pulled away.

During the short journey home neither of them spoke. As soon as he unlocked the door, she shot upstairs, and when he called her to come and have her hot chocolate, she ignored him. He found her already in bed with the lights out. Despite spending the next five minutes or so trying to persuade her to come back downstairs and talk to him, she refused.

He sat in silence at the kitchen table, his heart heavy. What had been the best day he'd had since her concert had turned sour. Had he done wrong by not telling her? He wanted to protect her, knowing she was still tetchy about Emily. He'd considered it best to see how things went with Deryth first. Huh, Deryth! How cunning Hannah had been in the car when she'd once again referred to her as Miss Morgan, thus re-establishing a sense of distance. He swallowed hard.

Or had he been weak? Had he known deep down she might take it like this and avoided confrontation? His mug of tea remained untouched next to her chocolate, a wrinkled skin forming over the top to remind him that he was supposed to protect her.

"Arrgh!" He tossed the milk down the sink, splashing the worktop in temper. It was so frustrating. He couldn't help but feel a little angry with Hannah, too. He'd dedicated himself to her this past decade. Didn't he deserve a little happiness? But thinking that way made him feel tremendous guilt.

It had nothing to do with Deryth, he was certain. She and Hannah got on like a house on fire. No, she wasn't ready to share his attention, that was the truth of it.

***

After he left, Hannah sobbed into her pillow. They'd all lied to her. It was obvious both Emrys and Anwen knew Dada'd gone on a date with Deryth. She'd put the clues together, like Velma from *Scooby Doo*. A wink here, a nod there, and she knew they were all in on it. Did they think she was stupid?

Why, though? She liked Deryth—a lot. All right, if she was honest she wouldn't want Dada to marry her—not yet anyway—but she wouldn't have minded him going out with her, not much in any case. It was all about trust. She certainly couldn't trust Mamma—she hadn't even rung to ask how the concert went. And now she couldn't trust Emrys, or Anwen, or Deryth, and especially not Dada. They'd all let her down by lying. And what about the wolf, Tarian? She'd seemed like a friend, like she might be one who'd look out for her, but she hadn't seen her in ages, so she probably couldn't trust her either.

***

Deryth was upset. Bleddyn had rung around nine to break the news, his voice little more than a whisper down the line. And they'd spent such a lovely afternoon together. He didn't deserve this, though neither did Hannah. They'd made the wrong decision in not telling her, that was all. Deryth hoped Hannah's tenacity would shine through and they would be able to stitch the wound back together.

Switching off the TV, she sat on the sofa and curled her legs beneath her. How on earth would she handle this on Monday? Should she tell Bethan what had happened? Her stomach churned at the prospect of doing so. It seemed the right thing to do since Bethan was Hannah's teacher and ought to be prepared in case she caused a scene.

She'd confided in no one other than her family as yet about her date with Bleddyn. The relationship was still new. It was uncanny, because the previous week Bethan had commented on the way she and Bleddyn had looked at each other as they chatted at the classroom door. She'd teased her about flirting with one of the dads, but Deryth rebuffed her, saying they'd known each other for some considerable time, and it was natural they'd grown more familiar with each other since she had so much to do with Hannah. She hadn't even admitted to Bethan that she'd done Hannah's hair for the concert, nor that she and Bleddyn had attended it together. She wasn't ready—not yet.

She poured a glass of wine and wrapped herself in a throw. As it was late September the evenings were getting chilly, but it was still too soon to put the heating on.

The first flush of wine warmed her insides and encouraged her mind to wander …

The first time the change had occurred had been the most traumatic experience of her life. When it was over,

Tadcu had sat her down and explained what had happened, ashamed he hadn't prepared her earlier. He hadn't expected it to happen so soon, he'd said—must have been the shock of the death that brought it on prematurely. And she'd learned to live with it ever since.

In some ways it was a gift; in others a curse. She shivered, and wrapped the throw around her more tightly, tucking it around her bare feet.

Morfydd's death had been the catalyst. She'd dealt with the death of the lambs and the calf, but seeing her beloved Morfydd lying there with her neck twisted in a grotesque manner, so that she faced the wrong direction to her body, had almost destroyed her. She'd loved that dog. She'd reared it from a pup, herself still a little girl, and was so proud of her when she'd given birth to the pups. Even now the memory brought tears to her eyes.

Eyes. Morfydd's had held hers. Unseeing, yet still pleading, and all she'd been able to do was promise to take care of her little ones. And so she had—Bronwen was evidence of that—and the rest they made sure were well homed.

As Tadcu had lifted Morfydd's limp body and wrapped her in an old blanket, she'd been overcome with grief and anger. It was the anger that had triggered the change. It wouldn't have happened if she hadn't been so utterly consumed with rage. At least not for another year or so, until she was an adult, according to Tadcu. But in truth it had always been there, lying dormant, waiting for someone or something to pull the trigger.

She'd been driven wild, blind with fury, and most of all intent on revenge.

Tadcu had stayed by her side throughout the whole thing, and had talked to her over and over about the repercussions of what had happened. She'd learn to control it, he promised—eventually. And so she had.

Once again it had become a curse, one she knew she had the power to break, at the right time and given the right circumstances. She needed to be certain it was what she wanted, nothing more. Certain it would be best for her, for Hannah, for all of them if she relinquished her power. What had happened tonight made her uncertain again. And that was because there remained a thread of doubt as to how best she might protect Hannah. Would it be best done by giving up her gift, or keeping it?

She'd wait and see. What would be would be, life had already taught her that.

Accusations

They'd had a little talk, her and Dada, so Hannah felt a bit better. When she remembered what had happened, it still made her tummy ache. She told Dada, but he insisted she had to go to school because having an achy tummy from feeling upset was not the same as having tummy ache from a bug.

He also told her he'd already spoken to Miss Morgan, so she needn't feel awkward about it at school. She still did, though. In fact, she stayed in the cloakroom for as long as possible, until she heard Miss Collins begin to call the register, then she sidled into class and busied herself with the contents of her pencil case. She could sense Miss Morgan's eyes on her, and her heart raced.

"Right, everyone. Come and sit on the carpet for a few moments. Megan has some special news she wants to share with you," Miss Collins said.

Hannah frowned. What now? This hardly ever happened. Usually, they went straight into the first lesson, English.

Megan stood at the front of the class, nibbling her bottom lip. Her face was a bit red, which made Hannah think she was either hot or embarrassed about something.

She joined the moving throng to sit on the carpeted area at the front of the classroom. A few of the girls whispered behind closed hands, and a few of the boys groaned and sighed because they didn't care what Megan had to say.

Miss Collins hushed them. "Go ahead, Megan, tell them your news."

Damn it. The lace on one of Hannah's trainers had come undone. She'd told Dada to tie a double knot. She hadn't yet mastered the art of tying shoelaces. She'd either have to ask one of the girls or Miss Morgan to retie it for her.

Somewhere in between twiddling the lace in a loop and seeing whether the person she sat next to was good at laces, she heard the name, Ife. She sprung to attention, all ears. Was she mistaken, or had Megan said Carys's friend, the talent spotter, had rung her mum at the weekend to offer Megan a part in a TV programme?

She glanced left, then right. All eyes were fixed on Megan who grinned like a Cheshire cat. Everyone clapped and cheered. So she had heard correctly.

"You stole Mamma's brooch!" The words flew from her mouth of their own accord.

Everyone gasped, apart from Megan who frowned.

"That wiped the smile off her face," she heard one of the boys mutter. It had to be Jack, because he didn't like Megan. Nevertheless, right now, Hannah felt bad. She clasped a hand over her offending mouth.

"What?" Megan was looking straight at her, and from the way her face crumpled Hannah knew she was upset.

Why couldn't she say sorry? Why couldn't she say she hadn't meant it? All eyes fixed on her. Her heart raced and her hands clenched and unclenched repeatedly, but still she couldn't find the *sorry* word, because she still wasn't certain. The tree creature had planted a seed of doubt, and it was in full bloom. So, instead of the *sorry* word, she found herself saying, "When you came to my house … you stole Mamma's brooch. The tree—" She shook her head. "S-someone told me." She put her hand over her mouth again, but it was too late. And part of her wasn't even sorry because lately everyone had let her down.

Then she burst into tears.

And Megan turned white.

Then everyone started gossiping. And before she knew what was happening, Miss Morgan had taken her by the elbow and whisked her out of the classroom, towards the library.

***

Miss Morgan was disappointed in her. Miss Collins was disappointed in her. Megan wasn't her friend any more. Hannah hadn't felt this miserable since? Since Saturday, when she'd discovered Dada had lied.

Even though Miss Morgan wrapped an arm around her shoulders, Hannah sensed she wasn't very pleased.

Some time later, once things had calmed down a bit, Megan was brought to the library, but Hannah still wasn't able to find the words, *I'm sorry*. They'd done a runner and were nowhere to be seen.

At home time, Dada was called in and told what had happened, but even then, she couldn't find those two words, because she wasn't sorry, therefore she couldn't say it. Simple as! The anger was a ball of fire, heating her inside like a volcano, and until it cooled down she couldn't think straight.

***

The tree creature stood at the edge of the wood and smiled as Hannah approached. Hannah felt no guilt about visiting The Lane tonight, she would defy them all and do as she pleased, and besides, she wanted to speak to her about the butterfly gown. If it really was made of butterfly wings then that was cruel, and Hannah would tell her so. She wasn't wearing it now though. Instead, she wore a plain white slip, a bit like an old-fashioned nightdress.

There was something else she wanted to do tonight too—to rid herself of Mamma's gown once and for all. It held too many memories and made her sad every time she took it out of the trunk. She didn't care what Dada would think of her decision. It belonged to her, and she would do as she wished. Brooch unpinned, she cosseted it inside her jewellery box and folded the gown as neatly as she could.

***

"Brought this for you. Thought you might be cold." In one hand Hannah held the silky, cream gown and in the other a woollen cardigan.

"How kind." The creature took the gown from Hannah's outstretched hand and held it to her face. "What a gorgeous scent."

A lump threatened Hannah's throat, and she swallowed hard. Parting with Mamma's gown had been a difficult decision in some ways, though all things considered she believed she'd be better off without it.

"This belonged to your mother." The creature inhaled, her eyes twinkling like moonlit stars.

A rook took flight from a nearby oak and landed on the creature's left shoulder, causing Hannah to startle. She'd never been in The Lane at night before. In fact, come to think of it, she hadn't even been in her garden after dark, at least not since they'd lived in this house.

They'd had a barbecue once at her old house, but that was a long time ago, when they had neighbours.

She held out the other hand and offered the cardigan. It belonged to Hannah, not Mamma, but it was too baggy, so it might fit the creature. The creature smiled and took it from her.

"Give me a moment." The creature disappeared behind the tree, leaving Hannah alone in the dark. She peered back the way she'd come, hoping she'd be able to find her way home again with only the moon to light the way. Never mind. She'd made it here, so why shouldn't she make it back?

The full moon shone brightly. It winked at her, encouraging her disobedience. As her eyes adjusted to the dark, she noticed something strange. All the way down the length of The Lane there appeared to be markings. Close to the fence, strange looping, swirling shapes shone ghostly white. She turned around and faced the top of The Lane. Yes, the markings were ahead of her too, about every five or so paces, she assumed. Looking down there was even one at her feet. What were they?

"Well? How do I look?" The creature stood before her, dressed in Mamma's gown.

"Amazing!" The creature's beauty stole Hannah's breath and she forgot about the white marks. "Like Mamma, when she was Eliza Doolittle." Hannah flushed with pleasure.

The creature seemed pleased, and Hannah's heart thawed a little. "What's your name?" She was surprised she'd not asked the creature before, but until now it hadn't entered her head.

"My name is Rhiamon. It means *Great Queen*."

"Wow! A queen? In this wood?"

Rhaimon smirked. "Oh, I'm not from here, child … but that's another story."

Hannah saw that the cardigan remained crumpled on the ground, as if its occupant had disappeared into thin air. Oh well, it would likely spoil the dress, and in any case, perhaps queens didn't feel the cold, especially magical ones. She remembered the swirling shapes now. "What are they?" She pointed towards the path.

Rhiamon's expression darkened, and the light in her eyes dimmed. "Evil, child. That's what they are, for they are the cause of my imprisonment."

Hannah screwed up her face. "Like prison?"

Rhiamon hesitated. "It's a long story, and not for the fainthearted."

Hannah didn't know what fainthearted meant. She'd heard of faint because ages ago she'd nearly fainted when she had flu, and also in the butterfly house. Perhaps it had something to do with her bad heart.

The creature, who might be a queen, Rhi—something didn't seem to want to talk about the white shapes at the moment.

"You've been let down, child. Your heart is hurting. I see pain in your eyes." Her voice was smooth as silk, comforting. Hannah placed a hand to her chest, at the place where she knew the scar lay. Did she imagine it, or did she feel a twinge of pain? Their eyes met, and for a moment she believed she saw Mamma's eyes, not the creature's. But it had been such a long time. How might she even remember what Mamma's eyes looked like? The place with the scar gave another stab.

"Those who are supposed to protect you have let you down. I see it all."

Hannah eyed her suspiciously. "How?"

Rhiamon crowed. "As your queen I see and hear everything that goes on around here, and what I don't see for myself gets relayed to me by my servants."

"Servants?"

Rhiamon waved a graceful arm in the direction of the wood. "The birds, the trees, the creatures. Tell me, what is it you most desire?"

The gown shimmered in the breeze. Hannah noticed how the silk clung to the creature's curves, the moonlight making it appear pearlescent. For a moment she stood transfixed, wooed by its shimmer. Dada had told her how pearls grew when they'd been at the beach, the day she'd been worrying about going back to school. She wanted to be a pearl like this creature, not a bit of grit. Would she ever grow into one so beautiful?

"Well?"

The creature sounded impatient. What was she waiting for? Ah yes, she'd asked Hannah what she desired. "I want everyone to stop lying." She reached out a small hand and stroked the silk of the gown, once more surprised by how cold the creature's skin felt. She wondered why the creature didn't put on the cardigan if she was cold.

Rhiamon's jaw tightened.

Hannah suddenly remembered what Emrys had told her about Bronwen's mother—she couldn't remember the dog's name because it was a hard word to say. Could this *queen* be the witch he talked about? Her suspicion grew by the second. "Did you kill Emrys's sheepdog?"

The bluntness of her question took the creature by surprise. Her eyes glinted black. Even the moon shied away, disappearing behind a cloud, before timidly peeping out again from one side.

"Huh! What nonsense has the old dewin been telling you? It is he who makes others suffer needlessly, not I."

Anger flashed upon the creature's face. *She's not used to people asking her difficult questions*, thought Hannah. But if she really was a queen it was understandable, because every queen in every story she'd ever read liked having her own way. Then again, so did witches.

"What's a dewin?"

The creature shook her head and huffed. "Doesn't matter. Forget I mentioned it." Her anger made Hannah nervous. She swallowed hard and took a deep breath, considering what to do next. She'd test her, that's what she'd do. In fact, she'd test all of them, then she'd decide who she could trust, because right now she was angry with them all, and if she spoke the truth, she was even a bit angry with herself. "I'd better go.' She wrapped her arms tight around her own middle, giving herself a hug. "Dada'd worry if he knew I was here."

"And your father cares, does he, child?"

"Of course." Hannah's anger made her feel invincible.

"Which is why he's having more fun with *her* than you, is it?"

Hannah felt sick. Part of her wanted to defend Dada, but the other part was still angry with him for lying. She'd better go, before she made the wrong decision. She glanced at the creature's bare feet. They had to be freezing. "I'll bring you shoes next time. Mamma's might fit, and they have high heels."

The corners of the creature's mouth twitched, though her eyes didn't smile. "How kind, and perhaps next time you might join me in the wood," she said, pointing a graceful arm towards the trees. "Tell you what—we'll have a midnight picnic by the light of the moon, and I'll tell you stories of long ago. How does that sound?"

Hannah had to admit, the creature's offer sounded tempting. "I'll think about it, but I'll be back soon—with shoes."

Hannah lay in bed shivering. Never before in the whole of her life had she sneaked outdoors at night. She felt brave, confident, grown up, and a bit thrilled, all at the same time. She'd got away with it, too. If she listened carefully, she was able to hear the rhythm of Dada's snores floating through the wall. Perhaps she would go again. Maybe she would take a picnic—if she could find a way of hiding the food in the right sort of place.

Her feet were freezing. She could do with one of Dada's hot water bottles. Perhaps if she pushed Teddy down the bed, he'd warm her feet. The moon had come out of hiding and was washing the deep sill with a pale, blue light. Through the cutout flowers of her lace curtain, the glass misted. Spooky! She giggled and wrapped her quilt more tightly round her middle.

THE BITE

It was Halloween, or Nos Calan Gaeaf, as Emrys called it. Hannah enjoyed this particular festival because she loved all things spooky. Best of all, it was Saturday, so she had two things to look forward to as Emrys was due to come and have a last tidy up in the garden before winter, and Aunty Ffion and Evan were coming later to celebrate Halloween at her house.

She'd mostly forgiven Emrys for lying about Miss Morgan and Dada because it was possible he hadn't known. She'd partly forgiven Dada because she was beginning to agree he deserved some adult company, though he was taking Miss Morgan out for dinner again tonight which made her feel a bit sick. In one way it was a good thing because that was why Aunty Ffion was coming over—to look after her, but in another way she was sad Dada wouldn't be there to celebrate Halloween. Why couldn't he and Miss Morgan stay in with the rest of them? Why did they have to go out on their own?

She and Dada had spent the morning decorating the house and the front garden, even though no one would come trick-or-treating because they didn't have any neighbours. The night before, they'd carved a great big pumpkin into a scary face. It sat patiently on the front doorstep, waiting for it to get dark, so it could have its candle lit and its pointy-toothed grin would light up.

"Why do you call Halloween the other thing?"

Emrys put down the rake and leaned against the sturdy trunk of the bare beech. "Well, bach, Nos Calan Gaeaf is the old Welsh name for Halloween see, goes right back to pagan times."

"What's pagan?"

He removed his flannel cap and scratched his head. "Pagan is a belief in something other than the usual gods. Think of it like this, me an' you are doing a last tidy in your garden today cos the season's changing. It'll soon be winter, won't it? Nos Calan Gaeaf means *first night of winter,* so it's a celebration of the changing of the season. But there's also a bit of magic involved."

"Ooh, I like magic." She grinned.

"Long ago folk believed at this time of year the boundary between this world and the next was a bit—well, a bit less obvious, so it was easier to communicate with those who had already passed on."

She frowned. "What's boundary?"

"Like a line—a marking. Like the fence around this garden or the fence in the lane—the one that separates the track from the wood. Boundaries can sometimes be seen, or they can be invisible, see."

She swallowed hard, remembering the white shapes that separated the wood from The Lane. "So why do we make lanterns?"

"Well, let me see … Back in the olden days, people would dress up in costumes as a disguise against ghosts. They'd carve lanterns to ward off evil spirits. Here, come up by the fence an' I'll tell you a bit more 'bout the invisible boundary, though you won't be able to see it in daylight."

Hannah felt a bit queasy. Nevertheless, she followed him to the wire fence.

"See over there," he pointed a chubby finger, mottled with age, "where the wood is fenced off?"

She nodded.

"Well, Hannah, it's a boundary, right?"

"Uh-huh."

"Well, bach, what you *can't* see is there's also an invisible boundary running alongside it. One that can only be seen at night. If it were dark, you'd be able to see all kinds of markings on the ground, white ones. They're Celtic symbols of protection."

Hannah gasped. He was definitely talking about the ghostly-white markings she'd seen a few nights back, when she'd been talking to the tree creature.

"Does it surprise you, bach?" Emrys said, noticing the shocked expression on her face.

She gave a small nod, afraid to raise her eyes in case he read the deception there.

"Remember I told you 'bout when me an' Deryth found her in the wood—the evil one who'd killed our dog, Morfydd?"

She was hardly likely to have forgotten that story, was she? In fact, she'd thought about it every day since. "Uh-huh."

"Those markings are how we manage to keep her there. They form a magical boundary. No wire fence would have done, not even barbed wire. She's a powerful one all right, I tell you." He shook his head. "Sapped the strength from both of us it did, weaving that magic. An' we only had one night to do it in."

"How come she doesn't escape? How come they shine in the dark?"

"So many questions, bach. Come on, let's go sit over by the apple tree an' I'll tell you 'bout the night we trapped her."

Although it hadn't rained for a few days the grass was still too wet to sit on, so instead they plonked down on the old pig bench. The pig bench had been left in the garden by the previous owner; hardly surprising given its rotten condition. It was a wonder it held their weight.

Hannah remembered asking Emrys about it during one of his first visits. He'd explained how pig benches were originally used for chopping the pig into pieces after slaughter. His explanation had horrified her, and she had refused to sit on it for some time, but it seemed a bit silly now. She still couldn't get the image of the poor pig's face out of her head whenever she did though. She shuddered.

"You cold? Want to go grab a coat?"

"No … it's this." Hannah pointed to the bench. "Gives me the willies." She liked the *willy* word, and this was one of those times when she believed she could get away with using it.

"Duw, duw, you have the knack of lifting my spirits!" He chuckled, which made her laugh too. "Right, bach, let's go back to where we left off last time …"

Hannah watched him, eager for the story to start.

" 'Member me telling you 'bout her killing my Morfydd?" His eyes clouded over. "Never seen our Deryth so upset. Took it hard she did. Changed her forever … in some ways."

"Cos she loved her?"

"That's right, bach. An' when we lose something we love we're never the same after, are we?"

***

Hannah had not interrupted as he relayed the story. Even now, as she helped Aunty Ffion arrange the chocolate whiskers on the black cat cake, she thought about it.

The witch had hidden in the wood after killing Morfydd. Deryth and Emrys had used their tracking skills and had found her asleep under the blackthorn, its blossoms already appearing despite the snow. *Curled up like a babi*, he'd said. *Not a hint of shame on her face*. How might anyone do something so bad and not feel ashamed? All right, so she could be a bit naughty at times, but she always felt ashamed, once she calmed down anyway.

She remembered calling Megan a thief, and her face reddened. Instinctively she touched her cheeks with her cool palms, smearing melted chocolate onto it in the process.

Emrys had told her how Deryth had shot off like a bullet after discovering Morfydd's body, and how he'd had to run to keep her in his sights. Hannah couldn't imagine Emrys running, what with his gammy knee. It had been close to nightfall, too, which hadn't made it any easier. Hannah pictured him running in the dark towards the wood, with Deryth miles ahead. How had Deryth known the witch would be hiding in the wood? She'd have to ask Emrys. Perhaps Deryth had a sixth sense, the same as Bronwen.

There—the cake was ready. "I'll go and put my costume on," she said, getting up from the table.

"Need a hand?"

"No thanks. I can do it." She didn't want Aunty Ffion following her upstairs because she wanted a few minutes to herself to study the symbols.

She opened the sketch pad, secretly squirrelled beneath her quilt, to the double page spread. Emrys had tried his best to explain the symbols to her, but she'd found it hard to understand, so she'd run inside and fetched her sketch pad for him to draw in. She remembered at least two from the night in The Lane. In fact, the symbol in the top right corner had been the one she'd almost stood on. The number three was important to the Celts, he'd told her, which she was pleased about because it was her favourite number. All the best stories seemed to contain the number three. *The Three Bears*, *The Three Billy Goats Gruff*, *The Three Little Pigs*.

Emrys had drawn a circle with three overlapping loops. Beneath it he'd written the word *triquetra,* followed by a dash and the words, *protects against evil spirits.* Hannah traced the loops with her finger, noticing how they kept on going round, never coming to a stop.

One thing he'd said had shocked her to the core, and she hadn't been able to get it out of her mind since. *Her name's Rhiamon,* he'd said, *it means witch.* So it didn't mean *queen* then—it meant *witch.* She'd been dying to ask him if he might be mistaken, if instead it might mean *great queen* like Rhiamon had said it did, but she couldn't because then he'd have known Hannah had met her. Now, she was more convinced than ever that the witch and the tree creature were one and the same.

Emrys had told her how they'd found the witch fast asleep beneath a blackthorn tree, the most evil of trees, he'd said, especially powerful when close to its sister, the hawthorn. Used by the Devil himself to prick the finger of his followers. He'd explained the pins of a blackthorn were extremely sharp and would cause a lot of bleeding, often turning a wound septic. Must never cut a blackthorn tree on All Hallows, or it'll bring great misfortune, he'd said.

Apparently, Rhiamon had strewn the needles of the blackthorn in a circle around where she lay to protect herself. Emrys and Deryth had worked tirelessly throughout the night, marking the boundary of the wood with protective symbols to prevent her escaping.

"What if it hadn't worked?" she'd asked.

"Well fortunately for us it did, bach, though we weren't certain until she woke."

"Was she mad?"

"Mad? You never heard the like of it! Cussing an' screaming, spitting an' hissing like the diafol himself."

Hannah closed the sketch book and tucked it beneath her quilt before donning the witch's costume Dada had bought for her to wear. She wished she'd chosen the skeleton one instead, but then it would have seemed as if she'd copied Evan, and she didn't want anyone thinking that.

***

Out of all the games they played, Hannah's favourite was *pin the wart on the witch.* By some stroke of luck she won, despite almost throwing up from being twirled round and round.

They got so hot and bothered they decided to take the fun outside. A little earlier, while it was still light, Uncle Aled had taken some string and a few balloons and hidden them around the garden. Now, she and Evan were searching for them by torchlight. The sound of spooky music drifted from the house, adding to the tension. They'd managed to keep Jipp indoors until now, but there was no way he was going to miss out on this fun. He stayed close, rounding her and Evan back together whenever they drifted apart. Her heart beat loud in her chest, and her tummy tingled with excitement.

She'd just found her third balloon when she heard the gate open. Dada and Deryth were back. Perhaps they'd help her find the rest. "Dada!"

He came towards her, smiling, Deryth in tow. "Had fun?"

"Yes, lots. We're finding Halloween balloons. Come and help," she said, taking him by the arm and pulling him deeper into the garden.

Now there were four of them, and because Dada was here she wasn't scared any longer.

"Jipp!"

It was Evan shouting. In chatting to Dada she hadn't noticed Jipp disappear. Her heart sank. What if he'd run off into The Lane, like before?

"Jipp!" She joined in the hunt. It was tricky finding her way around the furthest end of the garden by torchlight, but she hoped they'd find him there. But Jipp was nowhere to be seen, and Evan grew more and more frantic. Aunty Ffion and Uncle Aled joined the search, and the garden became a clamour of whistles and calls.

"I'll go round the back and take a look up the lane," Bleddyn said.

Hannah wanted to scream at him, but she didn't dare. It would seem too suspicious. "Please Jipp, please," she begged under her breath.

Moments later, to her immense relief, Jipp came darting across the grass towards them, trembling from head to foot.

Grabbing hold of his collar, Evan did his best to calm him down. "He's hurt. His leg's bleeding."

Jipp was led into the kitchen where he continued to yap with pain and fear. The whites of his eyes shone bright, and his body trembled all over, reminding Hannah of when Connor had pinned her to the classroom door. Evan was right, for there on Jipp's thigh was a nasty tear.

"Now, now. Don't fuss. Poor boy," Aunty Ffion cooed, as she cleaned the wound while Hannah watched on in alarm.

"Who did it to him?"

"I don't think anyone did it, Hannah, he probably snagged it on the barbed wire as he squeezed through the fence. Daft old dog, running off like that in the dark. What if we weren't able to find you, then you'd be in trouble, wouldn't you?" Ffion continued to talk to him as she dressed the wound, the familiarity of her voice soothing his spirits.

Hannah knew it hadn't been the barbed wire. It had to have been the witch. She must have bitten him, because she'd seen teeth marks. What a cruel thing to do. But if it was Rhiamon, then how come he was still alive? Emrys had said she'd killed Morfydd, so why not Jipp?

She stroked his head as Aunty Ffion bandaged his leg. She hated seeing him so upset.

"It'll be all right, Jipp, don't you worry." He whined softly at her words, and she felt his heartbeat through his fur. "Poor thing. If someone has done this to you, I'll kill them." Her anger was a fireball, ready to explode.

***

The witch's ladder had done the trick. All Rhiamon had needed to do was unravel several strands of wool from the girl's cardigan—the one she'd gifted her to keep her warm—before knotting them into a ladder formation. Entwined throughout were a few stray hairs belonging to the girl that she'd pulled from the wool of the garment. Upon tying the knots, she'd uttered the malediction and faced the ladder towards the girl's window. It hung from a spike of blackthorn, a few raven feathers added to its twists for good measure.

And the dog? The dog's injury had served as a ruse. Tempted though she'd been to snap its neck, she'd resisted, and instead had merely gouged a hole in its thigh, close to an artery, but not so close it would bleed out. She licked her lips, recalling the salty taste. They'd be convinced the dog's ailment would have been enough to upset the girl. Not in a million years would they guess Rhiamon had used the ladder in order to steal into her dreams. Fools! Still, if it would tempt *her* out of hiding then it would be worth it.

From the bough of the blackthorn, Rhiamon watched, delighting in every speck of anguish the girl's dreams delivered.

***

"No! Get away!" The wolf had Jipp pinned to the ground. The gaping hole in his throat spurted blood, covering his chest and pooling on the floor. Momentarily, the wolf stopped the attack and turned its attention to Hannah, its eyes lit like two red torches in the dark. Would it attack her? She was so consumed by rage, she couldn't think straight. "Leave him be!" She dived at the wolf, attempting to pull it off Jipp, but the wolf held Jipp down effortlessly with one front paw and clawed at her with the remaining one.

It was huge. The size of a horse, not a wolf—but it wasn't Tarian, she was certain. Her tummy hurt. She glanced down. Streaks of blood soaked her T-shirt. The wolf snarled a warning before once again turning its attention to the dog.

Jipp was dead. Hannah knew it. The huge wolf held him in its jaws, shaking him like a rag doll and snarling. Jipp's blood spattered her face as he was jerked back and forth in the wolf's powerful jaws. She screamed.

"It's all right, it's all right—it's just a dream."

She opened her eyes to see Dada sitting on the bed beside her. "He's dead!"

"You were dreaming, Hannah. It's all right."

She stared beyond him, blind with fear. "He's dead, Dada. The wolf killed him."

Dada reached across and switched on her lamp before cradling her in his arms. "Sh, sh, no one's dead, Hannah, you were dreaming." But she was inconsolable.

"The wolf killed Jipp—look!" She yanked her nightdress away from her body and examined it. No blood. How? It had soaked her front. She wiped her damp face with her hand and looked at her palm, expecting it to be covered in blood. Nothing. "Phone Aunty Ffion. He's dead!"

"Hannah, it's two in the morning. Aunty Ffion cleaned Jipp's wound, and bandaged it. He's fine, I promise."

"No! You have to phone her now!"

She struggled from his grasp and shot out of bed. Her face was white as a sheet and glistened with perspiration, and her hair was plastered to her head with sweat. She paused at the bedroom door, clenching and unclenching her fists, before heading for the stairs.

"Where are you going?"

"To ring her!"

He caught her by the shoulders and pulled her towards him, his voice shushing and soothing. "I'll ring first thing in the morning—I promise. Come on, let me tuck you in. I'll sit with you for a while. The cut on his leg upset you, that's all, and made you have a bad dream. Jipp'll be fine, I promise."

She shook herself free and darted downstairs to the phone, her eyes mad with fear.

"Oh, all right!" Taking the phone from her trembling hand, he dialled the number. "I hope Aunty Ffion will understand."

FEVER

Bleddyn opened his eyes a fraction and peered in the direction of the window. Despite the curtains being closed, he knew it was still raining, for the room felt heavy and grey.

He sat up and glanced at the clock—7:55. Thank goodness it was Sunday, or there'd be one hell of a rush to get her ready for school. Normally he'd have been awake for at least an hour, but after the night he'd had he was exhausted.

He'd lain beside her until gone four. No wonder he was shattered. She'd eventually dropped off, though even after having been assured Jipp was fine, she'd remained fretful. Such a shame, as she'd seemed happier lately and hadn't even protested when he told her he was going out with Deryth last night. Was it down to Jipp's injury, or was something else worrying her? He groaned. Why did it seem of late that no sooner would they get over one obstacle than another would present itself? In some ways it had been easier when she was a baby, at least then there'd been fewer emotional issues to deal with. He paused outside her bedroom door, listening. If she needed another hour or so he'd let her sleep.

When 9:30 came, and there was still no sign of her, he thought he'd better check. She was fast asleep. He stood over her, watching the rise and fall of her chest. God, he loved this child so much. His stomach twisted at the thought of her coming to harm. She was pale, and was he mistaken or did her breathing seem a little laboured? "Hannah?" She didn't stir. He stroked her free arm. "Hannah?"

Her eyes flickered briefly beneath the lids, but remained closed. Her lids were moist and so pale that tiny blue veins were visible beneath the skin. "You all right, Missie?"

His question met with a faint groan, little more than a sigh. She was beginning to worry him. "Hannah?" He shook her gently by the shoulder. Her eyes flickered open, and stared through him as if he were made of glass. "You all right, sweetheart?"

She gave a small moan before once more closing her eyes. Within seconds she appeared to have fallen fast asleep again.

Bleddyn rose slowly from the bed, so as not to disturb her. Was she ill or simply exhausted after the trauma of her nightmare? He wasn't certain. He watched her sleep for a few minutes longer, but she seemed peaceful. Perhaps he'd give her another half an hour then check again.

"Should I call an out of hours G.P.?" Bleddyn ran his hands through his hair, his mouth twitching with tension.

When he still hadn't been able to wake her fully, he'd panicked and rung Ffion. By the time she arrived, Hannah was awake but obviously unwell. Her temperature was 102, and although she was a bath of sweat, she was shivering. Neither Bleddyn nor Ffion managed to get any sensible conversation out of her.

"Perhaps you should call a doctor," Ffion said. "I'll try to get her to drink some water. Do you have any paracetamol?"

Bleddyn's hands shook as he waited in line for his call to be answered. Seeing her like this brought back all the old memories of when she was a baby. Calm down, Bledd—it's probably a virus, he told himself. He tried to take slow, deep breaths as he waited, remembering how he'd taught Hannah to do the same once she'd been old enough to understand. It had proved a useful way of calming her down whenever she got in a tizz.

After the paracetamol and water kicked in, she seemed a little better. She half listened to a story, but didn't engage in her usual manner. Bloody doctor still hadn't arrived. It was what—a good three hours or more since he'd phoned, and still nothing. They'd wanted him to take her to the surgery. It wasn't like him to lose his rag, but he'd told them in no uncertain terms, she wasn't well enough to leave the house.

She was fast asleep again, her chest rattling slightly, though her temperature had cooled a little. He'd hardly moved from her bedside all day.

***

Concealed within the protective arms of the alder, Rhiamon watched the comings and goings through the girl's bedroom window. There was no doubt other than the spell had worked, that was plain to see. Throughout the day the girl had been visited by several well-intentioned adults, though of course they could do little to help her. She rubbed her hands in glee. It was dusk and the lamplight in the girl's room afforded her a better view of the bedroom. Her father hardly left her side all day, his distress evident in his movements.

***

Once Jipp was dead, the witch hung him upside down from a high branch by a length of twisted ivy. Hannah tried so hard to move, but no matter how hard she tried she was frozen to the spot—an unwilling spectator of the grisly scene. She opened her mouth and tried to scream, but her lungs made no sound, not even a whisper, despite them burning with effort.

She couldn't cry, either. She wanted to, and she wanted to be sick, but could do neither. It was for all the world as if she were turned to stone. Stone felt no emotion: no sadness, no anger. Emotions were all she had left.

She didn't want to look, but despite all her effort she couldn't turn her face away, nor could she close her eyes to the horror, for they were frozen open. Hannah watched as Jipp's limp body swung in half rotation a few times before eventually settling. His head hung low, his tongue protruding grossly as she watched, horrified. The worst thing of all was his eyes remained open, staring at her, confused as to why she wasn't coming to his aid.

Oh, how longed to tell him how desperate she was to cut him down and carry him home. No matter how hard she tried, she couldn't even make her eyes communicate with him.

And now the witch had disappeared, leaving Hannah alone with Jipp's corpse. This might be Hannah's one opportunity to set him free, if only her feet would move. Perhaps the witch had performed some sort of magic spell on her. Hannah tried again, but still found herself rooted to the spot. She was exhausted by her efforts.

Then she heard Dada's voice, close by.

"It's all right, sweetheart," he was saying. Although she was pleased to hear him, she failed to understand why he didn't rescue her. It was so frustrating. She wasn't able to see him either, at least not properly. He was no more than a shadow at the edge of her vision. *Help me*, she tried to say, but no sound came out.

"You're so hot. Try to drink some water. It will cool you down."

He supported the glass in one hand, and her head in the other. She tried to drink. She'd do anything to make this stop. Cool water trickled down her front, reminding her of how Jipp's blood had trickled down his as the witch had hung him from the tree. It made her retch, but nothing came up. She sensed Dada nearby. He seemed to want to help but didn't seem able to. Her heart leapt. Had the witch done something to him, too? If so, they'd never get away from here. She was confused, because Dada's voice sounded calm. A little worried, yes, but not panicky.

Then a different voice spoke, a woman's. She listened carefully, still unable to move her head or body in order to see who it was. And it was getting dark in The Lane. The clouds had snuffed out the moon, leaving nothing more than a little star light. She recognized the voice—Aunty Ffion. She didn't want Aunty Ffion to see Jipp like this. She knew how much she loved him. It would break her heart. Hannah fought with the last of her strength to set herself free. *No!* In her head she screamed the word, but it came out as little more than a whimper. Why wasn't Aunty Ffion upset? Surely if she saw Jipp hanging there like that she'd be devastated. She sensed a little concern in the tone of Aunty Ffion's voice, just as she had with Dada's, but neither of them seemed to understand how dreadful the situation was. Did they not care? "Jipp," she tried to say over and over again, but the word came out as, "Je," all soft. Her brain felt fuzzy, like it was full of cotton wool, then, within moments, she lost consciousness.

The next thing she knew she was in her own bed. There were lots of people in her room, and they were all whispering. With a great effort she managed to open her eyes a fraction, but she couldn't see who was there because they were around the other side of the bed, and she didn't have enough strength to turn. She listened carefully. The first sound she recognized was a squeaky rasping sound coming from her chest. Each time she breathed it tickled, and it wasn't a nice tickle, it felt wrong.

Ah, there was Dada's voice, and a woman's, too, but it wasn't Aunty Ffion this time. Perhaps she'd finally seen Jipp's body and had carried him home. She wasn't in the wood now, was she? No, she was in her own bed. The cotton wool feeling in her head slowly began to clear.

"Hannah, this is Doctor Phillips." It was Dada's voice. She focussed hard to locate his face, and eventually it drifted into sight. Except it wasn't solid, there seemed to be a shadow all around him, as though he were made of smoke.

"I'm going to listen to your chest, Hannah."

She was aware of the doctor's cold fingers on her skin. Icy, like the tree creature's. It made her flinch.

"Sorry, sweetheart. It's cold outside. I'll try not to touch you, okay?"

Instead of fingers, the doctor held something hard and equally as cold to Hannah's chest, like a disc.

"Deep breath—that's it, in … out … good girl."

The smoky vision of Dada's face frowned with concern. She wanted him to feel better. She tried to smile, but her face didn't seem to want to do as it was told.

She was vaguely aware of the doctor examining other parts of her body—her tummy, her skin—but when she tried to look down Hannah's throat she retched, then vomited. The front of her was all wet and sticky, and it smelled bad.

Why wouldn't they let her sleep? Then she remembered about Jipp, and her stomach churned so she was sick again. "Jipp?" This time she got the word out. Dada's face grew a little clearer. He was telling her Jipp was fine. He had a cut on his leg, that was all. He must be lying because she'd seen him hanging dead from the tree.

"There's no rash, and her temperature's come down a little. Continue with the paracetamol, and try to keep her hydrated. I don't want to admit her yet, but if things are no better in the morning, give us a ring and we'll review the situation."

It was the doctor's voice. Hannah kind of had the feeling she was talking about whether or not she needed to go to hospital, but she didn't want to. She didn't have the energy to get off the bed, never mind go to hospital.

"I'm okay," she managed to say, thrilled to be able to make her voice heard. There! The smokiness of Dada's face cleared after she spoke. She'd be all right now she'd found her voice. She reached out a hand to touch his face, but she was too weak to lift it clear of the bed. Never mind, at last she was safe.

***

The sickness was into its third day, but little had changed. She'd neither worsened nor improved in health. Because Hannah was too weak to get out of bed, Bleddyn washed her where she lay, noticing the subtle changes of puberty as he did so. He shouldn't have to do this. It made him angry again with Emily. And Ffion had dared to raise the question of whether or not he should ring her to tell her how ill Hannah was. Over his dead body. It would be the last thing he'd do. She hadn't even had the decency to ring and ask how Hannah's concert had gone.

He was surprised the doctor had decided against admitting her, though as she was no worse, he supposed there was some logic in her decision. He'd been given the usual advice—plenty of fluids, keep a check on her temperature, and look out for any sign of a rash, but the doctor was pretty certain it was some kind of virus that would be over within a few days.

The delirium worried him most. It was for all the world as though she were only half with him, as if at the same time part of her was elsewhere. He'd not felt this concerned since her heart surgery, yet he had to admit, physically her symptoms were the same as any virus. Deryth and Emrys were visiting this evening. He hoped they might be able to lift her spirits.

CHOICES

"This will be the biggest decision of your life, and no one can make it for you. Listen to your heart, Deryth, not your head this time, that's my advice."

Deryth bit her lip. "I want to do what's best for all of us, Tadcu, and that's what makes it so hard."

They'd not long returned from visiting Hannah and were sitting at the breakfast bar in Deryth's kitchen, drinking tea. This needed to be a private conversation, one not even Anwen should be party to, since even she didn't realize the bigger picture. Deryth and Tadcu had kept their secrets to themselves her entire life.

"It's a tough call, Tadcu. With Bleddyn it feels right, and Hannah, too. I have no qualms about what my future might hold should things become more serious between us. I wish I was more certain about how best I might protect her, that's all. I mean what does she need most? A mother figure, or someone who can do more to keep her safe from the evil on her doorstep?" She shook her head. "The one thing I'm certain of is I can't do both; I won't do both. I always said, if ever I found *the one* I'd be prepared to give it all up. I never imagined it might happen like this."

"I'll still be able to help protect her, bach, make no mistake, but you must be certain it's what you want, because don't forget, there'll be no going back." He swirled the tea leaves at the bottom of his cup before turning it over and peering inside. He chuckled. "If there was a speck of doubt remaining—" He handed her the cup with the tea leaves displayed in the form of a cat. "Treachery this stands for. Those old Romas knew a thing or two about predicting the future. Do yours."

Deryth took the last sip before repeating the process with her own cup. A distinct crescent shape remained on the bottom. She handed it to him.

"Changes—that's what the crescent stands for. Seems apt, don't you think?"

The clock ticked away a few minutes of silence.

As soon as he left, she locked the door. For the first time in ages, she was afraid. She could talk to him about most things and had always appreciated his advice, so why had she chosen not to tell him what she'd seen from Hannah's bedroom window? To the untrained eye it may have appeared as nothing more than a twist of foliage in the tree, but she had no doubt other than what she'd seen was a witch's ladder. Her stomach tightened. So that was the reason Hannah was so sick. Yes, Emrys also had his suspicions that dark arts were involved, but he hadn't seen what she'd seen. He was getting old, and while his own magic was still strong, his physical capabilities were beginning to diminish. She must protect him, too. She would act upon this alone.

***

The silvery light of a waxing gibbous moon, along with the ghostly pathway of charms, assisted Tarian in her attempt to locate the witch's ladder at the edge of the wood. Warm, smoky breath created little clouds of determination as she journeyed, and her hackles bristled with anger. She paused beneath the blackthorn. She might have known the witch would choose such a malevolent specimen.

Positioned just inside the boundary of the wood the ladder hung from the blackthorn, bold as brass. It made no attempt to hide its wilful deed. Tarian's bowels churned. Hannah must have met with the witch, or how else would she have appropriated an item belonging to her? Standing on hind legs, she sniffed, but was not tall enough to unhook it. Even on hind legs her nose barely nudged the bottom knot. And in any case, she knew it would not be enough to remove the offending object—either the witch would need to unleash the charm, which was highly unlikely, or its victim would need to cast it into flames. The curse could be destroyed by no other means. Since Hannah was so sick, the latter would be an impossibility.

She stood back down and marked her scent on the trunk—the least she could do was make the witch aware of her presence. Now her suspicions were confirmed, she needed to carefully consider what to do next. She'd have liked nothing better than to search the wood and tear out the witch's eyes, but acting on impulse would put the child's life at risk, and besides, she'd promised Tadcu from the beginning that she would not try to kill the witch. They were protectors, not murderers. She lay on the cold, damp ground, facing Hannah's bedroom. The child was very sick; the situation did not bode well.

Sometime later, she saw Bleddyn leave the bedroom, his movements sad and slow and his expression bone-weary. Her heart bled for him. No matter how hard he tried, he would not be able to rescue Hannah from this torment. Hadn't they gone through enough turmoil without this? Leaving the door ajar, he reached in and switched off the light, plunging the room into darkness and ending Tarian's ability to observe the scene. She yawned and settled down beneath the blackthorn. She would not leave this place until she had formulated a plan. Hannah must not be left to suffer.

Suddenly the air grew icy cold. Tarian's nocturnal companions—the amorous fox, the screeching owl, the snuffling hedgehog, were silenced by the witch's sudden and unexpected appearance. Tarian bolted upright, ears erect and legs stiff as rods.

"So, you've come at last! I've not witnessed your presence here for some time. Have you been in hiding?"

Tarian caught a whiff of stale breath as Rhiamon spoke, and her innards recoiled. She'd never hated anyone as much as this witch. "Unleash your charm, witch, or you'll regret it."

Rhiamon raised a sullen eyebrow. "I've waited for this opportunity for such a long time, do you imagine I would give it up on your say so, thief?"

Tarian suppressed a snarl and licked back a trickle of saliva. She must do her best to stay calm, otherwise this would undoubtedly end badly for the child. This witch was devoid of feeling and cared for no one other than herself. Tarian fought to conceal her anger. Her repose beneath the blackthorn had conjured a few possibilities, but she'd not yet had time to formulate her plan well enough to feel confident of a successful outcome. "What is it you want? What good will it do to harm the child like this?"

Rhiamon raised her dark eyes to the heavens and bit her bottom lip. Eventually she spoke. "My freedom is all I desire. Undo your charms, and I shall undo mine. A life for a life, it's as simple as that." She studied the wolf, no trace of fear or shame in her demeanour.

Tarian's hackles stood on end. She had never feared this witch. In battle, she knew she would have the upper hand, but she'd made a promise.

"Do you think I trust you to keep your word, witch? Even if your freedom were granted, do you think I believe you would undo this malediction? Would you take your leave of this place and never return, or would you watch her suffer before moving on to destroy the lives of others?"

Rhiamon cackled and turned her nose to the air in a haughty gesture. "The choice is yours, thief, and the risk is yours, for if you do not grant me my freedom she will surely die. My spell of sickness will last for five sunsets, then her life will end."

Tarian spun full circle, attempting to quell her instinct to rip the witch's throat open. "How dare you call me a thief? And how dare you threaten the child like this? You shall be thwarted, witch, I vow, you will never know victory!" Her tone had risen to a piercing yelp, despite her desire to stay calm.

"Oh … but you are a thief! You stole my freedom, and you know in your heart you plan to steal from the girl, too."

It was the last straw. She lost control and snapped at the witch's hand, grazing the skin. Should she have drawn blood, she might not have been able to stop herself.

Rhiamon shook her head and examined the skin. "Tut, tut. Is that the best you can do?"

If it wasn't for the witch's ladder Tarian would have been unable to resist inflicting more damage, but with Hannah so sick, her only chance was to persuade the witch to destroy the malediction.

Rhiamon bit her lip, considering. "Grant me my freedom in exchange for the girl, and you shall hear no more from me. I shall give you until tomorrow to make your decision. Come to me at the witching hour and tell me what you intend to do … and remember, she will have just one more day to live should you decide against it.

***

Bleddyn woke with a start. The clock on his bedside cabinet said 3:30. He swung out of bed and stood on shaky legs and crept towards her room, silently praying to no particular god she would be sound asleep. Pausing at her door, he listened to her breathing. His stomach relaxed, and the pounding in his chest subsided. Dare he take a peek, or should he leave her? The temptation to check on her was overwhelming.

Hannah lay on her side, facing away from him. The pale, blue light cast by the moon shone on her face, creating a ghostly hue on her complexion. Nevertheless she seemed at peace, her breathing less rapid than it had been these past three days. He tiptoed closer. So delicate, otherworldly, almost. The urge to lift her into his arms was overwhelming, though he dared not. This was the most peaceful she'd been in days.

He lifted the lace at the window and peered into the inky blackness of the garden. Why did sickness seem so much more frightening during the night? Was it merely the fear of having less access to medical assistance, or was there some grander terror lurking in the dark corners? Something primeval, almost.

His eyes adjusted to the darkness outside until he could make out the roof of the shed, the holly laden with early winter berries, and in the far corner, the apple trees still bearing a few pieces of fruit. A flicker of movement in the direction of the lane caught his attention. For the briefest of moments, he imagined he saw a woman in the trees.

Emily? Impossible. As the creature darted from view, the shimmer of a long, pale gown caught his eye. It was Emily's gown—the one she'd given Hannah after the concert. How ridiculous, his sleep-deprived brain was playing tricks with his mind. Nevertheless, the hair on his arms stood on end. He would check her trunk tomorrow to be certain. But that would be illogical. No, what he needed was more sleep. He planted the lightest of kisses on her forehead and returned to his own room.

***

They'd all left, and Hannah was alone again in The Lane. She sat on the damp earth and faced skyward. Black as pitch. No moon, no stars, even the symbols along the track no longer glowed. Gradually her eyes grew accustomed to the dark that threatened to engulf her. Along with the others, her fear had also vanished. She felt calm, almost. She might yet allow the blackness to take her. At least then she'd be at peace.

Tentatively, she craned her neck in the direction of the tree from which she knew Jipp hung, glad that at least she was able to move again. Was he still there, or had they removed his body? She stood on legs that threatened to give way, her arms flailing in the dark in an attempt to locate him. He couldn't be far. Soon she located the tree trunk. Nothing. She was able to wrap her arms two thirds of the way around it without feeling him. She stretched as high as she could. Nothing. Nothing but tree bark. Such a relief. Or was it? She had no memory of either Dada or Aunty Ffion cutting him down from the tree, and if they had, surely they wouldn't have left her here, alone?

What was she to do? She could not see her hand in front of her face, so she had little option other than to curl in a ball on the ground and wait. But for what? What if nothing happened? What if daylight failed to return, and she was stuck in perpetual darkness? And why did the thought not scare her? She was exhausted, that was why. As long as she could lie here and sleep, she didn't care.

A whisper on the wind, the trace of a hand brushing against her forehead, the gentlest of touches. She opened her eyes. Mamma! She wore the gown, its pale shimmer the only source of light. Then she stood and, turning her face away, beckoned Hannah to follow her deeper into the wood.

"Wait, Mamma!"

But Mamma did not wait. Instead, she sped up, until she was no more than a distant speck of light. Hannah tried desperately to keep up, her bare feet snagging on roots, ankles twisting in the undulating floor of the wood, until she fell to the ground. And the blackness returned.

A Ladder, of Sorts

Tonight's full moon shone in Tarian's favour, comrade to any lycanthrope. She had made her decision, though it had been an agonising one. She would set the witch free. The child was too precious and had gone through too much heartbreak to be allowed to suffer further, though exactly how she was going to do this she wasn't sure. The hardest thing would be ensuring the witch stuck to her side of the bargain, and that in itself would be no mean feat. She would insist on witnessing the charm destroyed before setting her free. It would not be enough for the witch to utter a few words of magic over the charm, for there would be no opportunity to check on the child to ensure it had worked. No, the witch would need to untie the ladder's knots in front of her and set it alight. She'd be sure to get to the meeting place a little early so she might use her own alchemy to ignite a small fire. The bristles of her fur stood erect. She bore a primeval fear of fire, but the situation provided no alternative.

***

As on previous days since this sickness had taken hold, Bleddyn spent most of the day at Hannah's side. Was she a little better? It was difficult to tell. In some ways she seemed so, for she hadn't vomited all day, and the trembling had subsided a little, particularly during the afternoon and into the evening. However, she still seemed as distant, as if she had one foot in this world and one in the next.

He remained concerned about the fact she still slept for most of the day, sometimes muttering and murmuring in her sleep, and was unable to speak cohesively during the time she was awake. He worried about encephalitis, meningitis, and all sorts of other dreadful illnesses, but the G.P. had reassured him she suspected none of these, and that Hannah was merely exhausted from the virus. He was assured sleep was her body's way of healing. Why then did he remain unconvinced? Something was amiss.

Every time he considered the possibility of the cause of her sickness being something more sinister it made him sick to the guts, so he had come to a decision. If there was no improvement in the next two days, he'd demand a referral and would pay for a private one if necessary.

During the evening, he'd got her to drink a glass of milk. She'd kept it down, which pleased him, as previously she'd refused anything other than sips of water. However, apart from a few nibbles of toast, she'd not eaten in four days. He lifted her frail wrist as she slept, certain the flesh on her arms seemed thinner, looser, and she usually had a fair old appetite, especially for sweet things. As soon as she was well enough to eat, he'd let her have anything she wanted, even if it was a whole pack of jam doughnuts. "Come on, Hannah," he whispered. "Please get well." A lump formed in his throat, and he swallowed hard. Perhaps he'd go downstairs and try an hour of TV before turning in. She'd come to no harm when he'd slept in his own room the previous night, so he'd do the same tonight.

***

Having beseeched the Goddess Cerridwen for divine inspiration, Tarian was grateful that at least it had not rained for a few days, which meant the ground layer of the wood was dry. She arranged a circle of stones in front of the offending blackthorn in which to contain the flames.

Next, her mouth dry with anxiety, she collected a heap of pine needles, along with some old-man's beard and strips of dried bark from a dead birch, and piled them in the centre. For the spark she would need to beg the help of the sun god, Beli Mawr, and hope he was not yet asleep. If he should fail to come to her aid, she'd be at a loss. Her innards churned at the prospect of failure, and she suppressed the urge to vomit.

There—she was ready. She stood tall and faced the full moon, ears pointing forward, head and neck erect. Her plaintive howl was a plea, a plea for the gods and elements to come together and assist her in her plight. The creatures of the nighttime wood heard it, and those that had resisted the dark side chorused her plea with their own cry.

She hardly dared look. Was there a sensation of warmth behind her? Did she merely imagine the ground beneath her paws had brightened a shade? There came the undeniable crackle of flame. Ah, her charm had worked, for there upon the heap of tinder, the smallest flame danced proudly in the cool night air.

And then she came. Gown billowing in the breeze, Rhiamon stepped from the shadows, confident as a bird on the wing. Stopping a few paces before the fire, she faced the wolf, eye to eye and soul to soul.

Tarian had never feared the witch. Hated her, yes, but never feared. However, tonight she was afraid, for if her plan went awry the child would die. Now it was a waiting game to see who would make the first move.

"So you've come to a decision?" It was the witch who spoke first, her voice confident.

"I have, though it has not been easy." Tarian paused, nostrils flaring, each gasp misting in the chill of the breeze. "You shall be granted your freedom, witch, but not until the charm is destroyed."

"Ah! So you expect me to unloose the charm while you walk away?" The witch laughed, haughtily. "Do you take me for a fool, thief? No, this is what will happen … the ladder bears five knots. For each knot I untie, you shall remove a charm from the boundary. Once the ladder is undone, I shall put it to the flame, but not before you retreat into the distance. I will not take the risk of once more being ensnared."

The witch reviled Tarian to the core. Witnessing her smug demeanour made her want to pounce, but this time she'd been beaten. Why, oh why had Hannah given her something belonging to her? If she hadn't, the situation would never have occurred. It was unfair to blame Hannah, and she knew it. In all likelihood the witch had persuaded her to part with the item. What mattered most was that Hannah regained her health despite the fact that once the witch moved on, someone else, somewhere else, would surely be made to suffer.

"So be it, you have my word. But you must be gone from these parts, witch, and never return."

"Huh! Do you think I would ever again come close to this place of torment? Ten years you have stolen from me." She shuddered, and her pale face took on a waxy hue in the moonlight. "I assure you, thief, I shall never again set foot in this place." With feet as light as snowfall, she stepped towards the blackthorn and unhooked the ladder.

***

The tightness in Hannah's throat suddenly eased, and the sensation of being able to breathe caused her to stir. Sitting upright for the first time in days, she gazed around the room, her heavy eyes attempting to focus.

For a few moments she had no clue as to where she was, then, ever so slowly, she came to her senses. She was in her own bed, in her own house, and not in The Lane at all. Had she been sick? Her head swam and the blood pounded in her ears. Where was Dada? And what about Jipp and the witch? She remembered the dream she'd had about Mamma in the woods and felt sad.

She swivelled her legs and attempted to sit at the edge of the bed. Now that her head was beginning to clear, she panicked. Something was wrong. Dada needed her. She must go to him.

She tried to stand, but her legs gave way. Why would they not support her? Fear made her heart beat fast, and for a moment she believed she might faint. She sat at the edge of the bed facing the window—the little one with the lace curtain.

The cheerful face of the moon welcomed her back to the land of the living. Its left eye smiled, while its right winked at her sympathetically, acknowledging what she'd been through.

Moving her head too quickly made her feel nauseous, so, ever so slowly, she turned in the direction of The Lane. Was she mistaken, or could she see a fire burning? She leaned forward and lifted the lace. No, she was not mistaken. There, close to the boundary, a small fire danced, its nervous flames constantly on the move, as though it wanted out of there. What on earth was happening?

She picked up her clock in both hands and studied its luminous face. "The big hand's just past the twelve, and the little hand's bang on it," she whispered into the darkness. Twelve o'clock. Midnight, or as Emrys called it, the witching hour. Shivering with cold, she tried once more to stand, pleased to discover that this time, her legs obeyed her command. What if the fire spread and the whole wood burned to the ground? She should probably get Dada. He'd know what to do.

But she didn't want to wake Dada. An overwhelming sense of The Lane calling urged her towards the bedroom door. She felt certain she was needed. She must make it to The Lane, though why she couldn't say.

***

With one last knot to untie, both Tarian and the witch were on tenterhooks. Each attempted to brazen out the ceremony.

With each charm she removed, Tarian's insides churned. The pathway at the boundary to the lane opened up before her eyes, the ghostly-white symbols extinguished. A dark escape route for a dark being. As each protective symbol disappeared, the glint in the witch's eyes shone brighter. All that remained was for the witch to cast the malevolent object into the flames, and yet even now Tarian knew she could not trust her. If she could wheedle her way out of destroying it, she would.

***

Rhiamon gripped the woollen ladder tight, not wanting to let go. Might she trick the wolf by casting it into the flames then rescuing it before it was destroyed? She doubted it, for each flame danced excitedly, eager to be done with its task. Still, she had the old dewin's death to look forward to. What the wolf didn't know was that once free, her first port of call would be to the farm where she planned to slit the old man's throat while he slept. And what was more, she would do it with his own scythe. She'd stand over him and watch him bleed, witness him clutch his hands to his throat in a futile attempt to stem the flow. She'd wait until his heart stopped beating, until his face wore an alabaster death mask, then she would away to pastures new.

***

Hannah was upon them before they knew it, her face ashen with shock. Dressed in a flimsy white nightgown, she trembled with fear and cold.

Neither Tarian nor the witch heard her approach. A gasp escaped the witch's lips, and a yelp of surprise from the wolf, when she suddenly appeared.

The end of the woollen ladder poked from beneath the witch's palm, as though eager to escape, but the witch's grip was tight.

"Quick, Hannah, the ladder, take it from her hand!" She pounced on the witch, knocking her to the ground.

Hannah saw that the witch clung to something as though her life depended on it. Spitting and cursing the most foul of words, she hung on with all her might.

Hannah was frozen to the spot, utterly confused. What was the string-like thing held within her grasp? Why did the wolf want her to take it? She watched in horror as the witch fought back. The witch's nails tore at Tarian's face, succeeding in their aim, so that night-dark blood ran into her eyes, temporarily blinding her. But Tarian was the stronger opponent. She shook her huge head, sending drops of blood flying. Her sight clearing, she pinned the witch to the ground, one paw to hold steady each of Rhiamon's flailing limbs.

Suddenly Hannah knew what she must do. Terrified, she stepped towards the witch and prised her fingers open, forcing the string-like object from her grasp.

The witch's screams filled the air, causing every creature in the wood to join in the alarm call. The wailing filled Hannah's ears. Instinctively she let go of the witch's hand and covered her ears in an attempt to drown out the noise.

The wolf was speaking to her, its words urgent, but Hannah could not hear what was being said. She dared not uncover her ears for fear they might burst. She squeezed her eyes shut tight, attempting to further distance herself from the noise. Something tickled her cheek. Was it a creature of terror? Her heart beat so loud she worried it might stop. Her heart was weak. It shouldn't be put under such strain. Peeping through one eye, she attempted to see what was causing the tickle. It was the thing—the string-like thing the witch had been so desperate to hold on to that she now held in her right hand.

And suddenly she knew what she must do. Her heart might be weak, but her spirit was strong. Hadn't Dada always told her that? In one, deft movement, she flung the object onto the fire. The greedy flames devoured it instantly, hissing and crackling in their haste to consume it.

"Run, Hannah!"

Tarian's voice woke her from her trance. She found her feet and ran. She did not look back.

***

Glancing at the clock, Bleddyn was shocked to see it was approaching 7:30. He'd slept right through. What if her condition had worsened? Awash with guilt, he sprang out of bed, ignoring the ache in his back from having spent most of the past few days sitting at the edge of her bed.

He paused for a moment at her door, afraid to enter. "Hannah?" She looked better, her complexion more healthy. Dare he hope?

Her eyes flickered open. "Dada?"

He grinned down at her, attempting to put on a brave face. "How are you feeling, Missie?"

She sat up and yawned. "Better … lots better." She rubbed her eyes and yawned. "I've been asleep for a very long time, Dada … and the dreams! So many dreams."

Bleddyn hugged her close, breathing her in. "My goodness you had me worried." He stroked her hair tenderly, not wanting to let go.

"Can't breathe, Dada, you're snuffling me!" Her voice was a muffled vibration against his chest. He relaxed his hold and studied her face, noticing the sleepy, pink tint to her skin for the first time in days.

"Need a wee!" She swung her legs round the bed and attempted to stand.

"Wait! You might feel dizzy. You haven't been out of bed in five days." He took her arm, again noticing its thinness.

It was then he saw the stains on her nightgown. "Good grief! How on earth?" She was filthy. He'd noticed her hair matted as he'd stroked it, but had assumed it was because she'd hardly lifted her head from the pillow in days. He stared down at her feet, shocked at the amount of dirt and grit between her toes.

Her mouth fell open. "Need a wee!"

His hands still shook as he made the toast. How on earth had she got so dirty? She'd not been able to stand, never mind go outdoors—and at night! He should be ashamed of himself for being so negligent. She used to sleepwalk as a toddler but hadn't done so in years. From now on he'd have to make sure the doors were bolted at the top. Living in the country had made him complacent. Even now he couldn't believe she was sitting up reading a book, about to be spoiled with breakfast in bed.

***

Dada helped her to wash, in case she felt light-headed, but she didn't. In fact she felt quite well, a little weak with hunger perhaps, but nothing more. He'd brushed her hair and tied it in a ponytail. She'd wanted it washed, but he'd refused, saying it was far too soon. She grabbed the ponytail and sniffed. Yuk! It smelled sweaty and earthy. She was ravenous! She hoped he wouldn't be long with her toast and milk.

He thought she'd not been out of bed, but she had. She'd been in The Lane, and there'd been a fire. Had it actually happened, or was it a dream? It had to be real, or how else would her feet have got so filthy?

"What day is it, Dada?" She'd swallowed the first triangle of toast in three bites and was already devouring the second.

"Wednesday—you've been out for count since Saturday night. I've been frantic with worry." He leaned over and kissed her butter-smeared cheek.

She chewed noisily, her table manners forgotten in her hunger.

"Can I go to school?" She gulped down a mouthful of milk.

"Certainly not. We'll see how you are next week. I don't think you realize how sick you've been. Do you remember the doctor calling? She's been twice. She even considered sending you to hospital."

She paused in her chewing, her mouth twisted in contemplation. "Did she? I think I remember Deryth and Emrys coming. I'm not sure." She started on the third triangle of toast, a little less voraciously than the previous two.

"You've had lots of visitors—Aunty Ffion, Emrys, Deryth, but you were too ill to talk to them."

She nodded.

"You okay here if I go and ring them? They'll be thrilled to hear you're better. We've all been so worried."

"Fine. But I need to go to school soon. I need to say sorry to Megan, properly."

***

"Did you miss me?" Hannah attempted a cheeky wink in Deryth's direction, though she still hadn't mastered the skill.

Deryth hugged her close. "You bet, Missie."

Since when had Deryth started calling her Missie, like Dada? Hannah couldn't remember, it had just seemed to happen. It was as Deryth let her go, she noticed the scratch. She gasped. "How did that happen?" she said, pointing to Deryth's face.

Deryth pulled an imaginary stray hair from the sleeve of her black jumper. "Oh, it's nothing. I had an argument with the bathroom door when I went to the toilet in the middle of the night, that's all." She ruffled Hannah's hair, playfully. "Great to see you back to normal. You had us all worried, especially your father."

Hannah was still examining the scratch on Deryth's forehead. Two vertical scratches ran from her hairline all the way down to her eyebrows. Hannah wasn't convinced about the door story, so she huffed in reply. For a moment, she was reminded of when the witch had scratched at Tarian, how trickles of dark blood had run down her forehead and into the wolf's eyes. Deryth's expression was blank, Hannah knew she'd get no more from her on the subject, so she'd best drop it. "Deryth? When I come back to school I need to speak to Megan, okay?"

Deryth swallowed. "All right. If it's what you want. I'll take you both to the library first thing Monday morning."

"Yes. And I want to tell the class, too."

"Tell the class what?"

"That I'm sorry … and that Megan didn't steal my brooch." She stared at the floor, unable to meet Deryth's eyes.

"If you're sure it's what you want, then fine. You know I'll be there to support you."

Hannah nodded. "It is."

An Unexpected Gift

Instead of a Christmas concert, Hannah's school was holding an art sale to raise money for a local children's charity. This pleased her, as art was one of her best subjects, and it also meant she wouldn't need to learn any more lines.

Dada would be sure to buy her artwork. She'd painted a snowy evening scene of The Lane and was proud of it, though she hadn't told anyone where her inspiration had come from. She'd captured the moonlight and the way The Lane seemed to get narrower and narrower the higher it climbed. She'd had enough experience of seeing it by moonlight to know.

Once Dada bought it, she'd get him to mount it on her bedroom wall, right opposite her bed, so she could look at it last thing at night and as soon as she woke up without having to turn her head.

She hadn't included Tarian or the witch in the painting because, one—wolves and people were hard to get right, and two—she didn't want to be reminded of the witch every time she opened her eyes. She might steal into her dreams if there was a picture of her in the bedroom. She'd prefer to picture The Lane at peace, all snowy and hushed.

That way she'd sleep better. She was adding a little more snow to some of the winter-bare branches when a voice startled her and made her smudge the paint.

"It's fantastic, Hannah. Is it The Lane behind your house?"

Looking over her shoulder she was surprised to find Megan standing there, studying her work.

"No—it's just a snow picture." Why she didn't want anyone to know the subject of her painting she wasn't sure. Somehow it felt personal.

"Well, it's very good. I like the way you've painted the moon shining down on the tops of the trees," Megan said, pointing towards the silvery orb. "It's winking with one eye and smiling with the other."

They were back on the best of terms, her and Megan. Hannah was so glad she'd found the courage to apologize all those weeks back. It was lovely to have Megan as a friend again, and even though Ife had spotted Megan, and not Hannah, she no longer minded. "Thanks Meg. Show me what you've painted."

Megan groaned. 'Oh, I'm not as good as you at art. Mine's stupid."

Megan had attempted to draw a reindeer, but its right eye was in the wrong place which made it look cross-eyed. Hannah stifled a giggle. "Reindeer are difficult to draw, Meg. Why don't you try a snow picture. It's much easier."

"I wish I had, but it's not right to copy you." Megan frowned at her own painting.

"I don't mind. I'll help you if you like." *So, she isn't good at everything*, Hannah thought, as she helped Megan mix some colours. It was good to know, though she wished her no ill.

Hannah was mega excited because tonight she would sleep over at Aunty Ffion's for the first time without Dada. They were going to have hot dogs—vegetarian ones for her—and then they were going to watch *The Nativity*, the funny film featuring Mr. Poppy. It was her favourite.

Dada and Deryth were going away for the night, to a place called Bath, to visit a Christmas market. Hannah thought Bath was a strange name for a place and told Dada, so he explained about it being named after the Roman baths, which kind of made sense. She didn't mind Dada staying away for the night, but she did wonder if he and Deryth would have separate rooms at the hotel. She hoped so because she didn't like the idea of him cuddling up to her in the same bed. It grossed her out. She'd been going to ask him but thought better of it because lately she'd been getting better at not being personal, and in any case, she didn't suppose he'd have told her the truth, just what he believed she'd want to hear. She focussed on the fun evening ahead instead of the image of Dada and Deryth in the same bed.

Equally as exciting was that come Sunday afternoon, they were all going to Emrys's farm for tea. She couldn't wait to see Bronwen and Anwen again. She had the feeling something special was going to happen when they went there because she'd heard Dada and Emrys speaking in low voices the week before. She was desperate to know what it might be, but as she also liked surprises she'd decided against nagging. Never mind, even if there was no surprise, she'd still enjoy herself, because at least she'd get to eat cake.

It had been over a month since her illness. She hadn't forgotten the dreams, nor the battle in The Lane, but she tried not to dwell on it. Each night since, she'd peered into The Lane from her bedroom window to see if the magical symbols were back, but she couldn't quite see. She wouldn't go out in the dark to check, not after the last time.

If she hadn't seen the dirt on her feet and nightdress that morning she'd have thought it all a dream, but the evidence had been plain to see. In one way she hoped never to set eyes on the witch again, but in another way she'd have liked to give her a piece of her mind, as Emrys always said. Maybe one day, when she was brave enough.

***

As usual, Anwen's kitchen was roasting. The comforting heat from the cooking range contrasted sharply with the cold air outside and ruddied everyone's cheeks. Bronwen leapt upon Hannah immediately. Eyes half closed, Bronwen whined with pleasure as the two of them rubbed noses.

A rich, dark fruit cake sat in wait on the table alongside a plate of freshly baked scones. Hannah knew she was in for a treat. All five of them sat around the table, Deryth handing out paper napkins, while Anwen poured.

"Shall I tell her, or do you want to?" Emrys winked at Bleddyn.

Bleddyn grinned. "You tell her, Emrys. It's best coming from you."

Hannah glanced from one to the other and back again.

"Now then, bach, I hear you've been nagging your dad for a dog. Is that right?"

Hannah nodded, uncertain where the conversation was leading.

"Well, I've some news for you." He bent down to where Bronwen sat beside his chair and hugged her nose. "Old Bron's going to be a grandmother, aren't you, girl?" Bronwen whined with pleasure. "And we were wondering whether or not you might like one of the pups."

Hannah was dumbstruck. Her mouth fell open, but no words came out. She'd nagged Dada for ages about getting a dog, but he'd point-blank refused. Was she hearing correctly? She glanced at Bleddyn, expecting him to protest, and discovered that instead of frowning he was beaming.

"Really? No kidding?"

"Aye, really," Emrys said. "The pups are due around Christmas. The mother's over at a neighbour's farm across the way. I can take you there once they're born if you like. The farmer's willing for you to have the pick of the litter."

No words. Hannah leapt from her seat and hugged Emrys, then she hugged Dada. "A dog for Christmas! Can't believe it." Overwhelmed, she struggled to fight back the tears.

"Not for Christmas, Hannah. It can be your Christmas present, yes, but remember what I told you about how puppies shouldn't be taken from the mother until they're at least six weeks old?"

She nodded. The joy left her face as she remembered poor Bronwen's ordeal.

"So you'll be able to take it home 'bout mid-February, all right?"

"Tarian," she said aloud, without meaning to.

"What did you say?"

It was Dada.

"I'm going to name it Tarian."

***

Having not heard from her in three months, Bleddyn was surprised when Emily called out of the blue. A stretched silence followed initial greetings.

"So … I'll be in London for a few days the second week of December and wondered if you might like to bring Hannah for a visit."

Too dumbstruck to answer, he remained silent.

"You know … so I can give her a Christmas present."

He tried hard to quell the desire to yell down the

phone, and when at last he spoke his voice was terse. "As a matter of fact, she's been very ill. You didn't even ring to ask how her concert went." A tense silence ensued, each reluctant to break it.

Eventually Emily spoke. "Is she all right now?"

"Yes, she's fine."

"So … how does that sound? I guess the tenth would be best for me."

Best for her. It always came down to what was best for Emily. "I'll speak to Hannah and get back to you." He didn't trust himself to say more, so he put down the phone and tried to stifle his temper. He didn't want Hannah to be influenced by his feelings. In the end, he decided to wait until dinner was over before telling her.

"Will you come, too?" she asked. No excitement, instead she appeared a little nervous.

"Of course. I'll give you a few hours with Mamma, then we'll meet up again and come home. I won't bother booking a hotel this time. It will be far too busy so close to Christmas. Perhaps we can go by train. What d'you say?"

She hesitated. "Okay."

London

The weekend spent with Bleddyn was everything Deryth hoped it might be. It was hard to believe she'd known him a whole year. All right, so technically they'd only been seeing each other for three months, since she couldn't count the trip to Dinas Emrys or Hannah's concert as dates, but it was a year since Bleddyn and Hannah had moved to Wales.

Deryth remembered back to their first meeting, the day Hannah had started school. She'd read concern on his face as she'd seen Hannah out of the classroom at the end of the day. She'd known even then he was the caring type. She also remembered the first time he'd looked at her, like *really* looked at her. It had been back in the spring, and she'd needed to speak to him about Hannah seeming a little unhappy.

She'd sent Hannah to the library to retrieve her laptop in order to show him a story she was writing. It had been a ruse, as she'd wanted a word without Hannah being present. That had been the first time. She was certain he'd blushed as his eyes had held hers. Maybe she'd be brave enough to ask him about it one day.

She hadn't even known he was single then, in fact she'd assumed otherwise. It was Hannah who had brought the reality of their family situation to her attention. No holds barred there. She'd lost count of the times Hannah had her in stitches with her outspoken manner.

Closing the last hinge on the back of the picture frame, she turned it over and studied Hannah's painting. She'd offered to stay behind at school for an hour or so to get them all framed ready for tomorrow's Christmas art sale. Of course he'd be attending. How would she cope in a classroom full of people, knowing the weekend they'd had? Her face reddened.

Holding the painting at arm's length, she studied it closely. She was in no doubt that the subject was the lane. It wasn't half bad either, she'd even managed to get the perspective right. The lane climbed into the distance, narrowing as it did so. Fair play to her, and all from memory. It demonstrated how significant a place the lane had become in Hannah's life. Bless her, she'd kept it all to herself, confided in no one, not even Bleddyn or Tadcu. Didn't they say art was a great form of expressing one's experiences and emotions? Perhaps this was Hannah's way of dealing with things.

Why had she not included the witch or Tarian? Was it because they would have been too difficult to paint, or did she not want Bleddyn asking difficult questions?

She'd miss him this weekend. He and Hannah were going to London to visit Emily. Her stomach churned, but she allowed herself a little jealousy. It wasn't unusual to feel a bit insecure early on in a relationship? Early on … and yet it seemed as if she'd known him for ages. She was so comfortable in his company, so at ease. It felt natural. All right, so there had been a moment of awkwardness as they'd entered the hotel room for the first time, but even that had soon passed. Her cheeks reddened again, and she shivered with pleasure, remembering.

***

During the first hour of the train journey, Hannah hardly spoke. They hadn't taken the train in several years, and Bleddyn assumed she'd forgotten what it was like. Forehead pressed to the window, she studied the passing landscape, occasionally pointing out the odd building or animal but mostly she remained lost in her own little world.

Was it the unfamiliarity of the train ride, or because she would soon be seeing Emily that made her distant? Whatever the reason, he only managed to engage her in conversation by producing a chocolate croissant and milkshake from his bag. "So, what d'you think?" He leaned over and wiped a smear of chocolate from the corner of her mouth.

"Yummy!"

"I meant the train ride, silly billy," he laughed.

"Oh, cool."

Silence ensued, where once again she focussed on the passing fields. "When we get my pup, can we walk it every day?"

"Of course. Dogs need to be walked at least once a day. It's part of looking after them."

She nodded. "Can you and Emrys make the garden fence safer? Remember when Jipp got out?"

"Good thinking. We'll need to get it done pretty soon, won't we? I'm glad you reminded me."

She nodded, pleased. "Are we nearly there yet?"

Bleddyn smiled. "Not too far, about another hour."

"That's long!" She pouted. "Is Mamma meeting us at the station?"

"No. Remember I told you we were meeting her in Starbucks? We'll get off the train at Paddington, then we'll take an underground train to Covent Garden. Mamma's meeting us there."

"Like the bear?"

He frowned, puzzled for a moment before realizing what she meant. "Yes, like Paddington Bear. Do you remember how the family who found Paddington named him after the train station?"

She nodded, sleepily.

"Want to put your head on me and have a little sleep?" The drive to the station had taken the best part of an hour, then they'd waited for the train to Cardiff, followed by another wait for the London train. She already seemed dead beat.

"Yes." She cuddled in close, wrapping her right arm around his middle.

Bleddyn's stomach churned. Was he doing the right thing in bringing her to meet Emily, or would it ignite another round of negative emotions? It had been a difficult decision, with the two of them once again expected to do the travelling, but he couldn't deny her the chance to keep in contact with her mother, even if she was becoming less keen with each visit.

***

She'd not stopped frowning since they'd got off the train. She clung to the sleeve of his jacket, making it difficult to navigate a pathway through the throng of tourists and Christmas shoppers. Every time he visited this bloody city it got busier and busier. No wonder Hannah found it stressful. After the open expanses of their environment back home in Wales, it felt claustrophobic.

He was first to spot Emily, perched on a bar stool in the cafe window, a forlorn expression on her pale face. He waved, without smiling, and led Hannah inside. She clung to him like a limpet, refusing to look at Emily for a few moments.

"Hey, sweetheart, aren't you going to give Mamma a hug?"

Only then did she leave his side, though the cuddle was not exactly warm.

From her bag, Emily whipped out a pack of wet wipes and handed one to Hannah. "Here, give your face and hands a wipe. You're a bit grubby after the long train journey."

Bleddyn snatched the wipe from her. "She's fine. Her hands were wiped after she ate on the train." His voice was cold, anger evident in his tone. Hadn't she sent her straight to the bathroom when they'd visited in March? Good grief, had she developed a mania for cleanliness all of a sudden?

Hannah sensed the tension and pointed at her feet. "New shoes," she said, in an attempt to break the ice.

He'd have to try harder, for Hannah's sake. It wasn't her fault her mother was a narcissistic bitch. "Fancy hot chocolate? With whipped cream and marshmallows?"

She nodded. "I'll come, too."

So she wasn't comfortable enough to stay with Emily even for the short time he'd be at the counter. How on earth was he going to leave her for a few hours? Perhaps once they'd all sat chatting a while she'd relax a bit.

***

His nerves were frayed among the crowded streets around Covent Garden. The National Gallery wasn't far. He'd prefer to spend the afternoon there, where at least he'd have something interesting to look at instead of bloody shops. And he was missing Deryth. They'd seen each other every Saturday over the past few weeks, either at the farm or at his, or— He grinned, remembering back to the previous weekend. Meeting her was the best thing that had happened in his life since Hannah's birth. Dare he imagine a future with her?

***

When he picked Hannah up fifteen minutes before he was due, Emily seemed keen to get going. "I'm pleased to hear you're happy, truly I am," she said as they said goodbye.

At the time, her meaning didn't register. However, now they were on the train and he had a chance to mull it over he realized what she was getting at—his relationship with Deryth. So Hannah must have told her.

Hannah had shown no hint of emotion as she'd kissed Emily goodbye. He was unsure whether this made him glad or sad.

The rhythm of the train's motion made him sleepy. He closed his eyes and conjured Deryth's face to mind, sorry she'd already committed to Sunday lunch with a few old friends the following day. He'd have loved to see her. Still, it wasn't to be. Perhaps he'd invite her for supper one evening this week. He didn't think he could go two whole weeks without seeing her.

Hannah was fast asleep on his chest. His right arm ached from the weight of her head, but he didn't want to disturb her. He patted his jacket pocket with his free hand, checking the parcel was safe. Emily had passed it to him as they were leaving. Judging by its size and shape it was another bloody charm for her bracelet, the one she hadn't worn in ages. Jesus Christ, couldn't she be more original?

Decisions

The same question, every day, as soon as she came out of school. "Dada, has Emrys rung about the pups?"

"No, Hannah, he hasn't."

"But—"

"There's no point in butting. The pups will be born when they're good and ready. It's not the sort of thing you can make happen any quicker than nature intends."

Her shoulders sagged. He was regretting having told her about the puppies so long in advance, as she'd nagged the life out of him ever since. In the far corner of the kitchen sat an empty bed and an array of puppy toys. He had to admit, it looked a bit pathetic. After they'd bought it, she'd insisted on placing it in readiness for the pup's arrival. The bloody thing would be there until around the middle of February, as she wouldn't be able to bring the pup home until then. If she was this insufferable now, God help him after she'd chosen it. She still had little awareness of the passage of time in any real sense. All she remembered was Emrys saying the pups were due to be born around Christmas, so as the date drew close, the anxiousness mounted. Perhaps tonight's art sale would provide a temporary distraction.

***

They curled on the sofa together, enjoying a bedtime drink. Hannah's painting of the lane perched on top of the cabinet, propped up by a dictionary.

"I want it in my bedroom, Dada, on the wall opposite my bed."

"Then I won't get to see it. Why don't we hang it here, in the living room?"

She shook her head, determined. "No. My bedroom. You can see it when you come to wake me up."

He knew there was little point in arguing, she always got her way in such matters, and besides, now she was in a good mood he was considering raising the subject of Deryth staying over during the Christmas holidays. He didn't have to ponder the question for long, as her next words shocked him.

"Dada, can Deryth sleep over Christmas Eve?" Whipped cream trickled a channel down her chin and threatened to drip onto her top. With her index finger, she swiped it back into her mouth.

"We don't have a spare bed." His heart fluttered. Jeez! It was as if she'd read his mind.

"She can sleep in your bed. It's big enough."

How should he reply? He had to get this right. There must be no regrets later.

He took a deep breath. "And you wouldn't mind, would you?"

She shrugged. "No. We can all go together for dinner."

His sigh of relief had a sobbing quality. Christmas dinner this year was being hosted at Emrys's farm, and he and Hannah were invited. "Well, I'll ask her if you're certain you don't mind. We can all open our presents together on Christmas morning."

"Cool. I want to get Deryth something from me."

"Tell you what, how about we choose something from the craft gallery in town. She loves handmade things. We'll go and have a look on Saturday morning, shall we?"

She nodded. "Been saving. I'll show you." She leapt from the sofa and disappeared upstairs.

He released the breath he'd held captive. That was a weight off his shoulders.

***

He'd held out as long as possible, and in the end it was Deryth who persuaded him to bite the bullet.

"Get her a Pay As You Go, Bleddyn, I agree with you in principle, but she's not lying when she says all the other children have their own mobile."

It wasn't so much the running cost of a phone that concerned him. It was the fact that owning one at the age of ten might expose her to all sorts of issues. Still, he supposed he must move with the times.

The joy on her face as she opened it was worth it. She loved her gift from Deryth, too—a boxed set of art materials consisting of paints, pencils, pens and inks. That should keep her quiet for a bit.

Last, but not least, was the present from Emily. She'd deliberately left it until last. Was it because she considered it special, or because she didn't want any disappointment to spoil the happy mood?

The tiny box contained, as he'd guessed, another charm for her bracelet. He and Deryth waited in anticipation as she peeled away the sticky tape, both a little nervous as to how she might respond. They sat together on the sofa, while Hannah sat on the floor, surrounded by a heap of discarded Christmas wrapping paper. It had been a fabulous start to Christmas Day, and neither of them wanted the mood spoiled.

She held the charm between thumb and forefinger, a puzzled look on her face.

"Well, what is it?" Bleddyn asked.

She chewed her lip, a look of disappointment on her face. "A charm—for my bracelet."

"I guessed as much. Do you like it?"

She sucked air between her teeth, contemplating her reply.

"Well?" Bleddyn pushed her for an answer, the suspense getting to him. She'd gone quiet, contemplative.

She frowned, unsure what his question was, so he asked again. "Do you like it?"

She shrugged. "It's a butterfly."

***

It was like being part of one big family. Christmas lunch at the farm had been the highlight of his year, apart from meeting Deryth, of course. Yes, he felt at ease at Ffion's—they'd always been close—even when he lived in Peterborough, but with Deryth at his side, and the homely welcome at the farm, he felt more complete than he had in a long time.

As they were leaving, the phone rang. Anwen answered. "Well I never! Fancy that. And on Christmas Day, too." The kitchen fell silent. "Tomorrow? You sure? Around eleven? I'll tell Emrys." She beamed at Hannah. "The pups have been born, bach. Four of them by all accounts. Idris said you can go and choose the one you want in the morning."

Bronwen picked up on the excitement and worried at Anwen's legs. "Mam-gu Bronwen! Your Blodwen's gone and had her pups." Bronwen yapped excitedly as Anwen ruffled her ears. "She's a clever girl like you, she is. She knows look—" She nodded at Hannah. "Look at her face. She knows alright, don't you, girl?"

"Wowzers!" Hannah flapped her hands in excitement and let out a squeal that brought Bronwen to her side. "Can I go choose now?"

Everyone laughed. "In the morning, bach, give the poor Mam chance to get over the birth, and besides, it's almost dark."

"I'll pick you up afore eleven, bach," Emrys said, ruffling Hannah's hair. "Idris's place is just up the road—not far. Take us five minutes to get there."

***

Hannah lay in bed, wearing her new pyjamas as was customary at Christmas, and thinking about all the presents she'd received. She was crazy chuffed about her phone and Deryth's art set too, but Mamma's present? She still liked the bracelet, but sometimes it made her feel strange, sort of sad. And this particular charm made her even sadder. No, not sad … it made her think about the witch again, and she didn't want to think about her on Christmas Day. What was more, it made her wonder all over again if it was possible that Mamma and the witch knew each other. She shivered.

Without a shadow of doubt, the best present of all was still to come—her pup. Even now, she couldn't believe it. Tonight she wouldn't sleep a wink because tomorrow she'd get to choose it. How could she possibly sleep knowing that? It would mean two nights without sleep as she'd hardly caught a wink the previous night, what with the excitement of it being Christmas Eve and the thrill of having Deryth sleep over for the first time. It wouldn't be the last time, she was certain. Deryth and Dada loved each other, she was sure—not loved like he loved her, but in a different way, and she was glad for him.

Tonight her bedroom was dark—very dark. Not even a sliver of moon shone at her window as the silly clouds were hugging it. Perhaps they were trying to keep it warm. She'd asked Dada to leave her lamp on, but he'd refused as it was past eleven before she'd gone to bed. Dare she switch it on? Better not. It would feel like cheating after the lovely day she'd had.

She turned onto her side and tucked her knees to her chest. As well as choosing her pup tomorrow, she hoped she might get a chance to speak to Emrys alone. She had something important to ask him, something no one else must know about. They wouldn't understand.

***

How on earth could she choose? All four pups squeaked and squealed constantly until their mother licked or fed them. Hannah was surprised to discover their eyes shut. Emrys said it was normal and that they wouldn't open them for about a week. Her hands trembled as she picked up each one in turn. She was so nervous she had to wipe the sweat from her palms onto her coat in between.

Blodwen had given birth to two boys and two girls. The fat one was cute, but he wouldn't leave his mother. Hannah supposed she'd best not choose that one as it might miss its mother too much, and then she'd feel guilty, and besides, Idris wanted to keep one of the male pups for the farm. She'd choose one of the females. But which one?

"Look at this little one, Hannah." Dada held the last of the four and turned its face towards her. She gasped. "Freckles! Like me."

He smiled. "Exactly what I thought."

The pup pawed the air blindly and whimpered. Hannah took the pup from his hands and kissed its tiny, pink nose. "Tarian," she whispered. "Can I have this one, please?"

***

Dada got out her easel from under the stairs, and she spent most of the afternoon painting a portrait of the puppy. It wasn't too difficult because Dada had taken a photo of it on his phone and printed it out, so she had something to copy.

Dada and Deryth were in the kitchen drinking tea and listening to the radio, but she was happy in the living room on her own. They were listening to *The Sounds of The Seventies* with someone called Johnnie Walker on Radio Two, and she didn't like the music. In fact, it was kind of depressing.

He'd helped her a little bit with the outline of the puppy because she kept getting the size of its head wrong. On her first attempt she made it too small, like a pinhead puppy, and on the second attempt she made it too big. Now, that looked weird! Like a collie version of Bitzer from *Shaun the Sheep*.

She dipped a thin brush in the black paint and ever so carefully added the freckles, focussing hard to avoid them turning into blobs.

When Dada had been sorting out the money and paperwork with Idris, she had a few minutes alone with Emrys and asked him the question that had been burning inside her these past weeks.

"Yes. She's still in the wood, bach," he'd said. "She's not been seen off yet. Like I said before, it was the blizzard that brought her an' it'll be the blizzard that takes her away. Nowt else."

Switching to a slightly thicker brush she dipped it into pink paint and started on the nose. She'd wanted to ask about the wolf, Tarian, whether or not she was safe, too. After all, hadn't she saved Hannah's life? Trouble was, Emrys didn't realize she knew about Tarian the wolf, only

Tarian the pup. She must wait and hope the witch hadn't managed to beat her that night.

***

While Hannah was busy painting, Deryth and Bleddyn had talked. He'd wanted to know if anything was bothering her, pressed her to say if something was on her mind, but she couldn't tell him. No one knew, except Tadcu, and he understood because he had his gifts, too. Or were they curses? There were times when it felt that way.

They'd grown closer since the visit to Bath, too suddenly perhaps. The storm inside her was reaching a pitch. She pictured it as a raging torrent, about to spill over the edge of the falls. The pool at the bottom was dark and deep. It swirled in temper, frothing and spitting. It would drown her if she succumbed to it.

So she must decide, once and for all. She stirred her coffee, the mini tornado at the centre of the mug in empathy with her feelings.

He'd been dreadfully nervous, his voice almost a stammer. "Do you think you might be able to make a life with me and Hannah?" he'd asked, his expression sad, yet hopeful.

She'd hesitated before replying, but not for the reason he imagined. "Yes," she'd answered, "I do."

His face had brightened. He'd grazed her cheek with a kiss. "There's something important I have to say, Deryth, and I want you to feel free to consider it without remorse."

She waited.

He took a deep breath. "Thing is, I don't want any more children." A frown had settled on his face as he'd spoken, but he insisted it must be said, because he did not want to disillusion her.

"Me neither. I love Hannah, Bleddyn. I have no desire to have any children of my own—never have."

The muscles in his face had relaxed, and he kissed her properly. "You sure? I mean you're still young enough—"

She placed a finger to his lips. "I'm certain. I've never wanted children … but I'm glad we have Hannah."

So her decision was final. A blood moon was on the horizon, less than a week away. The date had been stored in her mind for a long time it seemed. She'd do it then.

No regrets.

WOLF SKIN

The night sky was still and calm, holding its breath in anticipation of what was to come. Winter clouds that had hung around during the afternoon fled by twilight, not wishing to be accused of blighting the event. Throughout the evening Deryth and Tadcu prepared as best they could. Incantations spoken and old gods beseeched, she knew she was ready.

It was well past the witching hour as she made her way towards the menhir in the top field, the Beth ogham clutched tightly in her hand. Facing south, she sat on the cold, dank ground, her back to the stone. Watching. Waiting.

The archer, Sagittarius, aimed its arrow towards the Scorpion's heart, while Mars, the warmonger, egged it on. Were either aware of the personal battle raging within her, or were they too engrossed in grander schemes?

The night air was bitter without the clouds to temper it. She shivered and wrapped her coat more tightly round her middle, knowing it wasn't merely the cold that made her quake. Knees to chest, she curled up small—a speck of stardust among giants. She'd watched this spectacle a few years back, at this same spot, but that had been different—Tadcu was with her then, and it had been for the fun of it. He'd offered to come tonight, but she'd refused. Deep down, he knew this was something she needed to do alone …

Gradually, earth's dark shadow crept across the moon's surface, cloaking it in its embrace. Her heart clapped like the god Taranis's thunderbolt, her head spun as fast as his wheel. She remained crouched and huddled, afraid that should she give her limbs the go-ahead, they'd up and carry her home. Was this really what she wanted? To be free of her gift, her curse, and live like any other person on this earth? After all this time it wasn't an easy sacrifice.

She watched, entranced, as the moon reddened, as shades of copper turned crimson, warming the sky. The change from woman to wolf occurred as it had always done, except for the first time, at her bidding. Powerful. But this would be the last time she would experience such brute strength. As the moon became gorged in blood, she stood and howled in praise of its majesty one last time.

***

Asleep beneath the starlit sky, the plaintive cry woke the witch. What had she heard? As silent as a shadow, she got to her feet and peered beyond the canopy of trees. She listened again, but the howl was not repeated.

A cackle of mirth upon her lips, she leaned against the hawthorn, contemplating. The moon was a ball of fire, its ruddy face shone down on the wood, providing a spiritual hue of warmth. With darkened eyes she watched, mesmerized, as Earth's shadow slipped across its surface—a magician revealing its trick—until once again, its face shone silver. Had the wolf chosen this night to make its decision? A night swollen by a blood moon?

Dare she imagine the wolf might have sacrificed itself for the love of a human? If so, then she'd only have the old dewin to contend with in future. Once rid of him, she'd be free of this woodland prison, free to roam the world as she had before. How might she be certain? Bound within the wood there was no way to tell, apart from watching and waiting.

Summoning a murder of crows from out their sleeping bough, she whispered her instruction.

Bless the crows! Within minutes they returned to tell her the good news—that there, at the top of the field, lay the abandoned pelt of the wolf. In their haste to please her, their excited caws drowned one another out like a mob of rioters. Maybe she'd reward them with a few pickings from the carcass, its eyes perhaps? Huh! Of course not. She'd not have left those behind.

The murder of crows was not beyond her summons yet. A whistle to the badger cete quickly brought them to her majesty's side, their will at her command. The crows would need to show them the way to the pelt so they might retrieve it for her.

***

January was cold and dark. Hannah hated January. Each hour, each day, each week, dragged. She was desperate to bring her pup home, but the closer she got, the further away it seemed. She'd managed a sneaky visit with Emrys the previous weekend, but the time spent with the pups had flown.

She was amazed at how quickly Tarian had grown. Now a month old, her eyes were open and she was able to walk, though she stumbled like someone who'd drunk too much beer. "How old was I when I walked?" she asked Emrys.

"I don't know, bach, you'll have to ask your dad. About a year or so I imagine."

"A year! That's rubbish." She held Tarian aloft, their noses close to touching. "You're clever, aren't you? You can already walk."

The pup squealed with delight, her hazy eyes unable to focus properly on Hannah's face. And then, before she knew it, Emrys had announced it was time to go. "Two more weeks, bach an' you'll be able to take her home with you."

Pouting, she kissed the pup on its nose and laid her next to her mother's teat.

See, the one thing that still worried her was the thought of her pup escaping into The Lane. And it was such a shame, because if the witch hadn't been in the wood, The Lane would be a wonderful place to walk. As things stood, she wouldn't dare. She'd seen with her own eyes what the witch had done to poor Jipp, and she hadn't forgotten the fight with Tarian the wolf, either. In fact, she didn't think she'd ever be able to forget it. It had been one of the strangest nights of her life. Sometimes it still seemed like a dream, except deep down she knew it hadn't been, or how else would she have got better after the witch put a spell on her? And of course there'd been the dirt. No, it hadn't been a dream.

The idea came to her so clearly, she believed it must have been lurking all the time. She knew what she needed to do.

***

For two days and nights the wind was raw, merciless, vanquishing any trace of cloud. Dada reckoned it was below zero, which meant less than nothing. Hannah didn't understand how something could be less than nothing, like if she had no sweets left that was it—they'd gone. You couldn't have less than nothing. She didn't argue, though. Her mind was on more important things.

She hoped Dada wouldn't find out what she was about to do, but then again perhaps he'd be glad of it, glad she was able to give the thing up now it no longer meant anything to her. Seeing Mamma again had made her realize how much he and the rest of her family in Wales meant to her. And not just her family, but Deryth, Emrys and Anwen too, because they would be her family if Dada married Deryth. Ooh! The thought no longer made her tummy dance, except with excitement. She'd always wanted to be a bridesmaid.

He wouldn't be happy about her going to meet the witch again, not if he knew what she'd done to her. She'd wait until he was busy writing, then she'd go. It shouldn't take long. She placed her boots and coat by the door, ready to make a quick getaway should the opportunity arise.

***

Dusk had almost fallen before Dada settled down to work. In fact, she'd almost given up on her plan, but her pup was arriving in a few days, and she'd do anything to keep her safe.

Early evening sun sat low in the sky as she climbed The Lane. It shone through the trees, casting long shadows on the ground and blinding her whenever she glanced at it. She shivered. How come it was so cold when the sun shone this bright?

She took a few more strides, until she was level with the end of her garden wall, then stopped again, afraid to venture any further. She sat on the wall, just as she had done a long time ago, and waited. "Hurry up," she muttered. "I don't have long." Should the witch fail to come soon, she would have to return home, though judging by the silence in the wood she was indeed close by. It had taken a lot of soul-searching to find the courage to come again after what happened the last time. She hummed a tune to calm her mind, the sound of her own voice making her feel less lonely.

It was the snap that caught her attention—a deliberate sound, not an accident. Hannah raised her head and peered into the darkening wood. She remained seated, afraid to cross the track to the boundary, her vision impaired by the creeping dark.

And then she came. But it was not the witch. It was the wolf, Tarian. Huge paws pounded the frost-hardened ground, head bent low so Hannah was unable to see its eyes. Its stride was deliberate, assertive, so why did it not look at Hannah? Had it not noticed her in the dimness of The Lane?

Hannah was reminded of the first time they'd met, how afraid she'd been, knowing a wolf was close by. But she was no longer afraid, in fact Tarian's approach was a relief. Perhaps she wasn't ready to see the witch again. Might it be possible for the wolf to deliver her peace offering, or would it lead to another fight? Hannah didn't want that, the last one had sickened her to the core. Hand in pocket, she rotated the seed pearl brooch round and round in her fingers, taking comfort in its soothing warmth.

As the wolf neared the edge of the wood Hannah stood and crossed the width of The Lane in a few paces. "I'm glad you're safe. I've been worried ever since—" Why did Tarian still not look at her? Why was the wolf's head bowed low? Hands on hips, Hannah took a step back and watched, puzzled.

"I'm unharmed," the wolf whispered, its voice husky.

Hannah frowned. Maybe it had a sore throat. Did wolves even get sore throats? "I've come to ask a favour." Still it did not lift its head, nor did it sit. Instead, it stood on the spot like a statue of a wolf. Hannah's instinct warned her something was amiss.

"A favour, you say?"

Taking the brooch from her pocket, Hannah held it in front of her. "I don't want this any longer so—" Aware of the tremble in her hand she dropped her arm.

"What is it? It's so dark I can't see. Come closer."

Tentatively, Hannah stepped forward, her heart pounding in her chest.

The wolf stood, not on four legs but on hind legs. However, they were not the legs of a wolf but the legs of the witch.

Frozen with shock, Hannah stared in disbelief. The sound of the witch's cruel laughter erupted from inside the wolf's head. Its eyes were hollow—two, black holes in a lifeless face. Blind and dumb, it faced Hannah, unseeing and speechless. Its lower jaw hung open, hideous. And instead of the wolf's belly, she saw her mother's gown, pale and smooth.

"This is what has become of your precious wolf!" the witch said, her voice a spitting cackle of malice. "Oh, that it were still daylight so you might see more clearly!"

Shock. Disbelief. She was horrified. Despite the bitter wind she felt hot, her heart beat fast and her legs trembled. "You're cruel! How dare you?" Why did she not run? To fight back—that was what she wanted, to tear at the witch's face with her fingernails until she bled.

Seeing her distress the witch laughed harder, rejoicing in her trickery. She spun in a circle, the dance within the wolfskin bringing it back to life—the dance of the macabre. Until that moment Hannah had been too stunned to cry, but now the tears flowed like rain, constricting her throat.

"Oh, poor thing!" mocked the witch. "She cries like a bairn for the wolf, even though it would have eaten her given half a chance."

"N-no! It w-was my f-friend." Hannah's sobs racked her whole body. "I'll t-tell Emrys. He'll s-send you away." She wished Emrys was here. He'd help her without a doubt.

"Emrys? That old fool?" she scoffed, drawing closer so Hannah was able to see into the dark depths of her soul. Her eyes were as expressionless as the orbs of the dead wolf, her face triumphant with glee. Hannah had once considered her beautiful, but no one this cruel could ever be beautiful. The witch gestured towards the pelt. "With this one gone, I'll have no trouble dealing with him."

Raising a long finger to her chin, she pretended to consider her options. "Let me see … First, I'll pin his crippled old legs to the ground with a pitchfork, then I'll tear out his hair in handfuls before summoning the crows to pluck out his eyes and feeding them to the pigs!"

Hannah thought she might faint. Bent double, she retched onto the ground, a trail of saliva dangling from her mouth. The more distressed Hannah grew, the more joyful was the witch. She whooped with pleasure at the effect her words were having.

"Did you believe your precious wolf had beaten me that night?" She waited for Hannah to straighten again, so she might look her in the eye as she spoke. "Would you like to hear how it met its end? Well I shall tell you … I snuffed out its life like a candle in the wind while it begged for mercy." She cackled again as Hannah wiped her snot-streaked mouth in her coat sleeve, then mockingly, as though she were a baby, said, "No sooner had you run home to your Dada than I crushed its skull with a rock.

Oh, I wish you could have seen the way its brains leaked down its snout! In fact, you reminded me of it a moment ago." She pursed her lips and frowned. "What a spoilsport you were, disappearing before it ended."

Never before had Hannah felt such hatred; never before had she been so consumed with rage. From deep inside her there rose a guttural growl. Uncontrollable. Animalistic. No care for her own safety, her first instinct was to fight. Body rigid, fists clenched, she raised her eyes to the darkening sky and screamed into the void.

And before her eyes the storm clouds gathered, huge and black. Black as the raven. An icy wind buffeted her face, drying her tears and causing the wolf's fur to shimmer on the witch's back. With a primal scream, Hannah lunged at the witch, causing her to step back despite the fence that separated them.

The witch whooped with joy.

"Leave this wood," Hannah shouted. "You do not belong here!"

The witch's laughter turned to anger and she spat her words. "Do you not think that is what I want? For more than a decade I've wanted to be free of this place, free to go wherever I choose, but *they* refused to grant my wish." She tore off the wolf pelt and held it aloft. "The dewin and his grandchild, this wolf, refused to set me free." With teeth as sharp as blades, she bit into the neck of the pelt, tearing a strip from the skin before ripping with both hands until the whole head was free from the torso. Head dangling in one hand and body in the other, she spat on the ground.

And that was the final straw. With both hands, Hannah reached through the fence, grabbed the witch's wrist, and sank her nails into the flesh. Startled by the attack, the witch dropped the wolf's head to the ground where it rolled fleetingly, before coming to a halt inside the fence at Hannah's feet. It stared up at her, through unseeing dark holes.

Hannah's anger was a tempest. Blind with rage, blind as the wolf, she howled with fury and with both hands, clung tight to the witch's wrist. She dared not let go for fear of what the witch might do.

A bolt of lightning flashed across the sky, illuminating the scene. The witch thrashed about, attempting to loosen Hannah's grip, but failed. Possessed with a strength she did not know she had, Hannah clung on, digging her nails in deeper, the strength of her hold like a magnet to iron.

Her temper mirrored by the sky, its thunderous clouds rained shards of ice down on the witch, their glassy prongs piercing her bare neck and shoulders. And still Hannah refused to let go. With her free hand, the witch attempted to shelter her face from the storm's wrath, but to no avail. The weaker she became, the stronger Hannah grew. It was for all the world as if the witch's strength was being sapped by Hannah's powerful grip.

Eventually, Hannah sensed the wrist grow limp. Trickles of blood, black as tar in the dim light, where her nails had pierced the flesh. And the crystals of ice continued to lacerate her flimsily clad body as it contorted in panic. Only then did she let go.

Bare branches froze in shock as the scene unfolded in front of them. Razor-sharp icicles trembled with fear. And still the wind blew, fierce and bold, flailing the witch where she stood until she screamed for it to stop.

Hannah stood stock-still, rooted to the ground, as the elements continued their assault.

***

How was this possible? Moments earlier Rhiamon had been savouring the child's misery, when suddenly the tables had turned. Perhaps she'd underestimated this child, mistaken her innocence for weakness. Damn her own complacency! The child was turning out to be more of a lion than a lamb. With hindsight, she might have guessed. Hadn't the child held her mother's brooch in her hand as an offering just before she'd revealed who she really was?

It was as if the storm read her mind, for it scourged her relentlessly, whipping her skin raw. "You shall not take me back!" she cried to the wind, her voice thin and pathetic against its mighty roar.

Painful memories of ten years previous flashed before her—the strength of the squall, its violent temper. It had delivered her to this place, but not before having punished her for her past misdemeanours by tossing and turning her in its huge arms for weeks on end.

She must not let it take her again. To be free of this wood was all she wanted. Well, that and revenge on the old dewin. Surely it wasn't too much to ask considering everything he'd put her through? And for the sake of a few dead lambs and a calf? The bitch could not be counted, as hadn't it been about to attack Rhiamon when she'd stolen into the barn with the pups? No, that was an act of self-defence. It was so unfair! She must try another tack. Struggling to gain control of her voice, she spoke. "Calm yourself, wind, and I shall reward you with this child. You may take her wherever you desire, do with her whatever you will!"

Hannah failed to hear her words, for no sooner were they spoken than the squall devoured them. Rhiamon's ploy fell on deaf ears, for instead of doing her bidding, the wind blew harder, knocking her to the ground in a quivering heap. Her legs kicked at the earth in an attempt to gain hold, but the blizzard pinned her down and battered her body with another round of ice shards, until she was soaked to the skin and bleeding. She screamed in temper, arms flailing at thin air, her face a contorted mess.

As if from nowhere, a flurry of creatures arrived on the scene. Those who had previously witnessed her bullying, or who'd been victim to her tyranny, joined in the attack. A skulk of foxes tore at her hair with their powerful jaws, while a colony of voles, sick of skivvying, nibbled at the flesh on her bare calves, their razor-sharp incisors plucking the exposed sinew. Agony! She screamed and thrashed with all the strength she could muster, but the attack persisted.

The air became filled with a crescendo of bird calls—blackbirds, tits and dunnocks flocked from thin air, hovering above her head, the bravest among them diving for a spare morsel of flesh. A great buzzard joined the throng, its talons fixed greedily on her dark eyes.

Only the crows resisted. High in the trees, they bowed their black heads, like mourners at a funeral. Silent as the grave, their iridescent feathers quivered in the wind. So they would not come to her aid after all. Cowards! She might have known.

The air was filled with the riot of the persecuted, and those who had witnessed her cruelty this past decade were hellbent on revenge.

***

Hannah covered her ears against the noise. As much as she hated the witch, such torture was impossible to watch. For one last time, she looked into the face of the wolf. "I–I'm so sorry," she sobbed, then she found her feet and fled.

SNOW

When Bleddyn woke the next morning, he was astonished at the view outside the window. The snowdrift had to be three feet deep. With the back of his hand, he wiped the condensation from the glass to get a better look. It was coming down thick and fast, the flakes small and feisty, not big and slow. The kind of snow that stuck. Thank goodness he'd done the weekly shop the day before, or they'd have nothing in. It didn't look as if there'd be school today. Hannah would love it. The first thing she'd want to do was don her gear and go outside to play. He knew he'd have a battle on his hands, as he didn't like her playing out in snow with her chest the way it was. He'd let her sleep a bit longer. She'd seemed particularly grouchy the previous evening. He hoped she wasn't coming down with something again.

Quiet as a mouse, he opened the door to his bedroom and crept downstairs.

***

The cold light of dawn filtered through the window, rousing Hannah from a deep sleep. As in grief, the reality of what had happened in The Lane the previous evening was her first waking thought. When she'd returned home, she'd hidden in the shed for some time in order to calm herself. She hadn't wanted Dada to see her upset like that. She'd crouched in a corner, while the merciless wind continued to howl, and hail as loud as bullets had pelted the shed roof. But it was strange, because as she calmed, so did the wind, until by the time she went indoors it was no more than a chilly breeze. Even the stars grew confident enough to peep out from behind the clouds, albeit for a few seconds.

And Mamma's brooch? Well, she must have dropped it in The Lane after the witch appeared in the wolf's skin because it wasn't in her coat pocket when she got home. Good riddance! It held too many sad memories. Why she'd once considered it a precious object she had no idea. She shuddered, remembering how she'd needed to scrub the witch's dark blood from beneath her fingernails. "It's paint," she'd lied to Dada when he'd come out of his office to see what she was up to.

She turned onto her side, facing the window. In the half-gloom of the early winter morning she made out the wavy pattern of condensation sparkling on the glass.

Was Dada awake yet? She listened hard. Yes, he was clattering about in the kitchen, probably preparing her breakfast. She wasn't hungry in the least, because now she was fully awake she couldn't get the image of the witch dressed in Tarian's skin out of her mind. And what about the way she'd torn its magnificent head from its body? Thin sinewy strips of skin had dangled from the neck, like a garland of pink ribbons. It made her feel sick.

Tarian had saved Hannah's life, but Hannah hadn't been able to return the favour.

And where had the storm come from? She'd never seen the sky blacken so quickly, nor heard thunder rumble so loud. Jeez, the storm had been in a bad temper! And what of the icicles that peppered the witch like bullets from a gun? How had they not landed on Hannah? It was all so confusing. She lay there, considering all that had happened.

Was it possible her anger had caused the storm? Surely not. And yet never before had she felt so powerful, so fearless. How had her own small hands managed to grip the witch's arm so tightly? And they'd tingled as she'd done so, as if an electric current passed from the witch to her.

She groaned. The image of Tarian's severed head made her stomach churn. Her hatred towards the witch was a ball of fire, the flames licking her insides as they danced. Would she ever be able to get it out of her mind?

She must try to calm down, or she'd not be able to face Dada without confiding all that had happened. Taking deep breaths, she summoned her pup to mind. She'd be bringing her home in a few days' time. She'd be her mother and would look after her and love her forever.

Big, deep breaths, in … out, in … out.

There … that was better.

Dada had moved to the living room. In the distance, she heard the faint sound of the TV, which was strange, because he rarely watched TV on school days. Why hadn't he called her yet? She was sure it was Monday … Yes, she and Emrys had gone to Idris's on Saturday, and yesterday she'd returned to The Lane. She sang the "Singing Walrus, Days of the Week" song, just to be certain. Ah, perhaps today was teacher training and Dada had forgotten to tell her. That would be nice, as she'd have an extra day at home. Or would it? After what had happened, school would be a good way of helping to take her mind off things.

She pulled the quilt over her head, making a den. Her nose was freezing. How long could she stay under here without dying? How silly! She didn't want to die. She had her pup Tarian to look forward to soon. Had she done the right thing in naming the pup after the wolf? Might it not make it impossible for her to forget? No. It was the right decision. She'd remember the wolf as it looked when it was alive—noble, majestic. And wasn't she good at putting hurtful things to the back of her mind, the way she had with Mamma? She breathed deeply and tried to puff the warm air up her nose. She stuck one little finger up each nostril, warming the ice-cold cartilage. That was long enough. She'd have to poke her head back out. The lack of oxygen was beginning to make her feel a bit panicky.

Dada still hadn't called her. With one hand, she fumbled for the clock. The big hand was on the four and the little hand was on the eight. Four past eight? No, that didn't sound right. Why had Dada insisted on buying her this type of clock? It was old-fashioned and much more tricky than the other type, the type with the number, then the two dots and the other number. It had to be something past eight, which meant if there was school, she'd be late. She'd better go and find out, in case Dada had the days mixed up. Perhaps he thought it was Sunday.

Brrr! It was mighty cold this morning. Thank goodness Dada had remembered to leave her slippers beside the bed last night. Her feet sunk into the fur lining. I bet Tarian's feet never got cold, she thought sadly, recalling the violent images of the previous evening.

The air in her room felt strange—too still, as though the world was hushed beneath a thick blanket. She stood in front of her window and wiped the condensation away in a circular motion.

Snow! Her garden was full of snow. And it was still coming down. Nose pressed to the window, she studied the scene. The sky was a blanket of grey, the colour of Tarian's fur. Relentlessly the snow fell, creating a whiteout that blurred her vision. The water butt below the window had disappeared, and in its place stood a small, white mountain. She couldn't see the shed window either, as the snow was piled up on the sill. She wiped the window again. She'd never seen so much snow. The wind had blown it in great big drifts all around the patio. If she stepped outside it would probably reach her middle. So that was why Dada hadn't called her. There'd be no school in this.

The window had misted again. She cleared it with the palm of her hand, and faced towards The Lane. Winter-bare trees swayed in the wind, their scrawny arms burdened with the weight of the snow. The track was invisible, though there the snowfall wasn't as deep as in her garden. Tall black trunks stood strong against the wind, their starkness contrasting sharply with the rest of the world. Overcome by a sense of peace, her mind began to quiet.

A sudden movement at the window caused her to scare, but it was only her robin. It perched on the snow pile on the window sill and fixed its eyes on her, red feathers puffed out, all proud.

And Hannah knew.

When Emrys telephoned later that morning to say that because of the snow she might have to wait an extra day or so to collect her pup, she wasn't surprised. A little disappointed perhaps, after such a long wait, but Dada had prepared her for the likelihood of such news.

Nor was she surprised when Emrys whispered these words: "The witch has gone, bach. The blizzard's taken her at last."

Her robin had prepared her for such news.

"So the wood is safe now?" she asked. "I'll be able to walk Tar—" Her voice broke at the mention of Tarian's name, and tears sprang to her eyes.

"Yes, bach. You no longer have to worry about anything … and I mean *anything.* There are those we say good riddance to, like the witch, and then there are those we are sad to lose."

She hung on to every word, certain he was trying to tell her something important.

"Sometimes we think we lose someone, but they haven't really gone, not while we still remember them," he said.

After she put down the phone, she thought about his words. "I'll never forget you, Tarian," she whispered.

AROUND THE BEND

February 2012

No fresh snow had fallen for days. The persistent sun, along with the calming of Hannah's mind, had assisted the thaw. No longer dour and grey, the sky was a blissful blue. Cloudless.

Today was the first day she'd been allowed out to play. Dada had sworn she'd be buried up to her neck if she went out sooner. Filling her lungs with frosty air she ploughed on, determined to venture further along The Lane than ever before. Arrow-shaped footprints in the snow led the way. If the blackbird was brave enough to make the journey, then so was she. After all, there was nothing to fear now, other than fear itself.

The bend in The Lane drew close. Just a few more steps until she'd reach it.

Come on Hannah, you can do it.

There it was again, a mere whisper on the wind.

Was someone really calling her, or did she imagine it? Perhaps it was the sound of her padded hood, rubbing against her hair. She lowered the hood and listened.

Nothing.

Head down, she continued her journey.

Had she reached the bend? This spot was less familiar, but it was difficult to tell because the snow had hidden all the usual features, like the hollowed tree where the grey squirrel lived, the big boulder where she'd once spotted a pile of fox poo, and even the gap in the fence, unless Emrys had already mended it. But he couldn't have done so in this weather. Strange, because now she was here, The Lane didn't look bendy. There was only one way to tell, and that would be to turn around …

No house, no grey roof tiles, not even a smoking chimney. Her heart raced with excitement and trepidation, both at the same time. A little further, then she'd turn back.

Come on Hannah, you can do it.

She remembered the very first time she'd met the wolf. She'd been a different person then, with a different life. She paused for breath, remembering … Tarian of the wood. The story Tarian had told her all that time ago—the one about the little dog and the Devil—perhaps she'd been trying to warn Hannah about the witch but hadn't wanted to scare her. It made sense, now.

A few more steps. She raised her head and gazed into the distance. There stood Emrys's farmhouse. Two tall chimneys, heaped with snow, awarded her a double thumbs-up. She beamed, and returned the gesture.

She'd go no further, at least not today. When her pup was strong enough to walk this far, she and Dada would visit Emrys. Tarian the pup would like that. She'd be visiting her mam-gu, Bronwen.

Spotting a nearby twig jutting through the drift, she picked it up and drew in the snow, summoning to mind Emrys's sketches. Three spirals, linked at the centre—the past, the present, the future. A crude attempt maybe, but nonetheless sincere.

Without a second glance, she turned and retraced her footsteps.

GLOSSARY OF WELSH TERMS:

bach – little one

croeso – welcome

dewin – wizard

iawn – all right

tadcu – grandfather

duw, duw – Good God, colloquialism

diafol- devil

mam-gu - grandmother

ABOUT THE AUTHOR

Catherine McCarthy is the author of the novellas *Immortelle* and *Mosaic* and the novel *A Moonlit Path of Madness.* Her short fiction has been published in various anthologies and magazines, including those by Black Spot Books, Brigids Gate Press, and Dark Matter Ink.

In 2020 she won the Aberystwyth University Prize for her short fiction, a competition judged by the assistant editor of the Times Literary Supplement.

A former primary school teacher, she now weaves dark tales from her farmhouse in West Wales. Time away from the loom is spent hiking the Welsh coast path or huddled in an ancient graveyard reading Dylan Thomas or Poe.

Find her at
https://www.catherine-mccarthy-author.com/
or at
https://twitter.com/serialsemantic

ACKNOWLEDGEMENTS

Many years ago, in the very early stages of my teaching career, I had the pleasure of teaching a little boy named Daniel, the boy to whom this book is dedicated. Daniel had Down syndrome, but he also had an incredibly supportive family, a big personality, and a heart of gold. I always knew he would go far, and he has. He loved stories, and the last news I had of him was that he was working at his local library. This gave me such a thrill. I believe Daniel taught me as much as I taught him, and he was close in my thoughts as I wrote this story.

That said, a writer's journey can often be a lonely one, and yet there are many who help us along the way.

First of all, I would like to thank my husband, Tony. Without your vivid imagination and support this book would not exist. You are my first reader, my harshest critic, my best friend and my life.

Immense thanks and appreciation to Heather and Steve of Brigids Gate Press for believing in this story, as well as my editors, proofreader and beta readers. Your professionalism and friendship along the way have meant so much.

I must give a special mention to Mark Peters for his invaluable sensitivity edits. His keen eye and firsthand knowledge helped make *The Wolf and the Favour* a better book.

To my friends in the Twitter community, you are all incredible and inspire me every day.

Last, but not least, to each and every reader, my appreciation always. Without you, my work would have no purpose.

MORE FROM BRIGIDS GATE PRESS

A tragic accident, shrouded in mystery, leads to a family reunion in the hidden village of Little Hatchet, located in the smothering shadow of GodBeGone Wood, the home of the mythical Woodcutter and Grandma. Alec Eades rediscovers his bond with GodBeGone Wood and the future his father agreed to years ago as nefarious landowner Oliver Hayward schemes to raise money for the village by re-enacting part of the Woodcutter legend. Old wounds are reopened and ties of blood and friendship are tested to the extreme when the Woodcutter is summoned and Grandma returns.

Something is outside; in the fields, by the ditches, on the roads. Something old and cruel and vicious. When Luke Sheridan moves out of Dublin city to rural Kilcross with his wife and baby, he imagines the worst part will be his extended commute to work. They can look forward to enjoying the countryside and being part of a small community. After all, his old friend Declan Maguire lives in the house next door and is a Garda in the nearest town. But Declan's devilish attitude towards drink, drugs and women means trouble is never far from his door. And worse, gruesome murders and the appearance of sinister figures at night mean the countryside is becoming a very dangerous place to live. *Country Roads*—don't go outside alone.

Following the death of a loved one, Rachelle Collins visits Ferguson Estate, an expansive country mansion which holds many fond memories, and one sinister secret, within its walls. Throughout the course of a single, terrifying night, Rachelle must confront horrors, both psychological and tangible, to prove just how far she is willing to go to keep her family together.

Prepare for adventure as Juliana, a nineteen-year-old Brazilian, finds herself forced to run from an occult overlord, leaving her sister in peril. Temporarily safe, Juliana works to save money for Vilma's rescue—and along the way, meets Patrick, a rich-boy mountain climber with friends in high places.

Angus Addison wants to see his corporate flag on the summit of Mount Everest—carried there by the first woman in history—but the Himalayas are no joke. Failure could cost both sisters their lives.

Juliana weighs the risks and rewards—for even if she raises the cash, she still must figure a way to free Vilma from the same man she ran from—a man known to his disciples as The Farmer.

Visit our website at: www.brigidsgatepress.com